CARL

THE EIGHTH MAGE

TAMARA GERAEDS

FREE SOUL JUMPER ORIGIN STORY!

Looking for a series of stories with just as much action, twists, monsters and magic as *Cards of Death*? Look no further! *Soul Jumper* is the thing for you!

Subscribe to my newsletter now – through www.tamarageraeds.com – and you will receive a *Soul Jumper* origin story FOR FREE!

PREVIOUSLY, IN CARDS OF DEATH

We've saved five out of seven of the souls Satan is after, but he has another way of using the chosen souls to open the circles of Hell. Soon we'll have to face him. Our final battle…

Will we be ready? Mom is still missing, but we've gotten Jeep and D'Maeo back. Taylar turned evil, twice, and I'm a bit worried about that. I have no idea how to stop it when the time comes that he can't snap out of it. We've had no time to think of a solution for it, or to investigate this further, because there's so much going on. Angels have gone missing from Heaven, and one was even killed. Quinn is afraid the missing angels have crossed over to Lucifer's side. He is trying to locate them, so I'm hoping to get good news from him soon. Meanwhile, Heaven is already under attack, and I have no idea how to help. I need to come up with something though, because Quinn told me I am also destined to save Heaven.

Even if I did, I wouldn't know when to do it. Everything on Earth is spinning out of control faster than before. Beelzebub came through the black portal in the silver mine. We drove him back using the Bell of Izme and some holy water, but he almost took out Vicky. Since then, she's been a bit distant.

One of the books we took from Shelton Banks' mansion gave us some important info on Jeep's wife: *Charlotte was a powerful magician. After a couple of mages asked her to join the Devil's army, Charlotte renounced her powers. Her magic can be summoned by a powerful mage with the help of her husband, with whom she still has a strong connection. To harness these powers, one will need an empty body...* 'Empty', in this case, means a body without magical powers. We could only think of one person without powers that we truly trust: Mom. I'm no too thrilled to transfer Charlotte's powers to her, since that means she'll be smack in the middle of our battle with Satan, but I guess we don't have much choice if we want to win this. We can use all the fire power we can get.

Our visit to Shelton Banks' house had another positive outcome. We found Jeep, and he was released from the burden of the angry mage ghosts inside his tattoos. It's weird seeing him without the moving tattoos. So weird that I sometimes think I can still see them move.

Getting rid of the mage ghosts wasn't easy, but eventually we got something good out of it: one of them gave us Shelton Banks' true name. Using a spell, I astral projected myself to Shelton Banks, involuntarily creating a split vision so I could see him as well as my friends at home. Shelton's true name gave me the power to make him answer my questions.

I needed to know how to defeat Beelzebub. But making him lift the curse on Vicky, the one that pulls her toward the Shadow World, was more important, so I did that first. I also got some interesting information out of him when I asked him about the curse. He told me the Devil wants to get rid of Vicky because she inherited great power from her ancestor…

Unfortunately, Shelton Banks pushed my astral form away from him before I had the chance to ask him about Beelzebub. I can only hope I'll return to my body unharmed…

CHAPTER 1

Faint voices are coming from one side; the other has gone silent.

While my astral form flies through the air, all kinds of thoughts go through my head, barely audible above the pounding that bounces in all directions. *I should've known it would be too dangerous to approach Shelton Banks, even if it was only in the form of an astral projection. Why didn't I put more safety measures into my spell? What if he damaged my soul somehow?*

My astral form slows down, and the voices go quiet. My vision is still split, but only the left side, the eye of my astral self, has visibility. I try to make my body open its eyes. It doesn't respond. It's as if we're no longer connected.

I gulp for air, even though my current form doesn't need oxygen. *Don't panic. Don't panic,* I tell myself. *I'm not completely lost yet. There are still two visions, so some part of the connection must have remained intact.*

I take in everything around me, and when I blink several times, the incoherent shapes start to make sense.

I've returned to the annex, where my body is lying on the ground. Several shapes are hunched over it.

"Vicky," I whisper.

The shady person starts shaking my body. She can't hear me.

I send several commands to my body. *Move! Open your mouth. Open your eyes. Do something!*

Of course, it doesn't obey. It lies there, looking disturbingly empty.

When I drift closer, everything around me gets hazier again.

Suddenly I'm hovering near the ceiling. I reach out to grab something before I disappear in the next room. There's nothing to hold onto, even if my hands weren't see-through.

"Help!" I call out. "I'm here!"

The shapes move around the annex. None of them look up.

And then, I see something strange.

The people below me are all shapes of light, but some of them have black spots. One even has tufts of black crawling through them. *Evil?* I try to make out who they are. *Must be Gisella. She's the only one of us with evil powers. Although...*

I narrow my eyes at the figure standing behind the werecat-witch. This one is holding a staff. *Maël.* A small sliver of black moves inside her chest. *Nothing to worry about. That's the remnant of the black tree in the Shadow World. It's only a tiny bit of evil, which she can control.*

I try to find D'Maeo to check if the Black Void has really left him. My gaze falls on someone with a bowler hat. *Jeep.* His body shows not even a single speck of dark. The person moving his hand to his mouth over and over beside him must be Charlie. He's also clean. Kessley is no different. Her body seems to glow a bit more than the others. *Probably her cheerfulness. Or the booze running through her veins.*

My gaze moves along. And freezes, along with my astral body. The person standing next to Kessley, with his arm around her, must be Taylar. His misty form is a weird mixture of dark and light. The black and white slivers swirl around each other as if they're performing an intricate dance. You'd think it was a battle between good and evil, but the twirls and dives don't come across as hostile. Playful is a better description.

I'm so mesmerized and stunned by the intricate pattern the slivers inside Taylar weave that I don't notice myself drifting through the ceiling until it blocks my vision.

I throw my head forward to get a glimpse of Vicky's body. Too late. My astral form keeps floating up. There's no use in struggling. There's nothing to grab onto, and none of my movements have any effect.

Soon, I don't hear my friends' voices anymore. The air around me gets warmer as I keep ascending. It's not until I spot a light in the distance, getting bigger and bigger, that I realize what's going on.

I start to struggle against the force pulling me in. "No! Let go of me!"

This can't be happening. Not like this. Not now that we're so close.

Again, I search for something to hold on to. I try to use my powers to turn back. Lightning, ice, water, sunshine…. nothing works. I'm defenseless.

Eventually I stop fighting. It's better to save my strength, because I will not accept this fate. So far, I've accepted all of it. I was meant to lose my father, to see my mother suffer from fits and torture, to fight Lucifer, and to lose the girl I love. If that is my destiny, then so be it. But I will not leave this battle so close to the end. I will fight for my life and for that of everyone on Earth.

Now that I have stopped resisting, I'm pulled into the light fast. I close my eyes and wait.

The light gets brighter, but it's not painful. It's soothing and warm. It makes me want to lie down and forget about everything going on below.

I shake my head. *No, don't forget. They need you. Mom, Vicky, Taylar, Jeep, D'Maeo, Maël, Kessley, Charlie and Gisella. Even Mona. I can't leave them.*

"Welcome," a soft voice says as the light dims.

I open my eyes. A glowing man in a white robe is standing before me. Ginger hair falls upon his shoulders, and his face is covered in freckles. His huge reddish wings seem too big for his slender body. His smile is sweet, and he gives me a small bow. "Welcome to Heaven, Dante."

I straighten my shoulders when my feet finally touch solid ground again. Or almost solid, since the road consists of clouds.

I bow back to the angel and answer him with a simple, "No."

His smile falters. "What do you mean?"

With my arms folded, I look him in the eye. "I don't accept this. Send me back, please."

"Your time on Earth is up, Dante. I'm sorry."

I take him in from head to toe and step closer.

He frowns but doesn't move.

"Listen," I say. "We all want the same thing here. Heaven and Earth are under attack. I'm the chosen one; I can save them both. But I don't have time to return as a ghost and learn how to move stuff. I need to be alive. So send me back."

"I know who you are, but there are rules. Unfortunately."

I cock my head. "Is there anything in the rules about someone taking over Saint Peter's duties at the gates of Heaven? Because I met him, and he didn't look anything like you."

The angel's cheeks turn red. He stares at me with his too bright eyes, and I stare right back. I don't believe for a second that the normal rules still apply, and I'm pretty certain this angel has the power to send me back.

Finally, he licks his lips and opens his mouth. "You want to keep fighting, even when I don't return you to your body?"

I roll my eyes at him. "Of course. I'm the chosen one. That's my job. I keep fighting until Satan's ass is kicked."

He chuckles but pulls a straight face so fast I wonder if I imagined it. "The task of the chosen one ends when he dies. A new one will be appointed."

My mouth falls open. "You're joking, right? That's it? You give up, just like that?" I shake my head. "Well, I'm sorry, but I can't do that. That'll take way too long." I turn and start walking away from him. "If you won't help me, I'll find my way back myself. I've been here before, after all."

A stunned silence answers me.

I've taken five steps when I'm lifted off my feet again and drift back to the gates of Heaven, that are now visible behind the ginger angel.

I give him my foulest look and try to conjure ice above him. It doesn't work.

After another long stare, he finally nods. "Fine. You're right, everything has been turned upside down here. To be honest, I thought you'd be relieved to pass on the baton. I expected you to beg for your life; instead, you beg for the lives of everyone on Earth and in Heaven. You leave me no choice but to honor your request."

I grin at him, and he raises a finger. "However, if

13

you fail again, there will be no turning back. No turning into a ghost either. That will be the end. Do you understand?"

I wave his words away as if they don't mean anything, although I feel the weight of them pressing on my shoulders. *This will be my last chance. I cannot fail again.* "Fine, fine. Just hurry, please."

"One more thing." He slams his hands together and a book appears between them. He flicks through it at dazzling speed, then nods and slams it shut. "Yes, I thought so."

"What?" I ask impatiently.

He throws the book over his shoulder where it vanishes into thin air. "There is a rule I would like to honor."

"What rule?"

"Your choice to keep fighting Lucifer in order to save everyone grants you a reward." He paints a large circle in front of him with a swipe of his hand, and seven familiar faces pop up inside it. "If you beat Lucifer, one of these people can stay with you on Earth until their time to move on comes again. Who will you choose?"

My eyes almost pop out of my head. "For real?"

"I do not make jokes, Dante Banner. Choose the one who will not move on if you defeat Lucifer."

My gaze flicks from one face to another. Some of them are easy to dismiss. Maël, Taylar and Jeep all want to move on. They want to be with their loved ones who are already in Heaven. They want peace.

Taylar and Kessley will want to stay together. If I keep Kessley with me, they will be separated. That leaves only three people: Vicky, whom I can't live without anymore, Dad, who never had enough time with me and Mom, and D'Maeo, who found true love with Mona.

"The only way to choose is with your heart," the ginger angel says softly.

Maël, Taylar, Jeep and Kessley dissolve, and the other three faces grow. They smile at me, and my chest tightens. Pressure builds up behind my eyes.

I know who I want to keep the most. Without Vicky, my life will be empty. I want to spend the rest of my life with her. But this is not the time to be selfish. There are two people who deserve happiness more than anyone. Two people who have fought to keep the world a beautiful place for decades.

I'm sorry, Vicky. Mom, Dad. I can't choose myself over them. No matter how much I want to.

I take a deep breath and spit out the only logical choice. "D'Maeo."

The angel nods. "Consider it done."

He stretches his arms out in front of him and his wings behind him. When he moves his arms up, my body moves with them.

"Good luck, Dante," he whispers.

And before I can thank him, he pushes his wings forward. A wall of wind throws me back. I fall through the clouds and tumble down at frightening speed. Inside my head, several drums come to life.

The light above me gets smaller and smaller. I feel like struggling, but I don't. This is what I wanted, after all. I have to trust that this angel will put me back into my body safely.

If only it didn't feel like plummeting to my death.

CHAPTER 2

After a while, I slow down. I drop back through a familiar attic and into the annex of Darkwood Manor. My astral form comes to a halt and I try to open my eyes.

Nothing happens.

I do feel something, though. A hand is placed on my chest, and someone shakes my arm. "Dante? Are you back? Open your eyes." The pounding going on inside my head almost drowns out the voice.

"Am twying," I mumble. It's as if my lips and tongue are stuck, and my limbs weigh a ton.

With difficulty, I lift my hand and search for Vicky's. She grabs it and squeezes hard. "Are you back?"

I nod, or at least, I think I do. "Yes."

Tears burn in my eyes. *She seems like herself again, and now I gave her up. I'm going to lose her.*

"Did you get the information we need?"

"Give him some time to recover," D'Maeo says reproachfully.

The sound of his voice makes me smile. *At least I made two other people very happy.*

A soothing warmth spreads through me, and I relax.

"Is that better?"

Of course, I should've recognized the feeling of Mona's sparks doing their job. A little fairy godmother love works miracles.

"Much better," I answer, pushing the pain of my decision to the furthest corner of my mind. The drummers in my head cease their attempts to drive me crazy, and the heaviness leaves my limbs. I open my eyes and smile when I see only one image, no more split screen.

"How did it go?" Charlie asks, wringing his hands.

I sit up carefully. "Rather well. I got him to lift the curse on Vicky, *and...* he didn't kill me! Or, actually, he did, but I came back."

"You died?" Kessley shrieks.

"Yes, but only for a little while. And if I die again, it'll be for real. No coming back as a ghost for me. I'm already on borrowed time."

"That sucks," Taylar says wholeheartedly.

Jeep frowns. "Well, I wouldn't say it sucks that he got back."

Taylar rolls his eyes. "You know what I mean."

D'Maeo rubs his sideburns. "Saint Peter actually

decided it wasn't your time yet?"

I clear my throat. "Actually, *I* did. But I'd rather not talk about that anymore. I'm back, I'm in one piece, and Shelton Banks lifted the curse on Vicky."

Vicky lets go of my hand when I rub my head to drown out the last of the drums. "What about Beelzebub? Did Shelton Banks tell you how to defeat him?"

"Well, he had enough of the interrogation before I could make him answer that question, so we'll need to come up with another way to find out more about Beelzebub."

Vicky stands up abruptly and turns her back to me. "I can't believe you, Dante. I told you to ask him that question first. It was the most important one!"

I shake my head fervently but stop when the annex starts spinning around me. "I know you think it was, but I disagree. Keeping you from getting killed is more important. And more urgent."

"No, it isn't!"

I throw my hands in the air. "Yes, it is, Vicky!"

She turns back to me, her eyes fuming. "You don't need me to beat the Devil. But you do need to kill Beelzebub."

Despite her shouting, I keep calm. I knew she'd be angry, but I'm happy with the choice I made. Shelton Banks made it very clear that Vicky is important in our battle against Satan. "Yes, but you're wrong. You *are* important." I look up at the others. "Each of you is. It has been said to us many times that we were all chosen to do this. Keeping the team complete is our best shot at winning."

Vicky is still fuming; her nostrils move with every needless breath she takes out of habit. She stares at me until I break eye contact.

Charlie helps me up, and I brush the dirt from my clothes.

Maël steps closer. She takes me in from head to toe. "He told you something about Vicky, didn't he?"

I nod. "I asked him why they wanted Vicky out of the way so badly. He gave me an evasive answer about her great-great-great-grandmother and the powers she inherited from her."

"What?" If Vicky's frown was any deeper, her eyebrows would melt into one.

I fold my arms together with a wide grin. "Looks like it's a good thing I saved your ass."

Maël is now scrutinizing Vicky. "We need to find out what kind of powers you inherited. We will need them to beat Lucifer."

Jeep beckons us, and we follow him into the kitchen where he taps the book we couldn't decipher. "I bet that information is in here."

Everyone agrees, and I'm about to do the same when something weird grabs my attention. This time, I am certain it isn't my imagination. My breath catches in my throat, and I point at Jeep's arm. "Jeep... one of your tattoos is moving again."

It's not only the nasty grin that makes the skull on Jeep's lower arm creepy. There's no doubt about it...

it is moving. The mouth opens and closes, and the eyes blink.

Jeep's expression is a copy of mine, full of surprise and fear.

Vicky has momentarily forgotten about her anger with me. She apparates to the other side of the table and bends over Jeep's arm. "How is this possible?"

Jeep clenches his jaw and closes his eyes. "There's still a ghost trapped inside. He's trying to get out."

Gisella pulls some shadows to her while Maël rises to her feet and pulls her staff from under her cape. "Can you stop him?"

Jeep's head tilts in all directions as he fights the ghost mage inside his tattoo. "I'm not... sure." His hand presses down on the skull, but that only makes it move more frantically.

Everyone stands up, ready to fight. Mona, who was preparing some hot chocolate, puts everything down and awakens the sparks inside her. Maël raises her wand and points it at the tattooed ghost. Before she can utter a single word, a shadowlike shape pulls itself from Jeep's arm with so much force that it's propelled forward, against the edge of the table. The table moves back, hitting Maël at the other side, making her drop her wand. Jeep is pushed backward. His chair topples over, with him in it.

Maël scrambles to her feet first. She aims the tip of her staff at the form hovering above the table now. Again, the figure is faster. It shoots down and hits her in the chest. The rest of us pull out or conjure our weapons and aim it at the escaped ghost while D'Maeo bends over to try and grab it.

The shadow form rises to the ceiling and holds up two freshly grown arms. "Wait! I'm not here to hurt you!"

Everyone, except for Charlie, hesitates. A grease ball hits the figure square in the chest, and he's pushed back, slamming against the wall above the back door.

"Ouch."

I gesture to Charlie to lower his arm. Somehow 'ouch' doesn't sound like something an evil mage would say. Normally our enemies growl or shout threats when we hurt them. Still, a simple 'ouch' and an 'I'm not here to hurt you' aren't enough to convince me he's on our side. This might be a trick. He might've stayed behind on purpose, in case we found a way to take out the other seven mages that escaped Jeep's tattoos. Which we did.

With a lightning bolt still dancing eagerly on my palm, I walk over to him. Gisella's shadows stay close, in case I need back-up. I make the lightning float up to the ghost's neck and push his newly formed chin up with the sharp, sparkling tip. "Who are you, and why did you stay behind when the other mages escaped?"

The shadow takes on a more human shape with every passing second. I can now clearly make out a face of about fifteen years old, with dark, wavy hair and thick eyebrows, plus long arms and legs attached to a slender body. He stops plucking at the grease stuck to his chest and looks down at me. "Hi. I'm sorry I scared you." He holds out his hand as if he's oblivious to the weird situation and the lightning almost piercing his chin.

I place my hands on my waist and wait for him to answer my questions.

He pulls back his hand and smiles ruefully. "Right. I wouldn't trust me either." He nods at the unreadable book that is still lying on the table. "I can help you with that, if you like."

Jeep pulls the book closer to him. "No, thank you."

"Right," he says again. "Let me answer your questions first. Who am I, and why did I stay behind, locked in Jeep's tattoo." He points carefully at the lightning bolt. "Would you mind lowering that just a bit?"

With a simple finger movement, I lower the bolt half an inch. Gisella keeps her shadows where they are.

"My name is Dylan Maylord. I'm from England and—"

A cheer from Kessley interrupts him. "Yeah! Finally another Brit!" She lowers her head with a blush when the rest of the Shield frowns. "Sorry. Carry on."

Dylan smiles, and I have to admit, he seems pretty decent to me. However, looks can be deceiving, so I wait for him to tell us more.

"I think I wasn't released before because Shelton Banks' spell only worked on maleficent beings."

Taylar snorts. "Of course it did."

I ignore his comment and keep my eyes on the young mage. "If that's true, then how did you escape now?"

Dylan's gaze drifts to Jeep behind me. "When we were all still trapped, Jeep was fighting constantly to keep us there. As soon as the seven evil mages escaped, Jeep's hold over me started to fade. I kept quiet while he slowly let his guard down and voila!" He opens his arms. "Here I am!"

"How joyful," Jeep mumbles.

Vicky steps up next to me. "I still don't understand. If you're not evil, then why did the Keepers of Life trap you?"

"Well…" Dylan lowers his head. He suddenly looks uncomfortable, ashamed even. "I tend to be in the wrong place at the wrong time, even after death."

CHAPTER 3

The sad vibe coming from Dylan is so strong that I'm inclined to believe him.

"I was searching for the man who killed me when I came across Jeep fighting the mages, minutes before they were trapped in his tattoos," he tells us.

"Were you out for revenge?" Vicky asks, staring him in the eyes to read his feelings.

The young mage shakes his head. "Not at all. I wanted to tell my killer that it wasn't his fault. He killed himself because the guilt was eating him up. I tried to tell him sooner, but I couldn't." He bites his lip.

"He's telling the truth," Vicky states. Then to him: "Go on. Why couldn't you tell him before?"

"I kept ending up in the wrong place, like some sort of bad rerun of my life. When he died and became a ghost with unfinished business, like me, I thought it would be easier to find him and tell him what really happened."

When he doesn't continue, D'Maeo slams his hands together, as if to wake him up. "Well, tell us, what happened? How did you die?"

"I was out camping with some friends, and I went to take a p…" His gaze meets Vicky's again, and he blushes. "I mean, to relieve myself. Without realizing it, I wandered onto military grounds. A group of soldiers was practicing." He shrugs. "Wrong place, wrong time again. I was hit by a bullet. If I had gotten there ten minutes later, practice would've been over. If I had taken a different path through the trees, I wouldn't have ended up walking straight through the only hole in the fence. But I never had the chance to tell the shooter all of that. Guilt took over his life, and he ended it." He lowers his head and wipes a tear from his eye.

I frown at Vicky, asking her silently if he is telling the truth.

"Look at me," she says to Dylan, and he does.

The whole kitchen in silent as she reads his emotions.

"He feels sorrow, regret and guilt," she says after a minute or so.

Charlie wipes a couple of left-over nacho crumbs from the table and licks them from his hand. "Why didn't you use your powers to stop your bad luck? You're a mage, you could've cast a spell."

Dylan throws his hands up in defeat. "Wrong time,

wrong place. I rarely got to finish a spell, because no matter where I tried to cast it from, my ingredients were blown away by the wind, or there was a giant leak above my head, or… I don't even remember all of it. And I don't think I want to." He shakes his head. "The last time I tried, someone non-magical walked in on me. My best friend." He blinks away another tear. "He thought I was crazy, a satanist or something. We'd been friends since kindergarten, but he never wanted to speak to me again. And he told everyone at school that I was a freak."

"That sounds horrible," Kessley says sympathetically.

"It was, so I never tried to cast a spell again." He lets out a curt laugh. "I don't even know if I'm any good at them."

Jeep is getting impatient, judging by the sigh coming from behind me. "What happened when you saw me fighting those mages?"

"Well, I was passing by and saw that you were losing the fight. I wasn't sure what I could do, but I couldn't just walk by without at least trying to help. And I was dead already, so what could it hurt?" He chuckles. "My powers consist of lifting curses and undoing spells, so I knew they wouldn't be any good. I had to think fast, so I just dove right into the fight, trying to knock over as many mages as I could, in hopes of giving Jeep the upper hand. I managed to knock over three of them, but when I tried to get up, I couldn't. Someone…" He gestures at the book filled with deceased mages, "the Keepers of Life, as I found out recently, were pushing me toward Jeep's tattoo. I was sucked inside, and… well, you know the rest of the story."

I extinguish my lightning bolt and gesture at Dylan to come down. As soon as his feet touch the floor, Vicky stops him from moving by placing both hands on his shoulders. She looks him in the eyes once more, and we all await her verdict in suspense, Maël with her wand at the ready.

Finally, Vicky lets go of Dylan. "His emotions match his story. I think he's telling the truth."

Mona, who's been hovering around the kitchen counter, pushes us aside gently and holds out her hand to Dylan. "Then by all means, come sit down and eat something."

Dylan allows her to pull him along and set him down onto the chair next to Jeep. He looks up at her with a confused expression. "Eat? Why would I eat? I'm dead."

Several chuckles rise around the room. I even see a smile on Maël's face when she sits down again.

I grin at Dylan before walking back to my own seat at the head of the table. "Trust me, it will make you feel better. And you aren't the first ghost that needed convincing. The members of my Shield hadn't thought of it either."

Kessley shoots me an indignant look. "You never had to convince *me*."

I tilt my head while I think back and realize she's

right. "I stand corrected. You are a hardcore food lover."

A wide grin turns the corners of her mouth up. "I am."

Dylan is watching the conversation and Mona's movements with fascination. "I've never seen the living and the dead so comfortable together. I mean…" he shakes his head as if to get rid of his confusion, "I saw and heard a lot when I was trapped inside Jeep's tattoo, but everything was sort of… shrouded. Fuzzy and unclear. Sometimes I doubted it was all actually real. It was more like a dream. A very, very long dream."

Only now Jeep seems to realize how it must have been for Dylan to be trapped underneath his tattoos for so long. Guilt washes over his face.

Charlie voices our thoughts exactly. "I admire you, Dylan. I would've gone crazy, you know."

Dylan stares at a stain in the middle of the table. "Yeah… I think I did go crazy at some point. But when I finally stopped screaming and pounding, I was still trapped, so I figured it would be wiser to stay calm and wait for a chance to escape."

Jeep clears his throat. "I'm sorry."

Dylan turns his head to face him. "For what?"

"For keeping you locked up."

Dylan swats his words away. "That wasn't your fault. Nobody knew I got caught up in the fight. It was just bad luck, as usual. Don't worry about it. And frankly…" he bends over to the tattooed ghost, "I'm glad I ended up with you instead of with some boring guy who never experiences anything exciting."

The guilt and sorrow on Jeep's face are replaced by a glint in his eye. He laughs out loud and slaps Dylan on the back. Or at least, he tries to, but his hand goes straight through, and he slaps himself in the face.

Kessley doubles up with laughter. "Looks like Dylan needs some practice turning solid."

The mage blushes. "I know how to turn solid. I just haven't been able to do so in a couple of decades."

"I know, I'm sorry," Kessley hiccups.

"It's the booze," we say in unison.

Dylan relaxes again and turns in his chair when the smell of chicken wings fills the air.

Mona beams at him. "Getting hungry yet?"

He nods feverishly.

When Mona puts a basket in front of him and another in the middle of the table, I suppress the urge to grab a chicken wing. I've had so much to eat already today, and I need to stay fit. I crunch my teeth when the delicious smell lingers around me and rise to my feet. "I'm cold. I'm going to put some clothes on. I'll be right back."

Upstairs, I take off my pajamas and slip into some clean jeans and a simple white T-shirt. All of my sweaters are still at Mom's house, so I put a jacket over it. I slip the two notebooks and my athame behind my waistband and stick my Morningstar in my pocket.

When I walk back into the kitchen, Dylan is still ripping the meat from the bones as if he's afraid the animal will fly away. His basket is almost empty, and when he's done, he licks his lips and burps. "Oops. Sorry." He covers his mouth with his hand. "You were right, that does make me feel better. I forgot how good food can taste."

I glance at Mona sitting on D'Maeo's lap. "Food is great in itself, but Mona adds a little magic to hers to make you feel better, give you more energy."

"Really? I never noticed that. Probably because I never paid attention when Jeep was eating." He leans back in his chair and stares at the ceiling. Then he suddenly stands up and reaches for the book we can't read.

At first, I think he's tricked us. He *is* working for Shelton Banks, and he wants to take his books back. I see Maël and D'Maeo tensing too. But Dylan places the book in front of him and says, "I can try to get rid of the protection on this book for you."

I frown. "Gisella tried to lift it already. It didn't work. The spell on it must be really powerful or intricate. We think it consists of several layers."

Dylan rubs his hands together. "That shouldn't matter. I've got the ability to lift any curse or spell, remember?"

"We could've used that power a lot sooner," Vicky grumbles beside me.

"Let's be grateful that we have it now," Maël comments.

Vicky nods, and we all concentrate on Dylan and the book.

He flexes his fingers. Then he lets his hands hover above the book for a second before moving them in circles in opposite directions.

I watch the book closely. Nothing changes.

Dylan mumbles something that sounds like a curse and steps back. He cracks his neck, shakes his shoulders loose and rubs his hands together again.

He repeats his movements. Nothing.

I hold up my hands. "Forget it. It isn't working. The protection is too strong."

Dylan turns his wrists and hops in place, like a professional kickboxer getting ready for a fight. "Let me try one more time. I'm a little rusty. I haven't used my powers for a long time."

Reluctantly, I let him continue.

Dylan takes a couple of deep breaths, and although they won't give him any physical advantage now that he's dead, they do help him focus. For a while, he just stares at the book. The reflection of it in his eyes changes. It's as if several copies appear on top of the original. That's when Dylan starts to move his hands again. He flexes his fingers, lets his hands hover above the book and moves them in circles in opposite directions. Bit by bit, the letters blend together. Dylan's movements get bigger. The black stain is pulled apart and formed into different letters that spread over the page. I still can't read any of it.

Dylan seems to sense that his work isn't done yet.

He brings his face closer to the book and sucks in air. The letters are pulled into his mouth. He lifts his head and blows them out toward the ceiling, where they slowly dissolve. He repeats this process three times before straightening up. While he shakes his hands and breathes in and out a couple of times, the pages of the book flip themselves. On each page, English text is now visible. With a last twist of his wrist, Dylan closes the book. I gasp when I read the title embedded in dark letters into the front.

The Nine Circles of Hell

CHAPTER 4

Several of my friends bend over the book at the same time. They frown and sit back down, looking defeated.

"What?" I ask.

Charlie gestures despondently at the book. "It's about the nine circles of Hell. What good will that do us?"

"Really?" I almost snort. "You think this book won't help us?"

They nod, and I place my hands on my waist. "Okay, then why was it so well protected?"

Taylar shrugs. He suddenly looks exhausted. "Because Shelton Banks wanted to trick us into taking the wrong book?"

"No…" I shake my head and run my finger across the letters on the cover. "No, the other two books were useful too."

I refuse to believe he tricked us into taking an insignificant book.

"Look," I say. "There might be something in this book about keeping the circles of Hell closed. I say we check it out."

Gisella yawns and stands up. "Do whatever you want, but I'm going back to bed. I can barely keep my eyes open."

Charlie rises from his chair too. "I'm with Gis. It's the middle of the night. Even if there's something useful in there, we can't do anything with it until we've had some rest."

The others mumble their agreement except for Vicky, who remains silent. Dylan stands between us with hunched shoulders. Once everyone except Vicky has left the kitchen, I give him a smile. "Hey, don't feel bad. You did a great job. Whether this book holds important information or not, you helped us. It probably would've taken us hours or even days to figure out how to lift the protection on it."

The young mage nods. "Thanks for being so kind to me. I hope this book will help you somehow."

I flip through it aimlessly. "I hope so too. It worries me that Satan has a back-up plan." I barely glance at the text that flashes by as I turn page after page. Until my eye catches a familiar face. I pull the book closer and flip back until I find the picture. I tap it feverishly. "I know this woman!"

Vicky joins me and studies the picture. "How can you know her? It says here she lived centuries ago."

"Yes, but I saw her, in the memory that Charon showed me."

"Charon?" Dylan repeats, sounding puzzled.

"The ferryman of the Underworld," I explain. "He showed me a fight between Lucifer and his wife, Isabel."

Dylan's gaze shoots from the picture to Vicky and back. "She kind of looks like you."

We both turn our heads to him in surprise.

"Like me?" Vicky asks.

The mage nods and points out several features. "Look at the full lips, the piercing blue eyes, the dark eyebrows." He pauses. "And of course the black hair."

I follow his gaze and frown. "You're right. She does look like Vicky. I noticed something familiar about her when I saw her in that memory, but I didn't put it together." I take Vicky's hand. "She must be your great-great-great..." My voice fades as realization hits me. Vicky breathes in sharply at the same time.

We spit it out simultaneously. "She is the one Shelton Banks was talking about!"

"My great-great-great-grandmother," Vicky whispers. Her eyes are wide. "Do you think I'll be able to do what she did?"

I nod slowly. "That must have been what Shelton Banks was talking about. And also why he wanted to pull you into the Shadow World, where you wouldn't be able to cause any trouble."

She shakes her head. "I can't believe that."

"Why not?"

"Come on, Dante. I'm not that powerful! I'm just a simple empath."

I can't help but grin. "Well, apparently, you're much more than that."

Dylan slams his hands onto the table, and we both jump.

Immediately he seems to shrink. "I'm sorry. I didn't mean to startle you. I just want to know what's going on. What is it that Vicky can do?"

I tap the picture of Isabel. "It looks like Vicky is able to create the circles of Hell, like her great-grandmother did. So even if Lucifer is able to break them, Vicky can create new ones and lock him in again."

Dylan's mouth falls open. "Really?"

I feel like cheering and dancing, but I remain calm and only nod. "Yes, really. Vicky can make sure we win."

Vicky shakes her head. "Don't get too excited about this. I have no idea how to create those circles."

"You will, once you read…" I flip the pages of the book until I find a description, "… this." When I turn the book over to her, she quickly scans the lines.

She sighs. "That's still not a lot of information. And it doesn't mean I can do it."

I kiss her on the cheek. "Sure it does. You're awesome." I look up at the mage. "Right, Dylan?"

He blinks several times and clears his throat. "I'm

37

sorry, but… doesn't that also mean that Satan is her…" He pauses and wets his lips, "… great-great-great-grandfather?"

Vicky's mouth falls open, and she searches for support. I catch her before she falls and help her into a chair.

"That can't be true, can it?" she whispers. "I can't be re-related to… S-Satan. Even if Isabel was my great-grandmother, that-that doesn't mean any-anything." She's so shocked that she stutters. "She-she could have… had chil-children with someone else, right?" She reaches out to the book and starts flipping the pages rapidly. "Maybe there's more in here about Isabel. About her children."

Dylan and I watch in silence until I see something familiar. "Wait!"

Vicky's hand comes to a halt.

"Flip back a bit," I say, without taking my eyes off the book.

She does, and my hand shoots forward when I see the symbol again. "There!"

Vicky frowns at the symbol, consisting of a two-barred cross with an infinity symbol at the bottom. In each space of the lemniscate, there is a horizontal capital I.

I read the text below it. "The Leviathan cross is a symbol of satanism. A horizontal *I* inside the infinity symbol indicates birth, in this case pointing to the offspring of the Devil."

Vicky narrows her eyes. "Where have I seen this

before?"

An image flashes before my eye. "On the Book of a Thousand Deaths."

She nods feverishly. "Right! But we both had a feeling we'd seen it somewhere before, didn't we? But where?" She scratches her neck, and I watch her while I try to think.

Then I see it.

I suck in my breath, and both Vicky and Dylan turn their head.

Vicky lowers her hand. "You're shocked. Why?"

I swallow. "That symbol on your neck, the one your mother and grandmother also had…"

There's no need to finish my sentence. Vicky is already shaking her head. "No, that looks different."

I stick out my arm and push her hair up so I can examine it again. "You're right, it does look different, but it's the same symbol… except… it's only half of it."

Dylan joins us. He compares Vicky's symbol to the one in the book. It's a capital *I* with a smaller *I* horizontally attached to it, just under the top on the left side. The half of the lemniscate resembles a large raindrop. "It's definitely the same."

Vicky places both hands next to the book, leaning heavily on the table. "The Devil's blood runs through my veins."

"So what?" I say. "That doesn't mean you're evil. You could never be evil, babe." I try to keep the panic from my voice, but my words are still a bit shrill.

Vicky shivers, and I pull her close. I rock her and kiss her head until she calms down. Dylan keeps his eyes down and doesn't move a muscle. I feel sorry for him. He got sucked into Jeep's tattoo decades ago, and when he finally manages to escape and tries to help, he accidentally drops a bomb on us.

I reach out to him with one hand, and he looks up, startled. "You helped us a lot, Dylan. I'm sorry you had to suffer for years, but in the end, you did that for a reason. Without you, we might never have found out about this."

Dylan seems a little happier until Vicky pulls herself free and wipes the tears from her eyes. "I'm not sure I wanted to know."

With my finger, I catch a tear running down her cheek. "I can only imagine how hard it must be for you, but honestly…" I wait for her to meet my eye before I continue so she can read my emotions and know that I'm telling her the truth, "… I have never seen any evil in you."

She smiles weakly, and I stroke her cheek. "Try to think of this as good news. You probably inherited a lot from Isabel, who was a good person and who had great power. You've got that same power. All you need to do is find it within you." I bend toward her and kiss her on the lips. "And I know you will, because you are awesome."

She stares past me for a couple of seconds. Minutes maybe. Then she takes my hand, which is still resting against her cheek, squeezes it lovingly and straightens her shoulders. "You're right. This isn't bad news at all." She pulls the book toward her. "If I study this, we'll have a great back-up plan."

"Exactly. And now we finally know why the Devil wants to get you out of the way as much as me."

"And why my mother and grandmother were killed." She bites her lip. "They must have had the same power."

Dylan is staring at her neck again, or rather at her hair, which has fallen over it. "But why is the symbol not complete? Why is only half of it visible?"

We all look down at the book. Eventually, Vicky pulls the collar of her leather jacket up to cover the symbol. "Maybe the other half will show itself when I use the powers I inherited from him? Or the ones I got from Isabel?"

I rub my arms to drive out the cold that suddenly spreads through them. The thought of her being a great-great-granddaughter of the Devil does give me chills. "Maybe. But it doesn't really matter. The most important thing is that you have the power to create the circles of Hell. And Lucifer knows this too."

She tilts her head in thought. "He tried to get rid of me, like he did with my mother and grandmother, but he failed."

I wrap my arm around her. "And he will fail again and again, because we are stronger than he is."

She rests her head on my shoulder. "I hope so."

Dylan stretches his arms and legs. "Would you guys mind if I take a nap? Pulling myself from Jeep's tattoo sucked a lot of energy out of me, and I also used my powers for the first time in… well, I'm not sure how long, but it seems like forever."

I let go of Vicky. "Of course! We should all get some sleep, if we can. We'll need all of our energy to prepare for the next phase in this battle."

Vicky frowns. "What next phase?"

I close the book and shove it under my arm. "Can't you feel it? The tables are turning. Our chances of winning are getting bigger."

There's a violent crash somewhere above us, and instinctively, I conjure a lightning ball.

Vicky's shoulders sag. "You were saying?"

I cling to the book as if it's a lifebuoy. "Mona!"

More clanging and creaking answer me.

"Mona!" I call out again.

The fairy godmother appears in a cloud of sparks. "We're under attack!"

"Yes, I've noticed." I hold out the book to her. "Can you please keep this somewhere safe? The information inside is crucial for our survival."

"Of course." She grabs the book and slides it onto an invisible shelf in the air.

I call out a quick 'thank you' to her and hurry up the stairs, with Dylan on my heels.

CHAPTER 5

Vicky apparates upstairs, where we meet up again. I freeze when the mansion shudders. The noise is deafening, as if we're in the middle of a tornado. The others hurry from their rooms into the second-floor hallway, with their weapons drawn. Taylar isn't with them. His panicked voice wakes me from my frozen state.

We dash around the stairs to the third floor and come to an abrupt halt. Taylar is dangling upside down near the ceiling, swinging his arms frantically at the swirling demon that's holding him up.

The sound coming from the monster is a combination of swooshing, whistling and growling. A loud thrashing comes from the secret room, which the demon blocks with its broad, twisting body. It hasn't been able to cross the line of salt that I placed along the doorway to the secret room, but the line at the porthole must have been broken.

The porthole must not have been properly closed. They must have found a way to open the portal in the silver mine again and stumbled upon the open porthole. How could we let this happen? They will destroy Darkwood Manor!

The tornado demon closest to us takes a step forward and hurls Taylar at us. I hold up my hands to catch him, and brace myself, but the white-haired ghost turns transparent and flies right through me. Once Taylar has landed safely inside Vicky's room, we all charge.

I hit the whirlwind demon with frost while I approach. Vicky waves her sword, Gisella tries to pierce it with her blades and gel balls whizz around our ears. I can't hear much above the racket that the demons are making, but I'm sure Maël is trying to freeze it in time, or at least slow it down. D'Maeo has stretched out his hands to hold back the wind as much as he can while Mona changes into a sparkling whirlwind that hits the monster in the face over and over. Jeep's hands are moving rapidly, and I can already hear small footsteps coming up the stairs. Kessley is changing shape rapidly, trying to come up with the best one to attack.

When I manage to cover the demon's chest in ice, I dive forward to knock it over. Any hopes of the body shattering to pieces evaporate when I fall right through the whirling wind.

I land on my stomach in the secret room, where I find two more tornado demons. They're turning like maniacs, ripping the walls and ceiling apart. Wood splinters fly everywhere, and I roll over when part of the ceiling comes down. One of the demons shoots up to the upper floor before I can stop it.

"There's one upstairs!" I call out to the others.

Only now does the demon in the secret room notice me. It turns a little slower and takes me in with its tiny eyes that are like needle pins in the large, cloud-like head. Now that it has almost come to a halt, I can make out its two thick arms and broad shoulders. It almost hits its head against the ceiling, and it has no legs or feet. Its lower body ends in a funnel. Even when it's not moving, the noise coming from it is deafening. Without taking its eyes off me, it reaches for the ceiling and pushes.

I grit my teeth and envision ice covering the whole body. Behind me, the swirling decreases, which hopefully means that Maël's powers are working.

A quick glance to my left tells me the porthole is still open, and two more demons are approaching it rapidly. I need to stop them, or they'll rip us into little pieces along with the house.

The tornado figure in front of me is completely covered in ice now. It's trying to shake the cold shards off, but with each piece that falls off, a new bigger one appears. Meanwhile, I step closer to the porthole and take my Morningstar from my pocket. When the demon turns to me, I swing my weapon. The stick extends, and the spiked ball is catapulted forward while the chain attached to it unrolls. It knocks a hole in the lower body, and the monster collapses on the floor.

I don't wait to see what happens next. Instead, I take the last step toward the open porthole, grab it and pull it closed. A millisecond later, a wind demon slams into it full force. Quickly, I get onto my knees and restore the salt line. Now they won't be able to get inside, even if they manage to get the porthole open. Which will be nearly impossible since it is now invisible from the other side.

When I get back to my feet, Vicky yells, "Duck!"

I'm not sure she's talking to me, but I do it anyway. At the same time, I turn around. The tornado demon I knocked over has somehow put itself back together and is now looming over me.

The wind it creates cuts off my breath. A sword comes soaring at us, and I lean back to avoid it. I expect it to lodge itself in the demon's chest, but it flies through as if there's no monster at all. Once again, I hit it with ice. It's the best I can think of while I try to come up with a way to destroy it. Vicky comes soaring after her sword. She tries to kick the demon in the neck, but her foot slips right through. The wind catches it, and Vicky loses her balance. She is thrown around and lands upside down against the back wall.

Anger flares up inside me, and I push off, sending all of my power to my outstretched hands. The wind pulls at me ferociously, but my rage gives me so much strength that I reach the demon in two strides. Energy courses through me, and lightning explodes from my hands as I push them against the monster. It shudders violently and makes a sort of grinding noise.

"Incoming!" I hear from behind me. When I step aside, big chunks of grease soar past my head. They cling to the demon's head and torso. It raises its trembling arms to tear the sticky stuff off. I think hard about rays of burning sunlight shining down on the grease, heating it up. I imagine it melting and spreading over the demon's body, blinding the monster and burning it all over. I've never tried using sun before, but on impulse, I thought it might work, since sunshine is a part of the weather too. In my mind, the grease is dripping down, taking over the demon's body bit by bit. Charlie is still hurling gel at it, and it's really pissing off the monster.

Suddenly it bathes in bright light, and the grease quickly covers every part of the body.

Vicky has picked herself up and is staring at the monster that's clawing at its face and howling at the top of its lungs.

"I didn't know you could do that!" she yells at Charlie.

My best friend pulls a chocolate bar from his pocket with one hand without pausing his attack. "I'm not doing that…" he gives a curt nod in my direction, "he is."

"Nice work," she says to the both of us as she reaches down to pick up her sword. "Keep going."

Charlie has ripped the wrapper from the chocolate bar with his teeth and is chewing on a large piece. "I'll try."

"Make it lower its arms," she instructs us.

Charlie covers its middle in grease, and I aim my sunbeam at it. Frantically, the demon tries to swat the melting gel away. It doesn't notice Vicky jumping forward with her sword raised. She slices the head several times, cutting off the parts that are covered in grease. The growling of the monster is cut off abruptly as the pieces drop down to the ground. Then the whole body tilts. Vicky jumps out of the way just in time. When it hits the ground, it is ripped apart. The tornado pieces whirl in all directions, but they appear to be harmless. Lost.

"Keep the grease melting on the head!" Vicky calls out.

Above us, the noise is getting louder, and the wind seems to pick up. *If we don't hurry up, that third demon will rip the whole house apart. I hope the others will be able to stop it soon. But by the sound of it, they've got their hands full on the second demon.*

"Concentrate, Dante!" Vicky yells, and I focus on the sunshine again.

Vicky picks up the three pieces of the head, covered in gel, runs over to the porthole and peers through it. Taylar comes zooming past. "Let me help."

Kessley follows him and changes into some sort of ultra long dachshund that forms a shield with its body.

After another check for movement behind the

porthole, Taylar opens it. Vicky throws the parts of the head through the opening, and Taylar slams it closed again, locking it and checking it twice.

"Duck!" Kessley calls out.

We do, and a second later, a lopsided tornado slams into her. The blow sends the dachshund sliding toward the porthole, but she's able to withstand the pressure. The small tornado moves over the long body and hits the glass inside the porthole. As soon as Kessley sees that the demon has lost interest in us, she turns back into herself and takes off to help the others.

I sneak closer to see what the head parts are doing, but another deafening creak from above distracts me.

I exchange a worried look with Vicky. "We've got to stop that thing."

She nods. "I agree, but how?" She gestures at the dark swirls of wind still hitting the glass, and the other parts, turned into wind too in the meantime, doing the same in the silver mine. "It can't put itself back together, but it's still alive."

Taylar bumps into me. "Sorry, coming through! We've got another patient here!"

This time it's Gisella carrying unrecognizable pieces of a demon. When I glance over her shoulder, I see Maël standing close to the still body. She managed to freeze it in time completely. Jeep's skeletons are holding it down.

Taylar opens the porthole, Charlie hits the demon parts on the other side with grease to blind them and

Gisella tosses the pieces of the other demon on top of them.

"There." Taylar wipes his hands when he's closed the porthole again.

I study the still form of the headless demon. "Is there a way to kill-?"

My sentence is cut off when debris showers down on us. We all cover our heads as the rest of the ceiling gives in. The pull of the wind gets stronger.

I run over to Maël, dodging floorboards and pieces of plaster on my way. "Leave this one, it won't be able to reassemble itself. We'll deal with it later."

With a curt nod, she agrees.

"To the stairs!" I call out.

Charlie and Gisella carefully make their way through the secret room and into the hallway. The ghosts simply go transparent and run straight through the rubble.

Charlie gestures wildly at me as he sways left to avoid a falling piece of wood. "Go, go! Hurry!"

He lets out a pained grunt, but when I look back, he's still gesturing at us. "I'm fine!"

We hurry up the stairs, which are shaking heavily. I grip the handrail tightly and pull myself to the top of the stairs as fast as I can. What I see there takes my breath away.

All the walls of the attic have come down. Chunks of all kinds of material are swirling through the air. The third demon is standing under a large gap in the roof. It has grown so much that its head sticks through the gap. The funnel that makes up its lower body is turning at crazy speed, sucking in parts of the outer walls while the monster uses its arms to tear down the rest of the roof.

"Stop!" I yell without thinking.

The giant head made of wind turns to me. The eyes blink as if it's trying to figure out what to do with me. Then it pulls its arms in and turns its whole body into a giant vortex.

It was already a challenge to resist the pull from just the funnel. This is much worse.

"Hold on to something!" I holler above the whistling and squeaking.

But of course, with everything falling apart, there is nothing to hold on to.

"Forget this!" Vicky screams. "We should get out of here, figure out a way to beat these demons and come back later."

I nod. "Go downstairs, we'll follow!"

Before she can answer or apparate, we're both pulled into the tornado. Vaguely, I can make out the others swirling around me. I'm hit in the head by something solid, and everything gets hazy. The world turns upside-down, or maybe that's just me. I try to work out where I am, but there's so much swirling around me—people, floorboards, roof tiles, plaster, dust—that it's impossible to get a clear view. I conjure a lightning bolt but realize quickly there's no way I can throw it without hitting one of my friends. Instead, I reach out to grab any body part of the demon I can reach.

My hand simply slides through it…

My eyes search for Maël, but the people floating around me are no more than a blur. I can't tell whether she's holding her staff or not and if she's trying to freeze the demon. The noise around us drowns out her mumbling, if there is any.

I tell myself the monster will slow down any second now. Maël is the only one who can get us out of this, and she's strong enough to do it. But while I turn and turn, not slowing down one bit and getting dizzier and more nauseous by the second, I start to lose hope. For a moment, the air around me lights up with sparks, and I smile.

"We'll be fine, we'll be fine," I tell myself softly.

Then, the sparks are ripped apart like pieces of dust, and my heart sinks. Panic rises to my throat. *How on earth are we going to beat this demon?*

When someone takes my wrist, I scream. The hand that clutches my skin is cold. A vague face swims into view. I don't recognize it at first, but it looks human. The mouth is moving, but I can't make out what the words are above the howling of the tornado. I'm being pulled closer, and now I can make out a face. Dark brown eyes under heavy eyebrows. It's Dylan. To be honest, I forgot about him completely.

"Are you seeing this?" he yells.

I want to tell him I can't make out anything in this chaos, but when I follow his pointing finger, I see it.

I see it, and it is wonderful. And unbelievable. Amazing and also a bit creepy.

CHAPTER 6

Below us, the house is moving. But not because of the tornado raging over it, ripping the roof and walls apart. No, it seems like the house has woken up. The outer walls are moving by themselves, and a loud rumbling rises from the middle. The demon turns a little slower, and for a moment, I can see the eyes blinking in confusion.

"The mansion..." I can hear Vicky gasp, "it's alive!"

I nod speechlessly. *The demon angered it. And now that we can no longer protect it, the house is defending itself.*

The windows from the second and top floor rise like giant arms. From all sides, they close the demon in and try to grab it. Of course, that doesn't work, since wind isn't solid, but it gives us the opportunity to attack again.

Once we've landed on the floor, some of us a bit

harder than others, we charge as one. One look is enough to combine our forces. Sparks, grease and sunlight hit the demon all at once. Swords, blades and shields cut through the air. Maël is standing tall, with her wand held out in front of her. From the forest below, all kinds of animal skeletons run out. Kessley has turned herself into several big birds with sharp beaks. She's circling the demon, pecking it wherever she can. Dylan is throwing whatever he can grab toward the tornado. And even though the objects fly through it, it distracts it at least a bit.

Vicky is standing next to Charlie, feeding him an endless supply of cookies so he can keep going. Thanks to my sunshine, his grease is flowing over the demon's head and shoulders.

"Cover the funnel so we can push it over," Vicky suggests.

Charlie aims for the lower part, and I melt his grease again, making the funnel solid.

The animal zombies reach the demon and start gnawing through the grease. The monster collapses, and the mansion slams its window arms down on it. Over and over it hits the demon, in the face, in the chest.

Dylan steps back and shoots me a sideways glance. "I think your house is angry."

I can't help but grin. "Yeah, I can't blame it." I gesture at the roof tiles and debris around us. "Look at this mess. Just when we'd gotten so far with the renovations."

"Watch out!" He pushes me aside, and a giant whirlwind hand flattens him.

"No!" I yell, and I dive forward to push the arm out of the way. The force of the wind blows me away, but Charlie is there to cover it with gel. I melt it again, my rage heating it up more and faster than before. The demon groans in pain and pulls its arm back. From the corner of my eye, I see Darkwood Manor smacking it with all its might. It goes down, but I can't join the fight. I need to know if Dylan is okay.

The spot where he got squashed is empty, and I call out his name.

"I'm here!"

I turn, and relief washes over me. "Are you alright?"

"Yes, fine." He pats his chest and nods. "It seems like my instincts work fine. I apparated in a reflex."

He turns his head to the raging fight beside us. "Come on, lets help the others out."

I slap him on the back, grateful that he's okay and willing to fight with us.

"I'm running out of cookies!" Vicky yells as Charlie swallows another one almost whole.

Dylan doesn't hesitate. "I'll search the kitchen for more to eat." He disappears before I can thank him.

The house shakes violently, and when I look down, I realize it's standing up. I hit the floor hard but scramble up and concentrate on the sunlight again. The demon is lying on its back, skeletons crawling all over it and even inside it. The Kessley birds peck every spot they can reach while Taylar whirls around them to protect them from the demon's hands, that keep trying to swat them away. The funnel and head are still covered in scorching grease, and the house slams its hands down on it. Still, it keeps moving.

"How do you beat these things?" I call out to no one in particular. Maël is using her staff to catapult Jeep's zombies back whenever they are thrown off. Gisella is kicking and stabbing the demon wherever she can, using her catlike moves to stay out of its reach. Mona and D'Maeo are fighting side by side. Mona's sparks attack while D'Maeo blocks the power of the wind.

"I know!" Dylan yells, scrambling to his feet and handing Vicky two bags of sweets. "We need to cut off the supply of warm air."

I frown and reach out to the wall for support when the house moves again. "Why?"

"Because warm air is what feeds a tornado."

We all slide to the center of the room when the house tilts. When I turn to the raging demon, I freeze. In the wall I was leaning on only seconds ago, a giant hole appears. The plaster and wood form a ragged line around it, making it look like a huge mouth. The four arms formed by the windows reach out to the demon, but they go through it as the grease melts.

Jeep picks up his hat, that has landed next to me. "Did the house just slide us out of harm's way, or is that wishful thinking?"

"No, it did," I answer, still flabbergasted because of everything that's happening.

Gisella helps Charlie up and nudges me. "Come on, guys. Help the mansion grab that demon."

Charlie straightens his shoulders and throws his hair back. Vicky is by his side in the blink of an eye. She stuffs a handful of sweets into his mouth, and he starts chewing like a madman. Balls of grease shoot out of his hands at lightning speed. They hit the demon everywhere as the arms of Darkwood Manor pull back. I focus, and rays of sunlight warm up the grease once more. The mansion responds immediately. The demon struggles, but with grease in its eyes, it can't see what it's doing. One of its arms shoots out and hits the house, shattering a window. Darkwood Manor only grumbles loudly from below us, making what's left of the floor shake. Then the arms grab onto the gel-covered parts of the monster, lift it with ease, shake the skeletons off gently and hurl it into the giant mouth, which closes instantly and with a crunching sound. The mansion shudders, as if in disgust, before reaching down through the hole in the floor.

It seems to be searching for something, groaning with impatience as it fails to get what it wants.

Dylan and Jeep exchange a quick look, and the tattooed ghost nods. "We'll go check it out. See if we can help."

They disappear, and I hear them talking on the floor below us.

"Charlie! Dante! Can you give us a hand here?"

We walk to the edge of the hole and peer down. The two demons we beheaded are still trying to get through the porthole to reunite with their heads.

I look at Charlie. "Do you have enough fuel left?"

He flexes his fingers and licks his lips. "I've got a little bit left. And Vicky's got more sweets if I need them."

"Great. Let's go for it."

We hit the headless tornadoes with everything we've got. The mansion waits patiently, and it's not long before it's able to pull out the monsters. It tosses them at the wall too. The mouth swallows them quickly.

"Open the porthole," I instruct Jeep and D'Maeo. As soon as they do, the whirling heads shoot through, followed by another demon, which we hit with grease and sunlight immediately.

It tries to fly out of reach, but Jeep quickly sends his skeletons over to it while Maël slows it down. The zombies swarm over the monster like a group of hungry piranhas, sending it face first to the ground.

The house reaches down and picks it up. Soon, all of the demons are gone.

I close my eyes for a second. The constant focusing combined with a lack of sleep has drained me. I feel like I could sleep for a week. But I can't even sleep for the rest of the night, because my house is in pieces.

"Make sure that porthole is properly closed and

the line of salt intact," I say to Jeep and Dylan, still standing next to it.

They obey, but Vicky, standing next to me, shakes her head. "What does it matter? The house is ruined. We can't stay here."

I wipe the sweat from my forehead. Suddenly I'm exhausted. "I know."

I expect her to put her arms around me, but instead, she walks away and flops down onto the top step of the stairs.

I'm so stunned that I just stand there with my mouth slightly open. I swallow the lump in my throat that rises not only because of Darkwood Manor, but also because Vicky doesn't seem like herself. In the fight with the tornado demons, she really went for the kill, which made me think she had overcome whatever Beelzebub's attack caused inside her. But now...

Mona approaches me and pulls me into a hug. "I'm sorry. I know how much this house means to you. You inherited it from your father."

I breathe in her sweet smell and try to let go of my concerns, focusing on something else for a second. Something that's only a six on the scale of total disaster, instead of an eleven.

Mona lets go and takes in my trembling jaw. "You'll be okay."

"Sure," I say, trying to sound light and failing miserably. "But it does hurt. Darkwood Manor wasn't only Dad's house, it was also the place where I met five of my best friends." I spread my arms and try to steady my voice. "And look at it now. It turned out to be even better than I thought. It fought to save us, and it was destroyed because of it."

Another groan rises from beneath us, as if the mansion answers me.

I kneel down and stroke the floor. It feels kind of silly, but I'm not sure how else to express my gratitude. "Thank you so much for your help, Darkwood Manor. I'll come back to fix you. I promise."

The mansion lets out a high squeal and starts moving again. The sound makes me think of the creaking of an old man trying to stand up. The big arms reach out to us and pick us up. One by one, they put us outside in the protective circle.

"I've still got some clothes inside that I'd like to take with me," I say.

I make for the back door, but Maël stops me. "Wait."

"For what?" I ask, still grumpy because I lost the mansion.

"Look."

I follow her pointing finger, and my mouth falls open. I conjure a lightning ball in my hand when a cloud slides in front of the moon.

While Jeep steers the skeletons out of the kitchen door, the arms reach inside and pull out hands full of debris. Instead of chunking them on the lawn, they stick them back inside.

"What's it doing?" Kessley asks, landing behind me and changing back into her human form.

"I think…" My voice catches in my throat. "I think it's repairing itself."

We can't see what's going on inside, since the windows move up and down as arms. But soon, the house starts to pick up roof tiles. The holes in the walls are filled up, followed by the roof.

By the time it starts putting the roof tiles back in place, I'm smiling from ear to ear. "This house is even more amazing than I thought."

Eventually, the arms slide back in place, and the mansion stops moving. After a last creak, silence descends on us.

Charlie burps loudly. "Sorry." He rubs his stomach. "I had a bit too much."

I can't help but laugh. With relief, but also from shock. "A bit too much? You devoured a whole aisle of cookies and chocolate! And I'm glad you did, because without you, I'm not sure we would've been able to beat those tornado demons."

Gisella places her hands on her hips. "Are you kidding? That house could beat Satan himself!"

I open my mouth to object but realize she might be right. My hand flies to my mouth.

Gisella frowns at me. "What? What did I say?"

"You gave me an idea."

She rolls her eyes. "I was kidding."

"That might be, but you were making a good point."

Confusion meets me when I look around.

"You think Darkwood Manor could actually kill Satan?" Taylar asks incredulously.

I shake my head. "No, but it could definitely help us. Nobody but us, and maybe Dad, knows what this house can do. So if it comes to a fight…" I pause, still a little afraid to say it out loud. "I think we should lure him here."

Charlie shivers. "Lure him to us? Are you crazy?"

D'Maeo clears his throat, and all heads turn to him. "I think it is the only sensible thing to do." Mona, standing next to him, nods solemnly.

"Why?" Jeep asks. "Isn't it better to have a safe place to return to in case things go sideways? We could harbor a lot of people here, especially if we expand the protection on the house."

D'Maeo sends him a sad smile. "If Lucifer escapes Hell and we fail to send him back, there will be no safe place on Earth. If it comes to a face-to-face battle, we'll have to give it our all. And that includes Darkwood Manor. It can fight with us. It will help us, even if it is only as an element of surprise."

"I think your idea sucks," Vicky says, folding her arms.

Jeep is also not convinced. "So, you want to stop blocking the portal in the silver mine? Lure him through the porthole and let him enter our house?"

The old ghost rubs his sideburns. "We will block that portal as long as we can. But if Lucifer breaks through, and reaches Earth, our best option is to fight

63

him here. There will be no non-magical people in our way, and we'll be on familiar grounds."

"He'll need his back-up plan for sure." Charlie grins, holding up his hand for a high five.

I slap his hand and grin back. "Only two more souls to save. And with each soul he loses, he gets more desperate. I say we get some rest and track down their next target tomorrow."

Kessley rubs her hands with a worried expression on her face. "What if we run into more of those wind demons? Without the house, we'll have no chance against them."

I gesture at Dylan, who's been listening silently. "Sure we do. Dylan has a solution."

He goes a bit more transparent when all heads turn to him. "I might know of a way, yes," he says timidly.

I throw my ball of lightning in the air. "See? Everything will be fine. But now, I order you all to go to bed."

"Aye aye, sir!" Taylar and Charlie say in unison. Jeep taps his head with a 'goodnight' and vanishes, and soon the other ghosts follow. Except for Vicky, who walks back to the house with me, Charlie and Gisella, and Dylan, who stares at the sky longingly. "I think I'll stay here for a while, if you don't mind. It's great to be outside. I'm finally free, and for the first time in decades, I can be alone again. I'd like to enjoy that for a while."

"Sure!" I say, slapping him gently on the back. This time, my hand doesn't go through him. "Thanks again for your help. Stay inside the circle, where you'll be safe. And if you want to rest, you can take the room on the upper floor, back of the house. Nobody uses that."

"Thanks, Dante."

With a nod, I say goodbye. I meet Vicky at the back door. Charlie and Gisella have already gone upstairs.

I reach out for Vicky's hand as we climb the stairs, and she takes it.

"That was…" she searches for words, "… amazing. I knew this house was special, but I never expected anything like this."

"Me neither." We enter my bedroom, and I undress quickly.

Vicky watches me from under the covers. "Are you sure about your plan to lure Satan here? It sounds too dangerous to me."

I hop in beside her and stretch my arm above her head, inviting her to snuggle up to me like she always does. I'm careful to avoid her eyes, since this is a test.

After a short hesitation, she puts her head on my chest.

"We'll be okay. We're going to win this."

Her body stiffens up a bit. Or is that my imagination?

I kiss her on the temple. "Are you okay? You acted a bit weird earlier." That last comment slips out, and I bite my lip.

"I know, I'm sorry," she says, tracing her finger

along my side. "For a moment, I was too angry and heartbroken to function. I should've been there to comfort you."

She sounds sincere, and I'm too tired to worry about it. If I can't trust my own girlfriend anymore, who can I trust? When she continues to caress my side and chest, I drift off into a peaceful dream.

CHAPTER 7

I wake up feeling refreshed and optimistic. Vicky is still asleep, so I climb out of bed quietly and sneak downstairs. Kessley and Dylan are sitting at the kitchen table, whispering to each other.

"Is everyone else still upstairs?" I ask them softly.

They nod.

I sit down in D'Maeo's chair, which is closer to them than mine. "What were you talking about? I mean, if you want to tell me."

Kess smiles. "Sure, it's no secret. We were trying to come up with a way to solve Dylan's unfinished business. Now that he's no longer imprisoned, he should solve it as soon as possible, right?"

My finger taps on the table while I think that over. "Yes, I think so. Unfinished business is dangerous. Jeep's tattoo must have protected you up till now." I scrutinize him for a second. "Do you feel any different?"

He scratches his head. "Well, yeah, I feel free and happy, but that's because I'm no longer a prisoner and because I made some great friends."

"True," I say with a wink, "but is there anything else? Anything that doesn't feel good?"

He stares past me. "Well… I do feel a bit restless."

"That's it?"

"Yep, that's it."

"Good. I think that means we've got some time left to find the man who killed you… what was his name?"

"Armando Accardi. His father was Italian."

I rub my chin. "We'll have to see if we can find out where he is."

Dylan shakes his head. "You don't need to do that. You've got your hands full already. I'd rather help you instead of the other way around."

"That's so sweet!" Kessley calls out. Immediately, she covers her mouth. "Oops, sorry."

About a second later, the table fills up as the rest of the Shield appears one by one.

"Sorry," Kess says again. "I didn't mean to wake you all up."

Mona, the only one who seems rested and who looks perfect as always, points at the clock on the wall. "I'm glad you did. Have you seen the time?"

Charlie, coming down the stairs behind Gisella, rubs his rumbling belly. "No, but I'm guessing it's almost lunch."

"Eleven thirty, yes." Mona walks over to the stove.

"I was thinking pancakes. How does that sound?"

"Great!" several voices call out at once.

I stand up to make room for D'Maeo and take Vicky in my arms when I reach my own chair at the other head of the table. "You look tired."

She shakes me off. "I'll be fine. You got rid of the curses, remember?" It comes out blunt, and once again, my doubts rise to the surface. *Is something going on with her?*

After a big yawn, Jeep slams his fist onto the table. "What's our next step?"

Mona raises the spatula in her hand. "After lunch, I want to go see if Shelton Banks is back in prison."

Taylar flexes his arms and cracks his neck. "I still feel great, so I think our plan to get him convicted is working."

My muscles relax a little. "Well, that's one less thing to worry about."

Jeep twirls his hat in his hands. "I think our first priority should be to find and save the eighth soul."

Vicky drops into her chair. "Maybe we can split up again, because I really need to find out how to create the nine circles of Hell. There was something in the book about it, but it was a bit vague."

Blank stares answer her, and I realize the others don't know about Vicky's ancestor and her powers yet. Briefly, I meet Vicky's eyes and ask her silently which one of us is going to tell them. She closes her eyes for a second and gives me a small smile. "I've got something important to tell you guys."

She gives them a summary of what we found out and shows them the picture of Isabel, her great-great-grandmother, when Mona hands her the book. She sounds much happier about it than yesterday, and that only feeds my worries.

Gisella shakes her head at me. "I can't believe you didn't see the resemblance when Charon showed you the memory, Dante. Vicky looks so much like her."

I pull my thoughts back to the conversation. "She did remind me of someone, I just—"

Vicky puts her hand on my leg and squeezes gently, comfortingly. "He was in the Underworld, with the ferryman. He got sucked into a memory about Satan getting trapped in Hell. Anyone in that position would be overwhelmed and confused."

I send her a grateful and relieved smile. *I'm worrying too much. Vicky is tired, and she's still processing the responsibility that was dropped on her.*

The werecat-witch nods, her eyes on the book. "That's true."

I pat Vicky's hand. "At least now I know why Charon showed me that memory."

Suddenly, Vicky sits up straight. "Hey, maybe he also knows how it works."

I frown. "There's probably more about that in the book."

She shakes her head. "No, there isn't. All it says is that I need to wake up this power somehow, and then I'll know what to do."

My frown deepens. "How do you know? We only

read a couple of pages."

She gives me a quick kiss on the lips. "I went through the whole book this morning when everyone was still asleep. When I couldn't find anything more about it, I went back to bed."

Mona puts a plate in front of her, and Vicky breathes in the delicious smell.

"Eat this," the fairy godmother says. "It will make up for the lack of sleep."

Vicky slides her chair closer to the table and stuffs a forkful of pancake into her mouth. She chews with her eyes closed, and I can see Mona's magic dancing under her see-through skin.

"Oh my goodness, this is sooo good, Mona." She licks her lips several times. "You've outdone yourself."

A sad longing rises to my throat. I can almost hear Mom singing Abba while she throws the pancakes in the air. Suddenly I have difficulty swallowing. My vision gets blurry.

"What's the matter?" Mona places a hand on my shoulder. "I thought you liked pancakes?"

I wipe my eyes and smile at her. "I do like pancakes. I just wish someone was here baking them with you."

"Oh, honey, I miss her too." She wraps her arms around me, and sparks jump from her hands, spreading over my body rapidly. "She'll be back with us soon. I feel it in my gut."

"I hope you're right."

"Your premonition was promising, wasn't it?"

"Yes and no," I grumble.

Mona rubs my back. "We'll make sure only the good parts come true."

When she rises, I grab her and pull her back for a real hug. "Thank you, Mona," I whisper in her ear. "For taking care of us all, for sticking with me. For everything."

"I wouldn't want it any other way."

Once we've all got a pancake under our belts, we discuss our next plan.

"I think we should go and see Charon," Vicky says.

I rub my face briskly to chase away the last of the sadness lingering behind my eyes. "I'm not sure that's wise."

"Why not?"

"Well, he clearly stated he didn't want to see me in his world again. And he didn't want me to disturb any other worlds either."

"Of course not," D'Maeo says, standing up to take his empty plate back to Mona and steal a kiss. "It might be dangerous for him to be seen with you. He's supposed to be neutral."

I hand him my plate when he holds out his hand. "That's the other reason why I don't think we should see him. He *is* neutral. All he wants is for the worlds to keep their balance."

Maël gestures to the old ghost that she's had enough. She readjusts her cape before she turns to me. "Charon is fond of you. That is what he said. And not only that, he knows we need to win this to keep the balance in the universe."

I turn the cup of coffee in front of me around and around. "So, you think he won't mind it if we pay him a visit?"

The ghost queen wipes a bit of sugar from the corner of her mouth. "I think he will be pleased, but to be honest… you never know with Charon. He can be fickle."

"And by fickle you mean…" I pause, and when she doesn't answer, I finish my own sentence. "He can change his mind about me and lock me in the Underworld?"

She straightens the golden headpiece that rests on her curls. "Yes, that is what I mean."

"So it's a bad idea," I summarize.

D'Maeo suddenly sits up straight. "Not if you bring a gift. Charon loves gifts."

Kessley frowns. "How do you know?"

He smiles. "Stories."

"What kind of stories?"

Jeep leans back in his chair and folds his hands together behind his head. "Don't you guys know the story of Orpheus and Eurydice?"

"Sounds like something from Greek mythology," Charlie voices my thoughts.

D'Maeo shrugs. "Well, most of those stories are true. Haven't you figured that out yet?"

"All kinds of stories turn out to be true. Heaven,

Hell, angels, the Underworld." I bring my hands to my head and move them sideways, imitating an explosion with my mouth. "At this point, I'd believe anything."

Dylan leans on the table, closer to Jeep. "Tell us about Orpheus and Eurydice."

The tattooed ghost unfolds his hands and sits up straight. He takes off his hat and places it in front of him. His fingers follow the rim of the fabric. "The whole story is too long to tell now, but what's important to us is that Orpheus was a legendary magical singer. His singing could move the earth, literally. Nobody could resist it. When he met Eurydice, a nymph, he fell in love instantly. They got married, but soon after, fate struck. Eurydice was bitten by a snake, and she died."

"How sad," Kessley says, taking Taylar's hand and squeezing it.

"It was very sad. But Orpheus couldn't accept her death, so he went after her."

"He went to the Underworld?" Gisella asks.

"Exactly. And there he asked Charon to let him pass so he could get his wife back."

"And Charon said yes?" Vicky asks incredulously.

Jeep laughs. "Of course not. But then Orpheus started to sing." He raises his eyebrows at me, urging me to come to my own conclusions.

"His singing enchanted Charon?" I ask.

"Not literally. But Charon was so touched by his song that he decided to grant Orpheus passage." He raises a finger. "But only once. He had to find his own way back."

When he falls silent, I finally understand what he's saying. "You want me to sing to Charon?"

"Yes. He likes gifts, especially ones that come from the heart."

"I can sing from the heart, but it won't sound good."

"Sure it will," D'Maeo says. "You can cast a spell." He grins.

I slam my hand on the table. "Jeep! You're a genius!"

He points his thumb at D'Maeo. "Actually, he is. He's the one that came up with this."

"You're both genius!"

My eyes fall upon Maël sitting quietly next to the old ghost. She doesn't look very happy, and my elation fades quickly.

"Do you think it will work, Maël?" I ask her.

She looks up, startled. "Sorry, I was lost in thought for a moment. Yes, I think this will improve the odds of him helping us."

I take out my Book of Spells and flip to an empty page. "Okay… a spell that makes me sing like a nightingale."

"Not literally," Vicky warns me.

I snort at the thought of me chirping like a bird. "Don't worry, I'll phrase it well."

Gisella clears her throat. "You should probably sing together."

I exchange a quick look with Vicky, and when she slowly nods, I turn back to Jeep and D'Maeo. "Okay, and what do we sing then? Somehow I doubt a simple pop song will do the trick."

Charlie's lips form an amused grin. "It sounds like Charon is a sucker for a good love story, you know, so you should probably sing about yourselves."

"Why?" Kessley asks. "Their love isn't tragic."

D'Maeo pulls Mona onto his lap and sighs. "It will be, just like ours."

The whole table falls silent except for Kess, who shakes her head. "I don't get it."

Vicky's hand finds mine under the table, and our fingers entwine. I try to explain it to Kess, but my throat clogs up with emotions. Sorrow, grief, even anger. At Satan, at myself, at the universe.

Eventually, Maël speaks up. "As soon as our battle with Lucifer is over, we will all move on. Our job as a Shield will be completed."

Kessley's mouth falls open. She lowers her head. "So Dante and Vicky, D'Maeo and Mona, they will be separated."

"Exactly," D'Maeo says hoarsely.

"That *is* tragic. You were meant for each other."

"Yeah..." I breathe in and out slowly before bending over my Book of Spells. I should probably tell them about the deal I made to keep D'Maeo here, but I can't process Vicky's response to that right now. The only way to drown out the depressing thoughts is to focus on this spell. The writing of the lyrics for the song will be tough enough. Especially since it has to come from the heart.

Vicky moves her chair closer to mine. "I'll help you with the song."

I kiss her on the cheek and squeeze my eyes shut to hold back the tears.

I open my eyes again when I hear someone standing up. It's D'Maeo, at the other end of the table. "While you work on that spell, we should discuss a way to find the next soul and to fight the tornado demons."

"That would be great." I nod at the ghost mage. "Dylan knows how to beat the demons."

The young mage blushes. "I think so, yes."

Charlie rubs his hands together. "Great! Tell us."

Vicky moves a little closer to me when I bend over my notebook again. "You know, we'll figure something out," she whispers.

I rest my head against hers, glad that she acts like herself again. "I hope so."

"We will," she insists. "After all, I'm the great-great-granddaughter of the Devil himself. I should be able to find a way around death."

She smirks when I turn my head to her.

"I knew you'd find something positive about that." I kiss her again and sit up straight. "And now we've got work to do. I've got a spell and a song to write, and you guys have a soul and some demons to find."

"If only the Cards of Death were still delivered to us," Taylar says. "That would make things a whole lot easier."

"Don't worry about that," I say. "We found the last two souls without the cards; we can do it again."

CHAPTER 8

The others are still discussing a strategy to find the tornado demons and take them out when Vicky and I finish the spell and song. We've written it to the music of *Nothing compares 2 U*, a song that used to bring Mom to tears after Dad left.

When I came up with the idea of using this song, I told Vicky I could keep most of the original lyrics, since they're pretty fitting. But she rejected that immediately, telling me a song with our own lyrics would make a better impression, and I had to agree.

Vicky wrote her parts, and I wrote mine, and when we read each other's lines, we both had to wipe away some tears. I guess that's a good sign.

Now, I stand up and pick up my Book of Spells. "Let's go to the annex to set everything up."

Vicky agrees. The others barely notice us leaving; they're so wrapped up in their discussion.

The set-up for this spell is easy and takes us only a couple of minutes. Then we stand in the middle of the circle of herbs we made and each take a deep breath. Vicky grabs my hand when I hold up my Book of Spells. I count down from three and we say the words together.

"Take our voices, one by one,
and turn them into something strong."

We both light a candle before continuing.

"Mesmerizing we will be,
when we make the ferryman see.
Make him hear our desperate call
of how our love can conquer all."

We light the other two candles and finish together.

"Change our voices, change them now,
and let our song be heard somehow."

The candle flames stretch and free themselves from their wicks. They whirl around us and push us closer together. I smile at Vicky as the flames light up her whole body, shining through her like an angelic light. Then the flames dive over our heads and into our mouths. Heat spreads through my throat, and I feel a sudden urge to sing. I quickly take the folded piece of paper on which we scribbled our lyrics, and hold it up for both of us to read.

The first lines burst out of me like fireworks, lights included.

"I've been longing for you, my whole life.
I never thought that we would meet."

I can hear silence descending on the kitchen before Vicky continues.

"I saw you lying there and fell in love.
And I knew you were the one."

Her voice is like nothing I've ever heard before, even more beautiful than mine. It's as if all other sound around us ceases, as if we suck everything into a vacuum where only our voices can be heard. Before I open my mouth to sing the next lines, I see our friends appearing one by one in the doorway. Their eyes are wide, their mouths open in awe.

"Then the world slowly began to tumble down.
You were there to keep me alive."

I turn my head and Vicky's gaze sucks me in. The next lines come out a bit hoarse.

"We faced all of the threats and dangers
side by side.
And you were there, yes you were there

when I needed you the most."

Heat and cold shoot through my heart when our voices entwine.

"But soon we'll move on,
soon we'll move on, alone."

All I see now is Vicky's face. Her beautiful face and her piercing blue eyes. They reflect everything I feel. Love, happiness, sorrow, longing, regret. I keep singing, but I don't even know what the words are anymore. The spell has taken over my voice, but my thoughts are only with her. With how much she means to me, how much I want her with me forever. My heart contracts painfully when I try to imagine my life without her. It's empty, worthless. I'd rather go with her than stay here without her. And once again I ask myself: why, out of all the girls I ever met, did I have to fall for the one who died?

Her lips stop moving, and she bends closer to me. We kiss like we never kissed before, and all my emotions blur together. It's such an overload of feelings that I struggle for air when she releases me. She seems to be equally shaken, and we lean on each other until the feeling passes. A dull throbbing is left behind in my heart when sound starts to trickle into my ears again. Not that there's much sound at all. There's only a soft creak, like a moan, made by the house, the gentle rustling of the wind outside and a collective sigh coming from the doorway.

We hold each other tightly before looking around.

Charlie is the first one to speak. "Wow," he says. "Just… wow, you know?"

Gisella, holding his hand, nods silently.

Kessley rubs her arms. "Yeah, that was intense." Taylar wraps his arms around her from behind.

Mona and D'Maeo are also huddled closely together, and Jeep is gently rubbing Maël's back. Dylan seems a bit lost, staring at the floor.

I want to walk over to them to give them all a hug, but a loud rumbling stops me in my tracks.

Just outside the herb circle, the air splits open to reveal a dark world with swirling rivers in the sky.

Water trickles in from the bottom of the portal and forms a large puddle on the annex floor. The bough of Charon's creepy skull- and bone-covered boat breaks through. The hand with the lantern on the high bow stops inches from my nose, but I don't step back. Charon is neutral; we have nothing to fear from him. And if he had evil intentions, he wouldn't have been able to find Darkwood Manor.

I bow when the figure of the ferryman, clad in a black, ripped-up robe, comes into view. "Charon, it's an honor to see you again."

A chuckle rises from deep within his throat. "It's nice to see you again too, Dante. But to you it can't be a surprise. I watched you cast the spell, heard you put in a line to make me hear your song. You wanted me to come here."

83

I nod. "I knew you didn't want me to enter your world again before I died, so…"

He smiles his creepy smile. "You're a smart boy. I like your confidence too. You had no way of knowing if I would come."

Vicky clears her throat. "How did you watch us?"

Charon spreads his arms. "I have my ways."

I think of the Lake of Remembrance that he showed me. The lake in which he keeps memories of countless dead people. He must have more lakes like that one. A lake in which he can see what the living are doing maybe. If only I could take a peek in it. See what Trevor is up to and check on Mom…

"I suspect you want something in exchange for that mesmerizing song," he states in his raspy voice. His sunken eyes bore into mine from under his dark hood. "Tell me what it is."

My friends have never been so quiet. It's like they're afraid to move. Even Gisella and Kessley don't make a sound. I'm grateful for that, since Charon can be grumpy about people interfering in his business or interrupting him. He wasn't too happy when I accidentally got stuck in a strange world. Of course, I did disturb the balance of the universe with the portal I made, so he had a right to be angry, but still… an angry Charon gives me the creeps. Even a friendly Charon is frightening.

I suppress a shiver when I look him in the eyes. "We were hoping you could tell us how to activate Vicky's powers."

His lipless mouth grows wider into something that resembles a smile. "Oh, you finally understand why I showed you the memory of Lucifer and Isabel."

"I do, and I'm grateful for the chance to see that. But Vicky has no idea how to do what Isabel did, and her birthmark is only half visible. We were hoping you could give us some advice."

"And a way to defeat Beelzebub," Vicky adds.

Even without eyebrows, I can tell Charon is frowning when he turns to Vicky. I want to nudge her, tell her to keep quiet, but I can't without the ferryman noticing.

Vicky has no trouble looking at him. Her back remains straight, and she doesn't tense up at all.

"You are so much like her," Charon says. To my surprise, he sounds pleased, affectionate even.

"You knew Isabel?" Vicky asks.

Charon leans on his staff with the bones wrapped around it. "Oh yes, I've been around for a long, long time. I saw Lucifer fall from Heaven. Watched him build an empire. Watched him change more and more into the monster he is today."

Vicky frowns. "And you didn't stop him?"

Charon leans forward. "My dear, stopping him would have tipped the balance in the universe. As much as I hate to say it, we need evil as much as we need good." He adjusts his hood with a bony hand, giving us a glimpse of his sunken eyes. "But now, evil is rising to the surface again, and once more we need a powerful woman to lock the king of Hell in a prison made of circles."

"So you'll help us?" I ask tentatively.

He gives us a small bow. "Yes, I will help you, just like I helped Isabel many centuries ago."

CHAPTER 9

Charon slides back and beckons us. "Please, step into the boat."

Vicky obeys without hesitation. I look back at my friends, still standing silently in the doorway. "Will you be okay?"

"Of course," D'Maeo answers. "We will continue our search for the next soul."

"What must happen, will happen," Charon says cryptically.

I step inside the boat. "Be careful," I tell my friends.

"You too," Charlie says, putting his arm tighter around Gisella.

The water rises and takes us back through the portal, which closes behind us fast. The air in the Underworld is cold, and I can barely see anything in the dim light that shines above the rivers in the sky.

Sharp mountains I don't remember rise in the distance, and when I see the surface moving, an image of crawling bodies pops into my mind, like the ones slithering through the rivers above us.

The light from the lantern hanging from the bow is also faint, and I pull in my arms when a cold mist touches me. *Not this again.* I clearly remember the way the mist tried to grab me when I was here before. Staying close to Charon is the only way I know to prevent it from reaching me, so I shuffle a little closer to him. He looks down at me when his rags touch my hand and smiles. I try to smile back, but my lips don't cooperate. This world makes me uncomfortable; *he* makes me uncomfortable. I can't imagine coming here after I die, crossing the river Lethe and facing where I will end up. All of my memories will be taken by this river and transported to the Lake of Remembrance. *Does that mean I won't remember anything from my life? Will I forget about my friends, Vicky, Mom and Dad? Will I forget I fought the Devil?*

A cold hand touches my shoulder, and this time, I can't stop the shiver running through me.

"Do not worry," Charon says. "You are destined for great things. You both are." He nods at Vicky, who is watching our surroundings with interest rather than fear. "You have already accomplished so much, and there is more to come. I feel it, here." His skeleton hand lets go of my shoulder and taps the place where his heart is, if he has one. "The river Lethe will take the memories of each soul that passes it, but those are only copies. You will remember it all. Each victory and defeat, each joyful and dismal event, each heartbreak."

I rub my arms at the thought of losing Vicky and hope he can read my mind again. If anyone can keep Vicky from moving on, it's him.

Charon shakes his head. "Your face is an open book, Dante. Do not show this to your enemies. They will use it against you."

Honestly, I don't think it will make much difference, since it's no secret that Vicky and I are together, but I wouldn't dare go against Charon, so I nod vaguely.

His face softens. "I can only help you with one problem, Dante. If I do more, my position in this universe will be threatened. Nobody likes it when neutral beings interfere too much."

I almost groan. *Why does everything have to be so difficult? Charon could probably solve this whole battle with one snap of his fingers. Why isn't he the one chosen to keep the balance?* I ball my fists until my fingers protest. When I look up again, Charon is watching me closely, leaning on his staff. There's a twinkle in his eyes.

"You still don't understand how all of this works, do you?"

I'm not sure how to answer that. I mean, there's a lot I still don't know, but I do know that Charon is powerful. He could end the battle easily.

Vicky grabs my hand without speaking, and I glance at her.

"We were born to do this, babe," she says. "Have faith in us."

"But—"

"Let me explain something to you," Charon interrupts me. He straightens up and waves his staff, indicating the vast world around us. "I am the ruler of the Underworld. I am powerful, in a way. But my power does not reach beyond this world. In reality, I am no more than a guide."

I watch the rivers meander above us and shiver when I see the bodies that reach out from them. I tear my gaze away and look at the ferryman. "Your power does reach beyond this world, doesn't it? You pulled me from another world when I got stuck, and you gave me back my memories when they were stolen. You can open portals into different worlds. There must be more that you can do. More than me."

Charon chuckles and places his bony hand on my shoulder again. "Dear, dear boy. Do you still not see it?"

He's starting to get on my nerves. *Why doesn't he just tell me what he means?*

Vicky squeezes my hand. "I see it."

My confusion grows when they exchange a knowing look. Vicky smiles at me and pulls me close. "You still don't see how powerful you are, babe. You still don't truly believe in yourself."

"Sure I do. I believe we can beat the Devil. We've all grown so much; we trained a lot and..." I fall silent when she places her finger against my lips.

"Not we, Dante. You. This is about you."

I pull back. "No, we were talking about Charon. About him being able to end this fight all by himself."

The ferryman is still looking at me like I'm a six-year-old who doesn't understand why two plus two equals four. "After eons of existence, I know my strengths and weaknesses. I know my limits, and yes, they are there. Everyone has limits. You are right, I can reach beyond my own world, but my powers there are limited. I can influence memories because all memories eventually end up in my world." He waves at the dark around us. "This world. But you can influence memories too. You can not only cast spells but write them yourself. Sure, you are still training, learning, but the power to accomplish almost anything is within you."

I open my mouth to answer, but he carries on.

"And I can open portals, but so can you. The difference is…" He leans closer and pushes his finger against my chest. "You have power in every world. Mine is confined to the Underworld. This is why I am the guide, and you are the chosen one."

I rub the place where he poked me. "You're serious."

"Very."

They both look at me expectantly.

"What?" I ask.

"You need to choose. What is it you want from me the most?"

I bite my lip. Of course, I already know what I

need to choose, but it's not easy to say it out loud. It feels a bit like betraying Vicky.

She reaches out to rub my back, and I blink to get rid of the image of her walking into the light. "You know what I'll choose. There's only one right answer." I take a deep breath and look Charon in the eye. "Please show us how to activate Vicky's power to create the nine circles of Hell."

The ferryman pushes his staff into the water, and the boat comes to a sudden halt. "With pleasure."

He steps out of the boat without lifting his feet, or so it seems, and beckons us. "Come on."

We follow close behind to make sure the mist doesn't grab onto us. There's no water where the ferryman steps, but I sink into it up to my ankles. I don't complain as long as there are no hands reaching out to me. The moaning far above us sends shivers down my back. I try to think happier thoughts, but everything here is so dark and gloomy. The sky is made up of shades of black and gray, and the ground is equally dark. If you're not careful, it will suck every bit of joy out of you.

We walk over an uneven path. Below the mist, I can feel small rocks with something soft in between. I can only hope it's grass or moss, but after the skull path in that unknown world we visited, I have a hard time believing it's something as innocent as that.

After several silent minutes, Charon looks over his shoulder. "You know, the mist feeds on fear. It leaves the confident alone."

I frown down at the claws of grayish white trying to grab my ankles. "It does?"

"Watch Vicky if you don't believe me."

I glance sideways and stumble over a bigger rock. When I land on the rocky ground, the mist swirls around me eagerly, but it doesn't touch me. It doesn't try to swallow me like last time. When I sit up, it creeps nearer. I squint down between the slivers and try to see what the soft stuff on the path is.

It's like ordinary mud, except that it moves. I bend down for a closer look and see the mud moving. It's painting patterns around my feet.

I hold out my hand to touch it. "It's beautiful…"

"Don't do that," Charon says, briskly pulling me back up. "It will suck you in if you get too close."

Vicky steadies me as I sway on my feet, suppressing the urge to reach down again. The mist pulls back as soon as she touches me. There's a clear space around her.

"You've grown more confident." There's amusement in Charon's voice, but it's replaced by a reproachful tone. "But it's not enough yet." He twirls his staff on the ground in thought. "I may have a solution for that." He lifts his staff again, and the hole that was made fills itself up. "After I help Vicky claim her heritage."

"Sounds promising," I whisper to Vicky as we start walking again.

With every step I take, the pull from the mud lessens. *I wonder where it takes you if it pulls you in. Do you become part of the path? Turn into mud yourself? Or do you end up somewhere underneath it?* I'm afraid to ask, and the more I think about it, the closer the mist gets.

Vicky gently touches my fingers. "Relax. We're safe here."

After what feels like forever, the ferryman goes into a dark cave. I try to ignore the chill creeping up from the cold, slippery floor as we walk toward a light in the distance. I make sure I don't touch the rocky walls that spread a musky smell. I don't want to risk coming into contact with any more dangerous species here.

When we finally come to a halt, I find myself staring at Charon's skeleton boat. That's where the light was coming from.

"Charon?" I begin tentatively.

He turns to me with a bright smile. "Yes, Dante?"

"Why did we walk all the way here if your boat was going here anyway?"

"Because the mud needed some time to attach itself to Vicky."

"What do you..?" I look down at our feet so suddenly my neck protests. Vicky's are covered in grease.

She tries to shake it off, but Charon holds up his hand. "Don't do that. We need it for your transition."

I shiver at the word. "Is that dangerous?"

"Not at all. She needs to acknowledge her ancestry to awaken her full powers. This will result in a transition."

Vicky takes in the mud creating patterns on her legs. A mixture of fear and disgust pulls at the corners of her mouth. "A transition into what?"

"Into who you were always supposed to become."

I almost snort. *Great, that clears it up.*

Charon tilts his head. "You will have to trust me."

"I do," we say in unison.

"Good." He gestures at the water. "Please step in, Vicky."

She hesitates and he holds out his skinless hand to her. She takes it, and he guides her in.

"This is the Pool of Awakening. The water will help you accept your heritage. All you have to do is believe in the strength that lies within you." He lets go of her and slides back.

I do the same, even though I want nothing more than to rush into the water and pull Vicky out.

Vicky steps back further and further until only her head is still above the water. I can see the mud clinging to her face now, covering more and more of her skin.

Charon moves his staff sideways to block my way. "Whatever happens, do not interfere."

I swallow the lump that rises to my throat. *Did I make a mistake asking Charon for help?*

My heart beats twice as fast when the water starts to move restlessly. Waves crash into Vicky, who's standing in the middle of the pool like a statue. Her face shows determination and doubt at the same time.

The waves slam together and form into hands that

tip Vicky backwards and lift her out of the water horizontally. She closes her eyes when the mud covers her whole face.

Then it starts to pull at her lips and crawl into her nose. She shakes her head and struggles to free herself from the water's grip.

"Relax," Charon says calmly. "Let it examine you."

She obeys, and the dark grease slips inside her mouth and nose. Her body shudders, and her legs kick, but the water hands keep her in place.

Suddenly, Charon turns to me. "Listen carefully," he whispers. "There is something you need to handle soon."

For the first time since I met him, the ferryman sounds worried. He glances at Vicky's shaking form before continuing in that hushed tone that doesn't suit him. "She is fighting something evil inside her. A sliver of Hell. Something planted, if I am not mistaken, by Satan's right hand."

I gasp. *I knew it! Why did I brush my doubts off so easily?*

"If you don't act soon, Vicky will be a powerful enemy instead of a faithful ally."

"Thank you," I whisper back.

He gives me a curt nod and straightens up.

Vicky stops shaking. The grease flows back out, and she coughs.

I let out a relieved sigh.

But it isn't over yet. One of the water hands reaches for the lantern on the bow of the boat. It carries it over to Vicky's suspended body and presses it against her side.

The mud immediately catches fire, and within seconds, she's completely covered in flames. Her arms and legs jerk as she tries to free herself. Her mouth opens in a scream that sends shivers down my back. I expect her to turn more transparent, to make the fire go through her harmlessly, but her skin only gets clearer. The flames tear at her clothes, her hair smokes, and fire engulfs her face.

Charon raises his staff a bit higher to stop me from diving forward. "Remember, Vicky, you are related to Lucifer; you can withstand any amount of fire. There is no need to fear it. Accept your ancestry."

When Vicky stops screaming, I can only think one thing, which I repeat over and over in my head. *Please don't let her burn, please don't let her burn.*

The flames crackle as they spread. The heat provokes drops of sweat on my forehead, but I don't wipe them away. I'm afraid that if I lose sight of her for one second, she will turn to ash.

"The fire cannot harm you," Charon says in his deep voice. It sounds as if he's hypnotizing her.

And finally, it works. She listens, and she believes.

The corners of her mouth slowly move up. The hands of water push her into a standing position. When she opens her eyes, they glow red for a moment. The hands let go, and she stands there, on the water, completely covered in fire, and smiling. To my relief, it's a sweet smile, not an evil one. Her eyes have returned to their normal light blue. She spreads her arms and performs and elegant turn, like a ballerina. The flames die out as she whirls, and I blink. Even in the dim light of the lantern, which is back on the bow of the boat, she seems brighter. As if a light shines from within her.

She crosses her arms over her chest and sinks into the water. The waves around her get clearer and clearer, as if the darkness seeps out of the Pool. A weight is lifted from my shoulders bit by bit as I watch it happen. I was already afraid there would be darkness within her somewhere, even before Charon told me there really is. Hidden, but ready to strike. A perfect spy in our midst, impossible to beat once she's fully turned. But now that I see her light up the entire Pool of Awakening, I know there is still hope. The water turns her around and around calmly. She comes to a halt with her back to me and Charon. The waves lift her hair, and I can see the incomplete symbol on her neck.

A red line, like a laser, shoots up from below and crawls toward her. It starts to burn lines onto her skin, like a tattoo gun, making the symbol whole inch by inch. The drop at the bottom becomes a lemniscate, and between it and the horizontal *I*, another *I* is drawn. As soon as the laser beam is done, it bursts into hundreds of red specks. The symbol glows red too, and then Vicky shoots up, out of the water. Her head falls backwards, and she spreads her arms again. Without looking, she lands next to the water line, steadily on two feet. Slowly, she brings down her arms and breathes out, lowering her head again. When she opens her eyes, they are a brighter blue than before. I didn't think that was possible, but now it's as if power glows inside them.

She cracks her neck and smiles at us. "I feel great."

"You look great," I say. "Even better than before."

She gestures at my feet. "Throw a rock at me."

My eyebrow shoots up. "What? Why?"

"Just do it."

"Okay…" I pick up a small rock, hold it up and hurl it at her when she nods encouragingly. My heartbeat pounds inside my head, sending a warning with every throb. *She'll kill you, she'll kill you.*

The rock is an inch from her face. She doesn't do anything to stop it from hitting her. Her arms hang by her sides, she doesn't step aside, and she doesn't turn more transparent to make it fly through her. Still… the rock doesn't hit her. It comes to a halt midair. When she narrows her eyes, the rock starts turning, faster and faster, until it's no more than a blur.

"Duck," she tells me, and I obey.

The rock soars over my head and slams into the wall behind me. A small avalanche falls down and stops at my heels.

Charon chuckles. "Well done, my child."

The tension leaves my body. *If Charon doesn't sense any immediate danger, I should be fine.*

I straighten up and gape at my girl, trying to hide

the fact that she scared the shit out of me. "How did you do that? You didn't even move a finger!"

She taps the side of her head.

My mouth is still half open. "You got all that power just by accepting your ancestry?"

Charon gestures for her to turn around. He lifts her hair with his staff, giving us another look at the full symbol. He nods contently and slides back. "Embracing who you are can give someone a great deal of power. Especially if you embrace the good as well as the bad. Nobody is perfect."

Vicky flattens her hair and turns around to face us. "I've accepted that the Devil's blood runs through my veins, but I refuse to give the evil molecules inside it any power."

Charon's face lights up. "I always knew you were more Isabel's great-granddaughter than Lucifer's."

A sudden urge to hug her falls over me, and I give in to it. As soon as I touch her, I pull back though.

"What?" she asks.

"Your skin!" Carefully, I stroke her cheek. "It's warm!"

Her eyes light up. "It is?" She touches her own hand and grins. "I guess I'm more alive now."

My heart flutters at the thought that this could be a first step to keeping her with me. Of course, Charon feels the need to crush that hope with force.

"You're not," he says. "What you're feeling is the Devil's powers running through your veins. His blood has grown hot over the centuries. This is why you're

100

immune to fire now."

Vicky throws her hair over her shoulder. "That's still pretty awesome."

I can't argue with that, and even if I could, there's no time to do so, because Charon has turned around and is making his way out of the cave. "Follow me," he simply says.

CHAPTER 10

This time we don't go far. Charon stands still right outside the cave. He looks around before turning to us. "This spot will do. You might want to get ready for battle."

"What? Why?" I step back and reach for my Morningstar.

"Because I'm opening a portal to Hell."

I want to ask why again, but he is already stretching his arms out in front of him. The air he touches moves. His hands draw the darkness in. A large circle comes to life, light pulsing from its center.

I grab my athame with my free hand. "Be careful."

The light explodes, and once my eyes get used to the sudden brightness, I get a view of what's inside the circle: the smoldering world I've seen in my premonitions too often.

Charon gestures at it calmly. "Hurry inside now.

Behind that rock, you will find your mother. Good luck."

"What?"

It's the only word left that I'm able to produce. I have no clue what's going on anymore.

"Aren't you coming with us?" Vicky asks, throwing a tentative look through the portal.

Charon leans on his stick lazily, as if he's not standing in front of a gateway into the most dangerous realm of all. "Even if I wanted to, I could not. I am merely a guide, remember?"

I finally manage to form a coherent sentence. "Why are you sending us in there?"

"Because you need more confidence. And your mother can give you that."

I glance inside Hell and lick my lips. *It doesn't really matter what his reasons are, does it? I'm given the chance to get Mom back. I'll take it, no matter how dangerous it is.*

Charon waves his staff at the portal. "Go now. I will keep this door open until you get back."

Vicky shows her bravery by stepping through first. I follow close behind, not wanting to leave her in there on her own.

Images from my premonitions fill my vision, and I shake my head to lose them. While I catch up with Vicky, I turn my head in all directions, scanning our surroundings carefully. Sweat is already dripping down my temples and back, and I can't keep my feet on the cracked ground for long, because it's just as scorching hot as I remember. My palms are so wet that I can barely hold on to my weapons. After a couple of steps, I put away my athame and conjure a lightning bolt instead. Much easier to hold on to.

We both freeze when a loud moaning echoes through the air. We position ourselves back-to-back and turn slowly, taking in every inch of the vast, dry landscape. When nothing approaches, Vicky glances at me. "Are you okay? You seem a little... overheated."

Her sincere concern comforts me. *There's still time to kill the evil inside her. Charon wouldn't have sent us in here if there wasn't.* I wipe some sweat from my eyes with the back of my hand, and blink. "I'll manage, even though I'm not fire and heat proof, like you."

I keep moving from one foot to the other to prevent my soles from burning while she stands still. There's not a drop of sweat on her face.

"Let's keep going," I urge her. "I want to get out of here as soon as possible."

After several more feet, we finally reach the rock Charon pointed out. It seemed so close by, but it must have taken us at least five minutes to reach. We both stop to listen intently for sounds coming from the other side of it. If Mom is there, she's bound to have company, of the not so nice kind. We're actually lucky to have gotten this far without bumping into a demon of some sort. Or the man himself.

I suppress a shiver. I don't want to think about what Satan has done to my mother. Or the state we'll find her in.

Vicky beckons me. We've waited long enough. There are no sounds, save for the occasional moaning coming from afar and the crackling of fire in the distance.

We step around the rock with our weapons raised. At first, I think Charon was mistaken. There's no one here. But then I hear the shuffling of feet and someone mumbling softly.

"Mom!" It comes out as a whispered shout while I dive forward and drop down on my knees, clutching the bars of her underground prison with both hands, even though they're hot too.

Vicky manages to grab my folded-up Morningstar before it falls down.

Mom looks up, startled. A deep frown appears in her forehead. "Dante? What are you doing? Did you make a hole in the ceiling?"

"Are you okay?" I ask.

She throws me a smile, but it's fake. Robot-like. "Of course. You know how happy I am. But I would like to see more of you, honey."

"I'm afraid she's more brainwashed than the last time we saw her," Vicky whispers to me.

I swallow the worry that climbs up into my throat. "Would you like to go on a trip with me, Mom?"

Regret falls over her face, and she lowers her head. "I would, honey, but I promised Trevor I'd wait for him here."

"Oh, it's fine," I tell her, trying to sound cheerful. "He'll be there too. He asked me to come pick you

105

up."

She looks up again, and now her smile is genuine. "He did? That is lovely!"

I pull the bars as hard as I can, but of course, they don't move an inch. With a grunt of pain, I pull my hands back and blow on them to cool them down.

Vicky gently pushes me aside. "Let me try." She pulls up, left and right, but nothing happens.

"What are you doing?" Mom asks, sounding a bit worried now.

"Just a little remodeling, Mom. It's a surprise for Trevor."

"How sweet of you!"

Vicky gives up. She stands up and rubs her sore hands. "You should try a spell."

I'm about to agree when someone clears their throat behind us.

We whirl around to face Trevor. He seems rather comfortable here, except for the sweat building up on his forehead. He's wearing comfortable pants this time, with a striped shirt on top. His black leather shoes are clean despite the dust and sand blowing up around us.

He folds his arms over his chest. "I'm impressed. I didn't think you'd find her here."

I copy his stance. "I didn't think you'd leave her here. I guess you don't love her that much after all."

His lower lip trembles in fury. "I love her more than anyone ever will."

"Then why did you lock her up, and in Hell of all

places?"

The earth elemental takes a step closer and prods me in the chest with his finger. His face turns half rocky as he tries to keep his temper. "Because there's no place as impenetrable as Hell."

Vicky snorts. "Impenetrable? Really? As you can see, there's no such thing."

Trevor steps sideways to block the cage. "You will not take her from me. She's happy here."

I conjure a lightning ball in my hand and hold it up. "I'll tell you what, if you lift the spell on her and she still wants to stay here, with you, I'll leave the both of you alone. If not…" I throw the ball into the air and catch it without taking my eyes off him.

Trevor's teeth crunch as he grinds them together in frustration. "She's not ready to truly love me yet. I'm working on it."

I raise an eyebrow. "Oh, I can tell. Lovely setting you've created."

His left cheek turns to stone. I'm really pissing him off. Maybe that's a bad idea, but I can't stop.

"She will never love you without a spell, Trevor. You know why?" I wait for any kind of response and get it in the form of a grunt. "Because you're a creep. And the fact that your best friend wants to destroy the world has something to do with it too."

To my surprise, it's Vicky who answers instead of Trevor. "No, there's more to him than that."

I turn my head to find out if she's kidding and find her looking Trevor in the eye. She must be reading his emotions and sensing something good inside him, even though her powers don't work on him. After all, she's a great non-magical empath too.

Trevor's rocky skin turns back to its soft human form, and my anger subsides a bit.

I wipe more sweat from my forehead. "There's something I need to tell you, Trevor. I had a premonition."

He looks at me expectantly. There's no judgment in his expression. Patiently, he waits for me to continue.

"I saw you, Mom and Lucifer, here in Hell. He told you to use Mom to get to me, and then he said…" I try to recall his exact words. "If you fail, you will suffer for eternity, and you will take your crush with you."

Trevor doesn't respond, but I see a small shiver running through him.

"Please let me take her home before it's too late. If she wants to see you, I won't stop her."

The earth elemental glances down through the bars and squeezes the bridge of his nose. "I can't."

"You have to, because I'm not risking her falling into Satan's hands. You promised to keep her safe, but you only made things worse. If you leave her here, she won't survive."

I try to keep the rising panic from my voice, but part of it seeps through. It makes Trevor look up.

When he doesn't speak, Vicky does. "He's telling the truth."

Trevor cracks his neck. "I believe you. And the way I see it, she is only in danger because you are still alive."

Before it sinks in what he means, he has changed into his full rock form. When he charges, I make a feeble attempt to hit him with my athame. But I'm too slow, and his transformed skin is too solid. The weapon bounces off as if it's made of rubber. Trevor knocks me over and pulls his arm back to punch me in the face. Vicky slams into him, but he pushes her off easily.

While he's distracted, I raise my hand to the side of his head. A lightning bolt hits him, and he tumbles sideways. I imagine large hail drops raining down on him. They fall from the sky but melt on their way down because of the scorching heat. Which is also burning right through my clothes…

With a burst of energy, combined with lightning from both hands, I push Trevor off of me. My hair and skin sizzle where it touched the ground.

"Why are we fighting, Trevor?" I ask when he jumps back to his feet. "We both want to keep Mom safe."

He turns his head briefly to check where Vicky is, but she's waiting for my cue.

"You want to take her from me," he fumes.

"And you want to take her from *me*," I counter.

"I've been good to her!"

My mouth falls open. "What? You put a spell on her!"

"Only temporarily." He shakes his head. "I can't let her go. I need more time to make her see we belong together."

This chatting is obviously getting us nowhere, so I prepare to hit him with a wave of cold water. I could use a little cool liquid myself anyway.

From the cage underground, Mom's voice drifts up. "Trevor? Dante? I'm ready to go."

A wave forms behind the earth elemental. It's about to slam into him when the ground trembles. I lose focus, and the wave falls down and changes into a sad, useless stream. Thundering footsteps draw near, and a worried frown forms between Trevor's solid eyebrows.

"The gate keepers," he mumbles.

The image of the warriors that pierced Mom's body when she was in Hell before flashes before my eyes. I saw them in a premonition, but it feels like I met them in person. I peer around the rock while Vicky keeps an eye on Trevor.

There they are. The two gate keepers of Hell. Giants with spikes all over their legs and horns on their heads. The sight of the staffs they carry makes me sick. I forgot how gruesome these were, covered in dried up blood and with a human spine wrapped around it. Flames reflect in their bright red chest plates as they stomp over to us.

I know one thing for sure: I do not want to see them up close.

I step back and take Vicky's hand. "We need to go,

now."

"What about your mother?"

I grind my teeth as I glance at Trevor. "She'll have to wait. And she'd better be alive and in one piece when I come back."

Strangely enough, Trevor looks just as scared as I feel. He tries to hide it by flexing his thick arms. "Don't expect me to change my mind. Susan is still mine."

"She'll never be yours," I hiss, digging my fingers into my upper legs and almost forgetting about the approaching gate keepers.

"She will," he insists. "But I've got to go now. Lots of work to do to create the perfect world for my love." And with that, he turns around and walks away fast.

The trembling under our feet gets worse. We hide with our backs against the rock.

"I'll be back, Mom," I whisper to the bars of her cage.

"I know, Dante. I have always believed in you," she says.

My heart contracts at the thought of leaving her here, but I can't imagine us taking on those gate keepers without help.

When I feel the rock shudder against my back, I beckon Vicky and start to move. We make our way slowly to the other side of the rock. I peer around it and see the heavy feet disappearing. Quickly, I move along. I squeeze Vicky's hand restlessly and barely dare to breathe. In the distance, I can see the portal. It's only a small dark spot, and you would probably miss it if you didn't know it was there.

The trembling has stopped, and Mom's voice calls out. "Oh hi! Have you seen Trevor? He was supposed to have a surprise for me."

I bite my lip and pray she won't mention me.

A low grunt answers her, followed by a short silence. I imagine the warriors scanning the surroundings and checking out the tracks on the ground. My blood freezes in my veins, even though heat still burns my skin. *The constant wind has suddenly dropped, leaving our tracks in the dry ground uncovered. They will lead the gate keepers right to us!*

I've barely finished my thought when there's a loud grunt from behind us.

A deep voice bellows something incomprehensible. It probably means something like 'intruders!'.

In a reflex, I grab Vicky's hand, spring to my feet and run as fast as I can.

The ground starts to tremble as the gate keepers give chase. It moves so much that we almost lose our balance.

"Can you create a wave to distract them?" Vicky asks.

"I'll try."

Without slowing down, I imagine a large wave rising up behind the red warriors and slamming down on them. In my head, they are lifted from their feet. I make another wave crash down on them from the other side.

The ground stops moving, the sound of their heavy footsteps ceases.

At that moment, Vicky comes to a sudden halt and turns around.

I want to ask her what she's doing, but then I see movement on the large rock we hid behind. One side rises slowly.

The gate keepers are shaking the water from their heads and rising to their feet, so I create another wave to make sure they stay down.

"Come on, let's go," I urge Vicky.

But she's staring at the rock as if she wants to burn a hole in it, gritting her teeth and balling her fists.

"We can't beat them," I continue. "We should get back to the portal before they get up again."

One of the warriors plants his staff into the cracked surface and pulls himself up in a sudden burst of energy. Steam rises from his nostrils as he growls at me and spits out more words I can't understand. Except for two that are pronounced clearly. "Chosen one."

Oh, great, they know who I am.

I hit them with another wave, but I've lost the element of surprise, and the warrior stays upright without much effort. His colleague rises to his feet too. They both point their staff at me, and I remember how they made Mom levitate in my premonition, right before they cursed her with red ash.

That same ash rises from the tips of their staffs and soars through the air, straight at me and Vicky.

I reach for Vicky's hand when the rock suddenly shoots into the sky. With a slight movement of her head, Vicky makes it fall down. It knocks the two warriors over as if they are bowling pins. The red ash evaporates, and Vicky's body goes limp. I catch her, take one look at the hand searching for the spine-covered staff, and lift my girl from the ground. With her hanging motionless in my arms, I hurry back to the portal. My heart pounds wildly in my chest. *Will I make it?* I try to conjure another wave, or something else to slow our pursuers down, but it's not easy to concentrate when Vicky is out cold and I'm the only one who can get us to safety. Staying upright is hard enough at this speed, and with the weight I'm carrying, and I need all of my self-restraint not to look back.

As I get closer to the portal, it becomes clearer, and once I'm only a couple of steps away from it, I can make out Charon's form. He's waiting patiently on the other side.

"Duck," he says calmly, and when I do, red ash soars over my head.

I expect the ferryman to block it or perform some kind of counterattack, but all he does is close the portal for a brief moment. The ash continues on its path and vanishes from sight as the portal reappears.

Charon beckons me. "Come on, quickly."

Two steps and I've reached him. I stumble through the portal and collapse against the outer wall of the cave, almost dropping Vicky. I manage to lay her down gently before my legs give in altogether.

The portal is already closed, and Charon nods at me contently. "You did well."

"Well?!" I take a couple of deep breaths. My lungs gratefully inhale the cold, damp air of this world. The burn marks on my skin from the hot ground in Hell tingle and pound.

"Yes, I'm proud of you."

"You're...? What... I... Mom..." I stumble over my words as I try to make sense of what he's saying.

Finally I gesture at Vicky's still form at my feet. "You call this well?" I point at the spot where the portal was only seconds ago. "And I left Mom behind!"

Charon nods patiently. "Yes, you had no other choice."

"You knew this was going to happen?" My voice rises in anger and disbelief. "Why did you send me there then?"

His gaze flicks from Vicky to me. "This was a final test for the both of you. To see if you were able to make the right choice in difficult times. Also, you needed to hear what your mother had to say about you. Her faith in you is stronger than the spell she's under."

I avert my eyes and bend over Vicky. "You knew we wouldn't be able to save her, and you still sent us in there." I caress Vicky's cheek and whisper to her. "Wake up, babe. We're safe."

"The toughest lessons are also the most valuable ones," the ferryman says. "And I sent you in there for another reason."

"Which is what?" I ask with a sigh.

"You needed to have that conversation with Trevor. He needed to know about your premonition. To make sure he'll make the right decision later."

I bite my lip and banish the image of Mom down there in that cage from my mind. "I'd rather have taken care of Trevor and have Mom here with us now." My voice trembles a bit, and suddenly I feel Charon's hand on my shoulder.

"Do not worry. Trevor is not ready to do the right thing yet, but he will be. Soon."

He squeezes my shoulder and waits for me to look up. "Trust me."

I nod. "I do." Then I wipe Vicky's hair from her forehead. "Will she be okay?"

The ferryman straightens up. "Yes. She used too much of her new powers. All she needs is a little rest." He lowers his voice. "And this is the perfect time to take care of that problem we talked about earlier."

I nod. "What about the circles of Hell? Does she know how to create them now?"

"She will soon."

He turns away from us and moves his staff. I can't see exactly what he's doing, but a new portal opens in front of him. Through it, I can see my bedroom at Darkwood Manor.

Charon slides aside and gestures at it. "I wish you luck in the final part of your battle, Dante. I will be watching you."

I feel the urge to shake his hand, to thank him, but that is such a human gesture, and it wouldn't show enough respect. Instead, I bow.

His hood hides most of his face, but I can see a glimpse of a smile on his skinless face before he bows back.

"Thank you for everything," I say. Then I bend over to take Vicky in my arms and carry her through the portal.

I lay her down gently on the bed, and when I turn back, the portal is gone.

I kiss Vicky on her temple, take off her shoes and cover her with the blanket.

"I'll be right back."

In the hallway, I softly call out to Mona. "Can you watch her for a minute, please? Call me immediately if she wakes up," I say when she appears.

She nods. "Sure."

When I'm halfway down the stairs, my friends are already waiting for me at the bottom.

Jeep is the first one to speak. "Where's Vicky?" There's worry in his voice.

"I put her to bed. She used a bit too much of her new powers." I give him a weak smile. "But she did save us by doing so. I'm not sure we could've escaped

Hell otherwise."

Several mouths fall open.

"You were in Hell?" Charlie asks.

I walk past them and slide down into my chair at the head of the table, suddenly too tired to stand. Everyone takes their usual seats while I search for a place to start.

One thing keeps rolling around in my head, and eventually I say it out loud. "I left Mom behind."

Then the tears start falling, and I don't try to keep them inside any longer.

CHAPTER 11

I calm down soon and give my friends a quick recap of what happened. I deliver the news about Beelzebub's influence in a whisper.

Jeep nods solemnly. "I also noticed a change in her, but it came and went, so I figured she was tired, like we all are."

"That's what I thought too." I glance at Taylar, remembering the dark and light parts swirling inside him. *Do we need to fear him too?*

"We should take care of this now, before she wakes up," Jeep interrupts my thoughts.

I take my notebook from behind my waistband and slam it onto the table. "I'll write a spell."

Jeep stands up. "I'll keep Mona company upstairs, if you don't mind."

"Good idea."

He vanishes, and D'Maeo and Maël follow him.

Kessley pushes her chair back abruptly. "Can I

make a snack for anyone?"

Of course, Charlie raises his hand first. "For me, please!"

I stare at the blank page in front of me and beg my brain to come up with a spell soon.

When it remains quiet, I look up. "Some coffee would be nice."

"Coming up!"

Dylan leans over the table toward me. "You know, I could help."

I drop my pen and smile at him. "I forgot! You can lift curses!"

His lips move up, but only a little. "I can, but a back-up spell would be nice. We're talking about Beelzebub here, and I'm still out of practice."

I take a sip from the coffee that Kess puts in front of me. "No problem. We can work together."

My mind finally wakes up, and the words start to spill out. I scribble them down quickly and ask Kessley to check the kitchen cabinets for the ingredients. She goes upstairs to pull the ones we're missing from Vicky's endless pocket.

"She's still out," is the first thing she says when she apparates back into the kitchen.

"Good." I gulp down the rest of my coffee and stand up. "I'm ready."

Kessley is a good assistant, but she can't take away my nerves. We set everything up around Vicky's bed. Kess mixes the herbs for me and creates a circle of salt. Meanwhile, I explain my plan to Dylan.

"Sounds good to me," he says when I finish.

I wish him luck, and Kessley hands me the bowl of herbs and a matchbox. Then she joins the others outside the circle, ready to intervene if anything goes wrong.

Dylan takes his place on Vicky's left side and takes a deep breath, out of habit. "Ready?"

"Ready," I confirm.

Dylan places his hands above Vicky's head. His gaze rests on her face. I wait for the reflection in his eyes to change. When it does, a shiver runs up my spine. A dark layer is lifted from Vicky's face. But only in his eyes. When I shift my gaze to Vicky, nothing has changed.

Dylan's hands start to move in circles, one going left, one right. This is my cue.

I light the black candle next to Vicky's head and the one at her feet and walk around the bed and around Dylan to light the other two. Meanwhile, the circles he draws are getting bigger.

I suppress the urge to check for changes in Vicky. I need to do my part, or this may not work.

Back at Vicky's other side, I sprinkle herbs over her body. The words of the spell leave my lips confidently.

"Powers of the universe,
take away this evil curse.
Strengthen the powers of this mage.
Remove the darkness and the rage."

My hands tremble slightly. It's time for the scariest part. Charon said she'd be immune to fire. This is the moment to find out.

Taylar and Kessley step closer with a bucket of water in their hands.

I light another match and drop it onto Vicky's chest before I lose the courage to do so.

There's a whoosh, and the flame grows. It's like dropping a lighter onto a trail of oil. The fire spreads over her body rapidly, and the room is filled with the smell of burnt spices. The dominating odor is thyme, which I used for purification.

When Vicky moves, Jeep jumps into the circle next to me. "Keep still, Vicky. They're curing you."

She obeys and closes her eyes. Jeep shoots me a sideways glance. "Continue."

Dylan has not paused for a second. His hands are moving inside the flames. His almost invisible state protects him from the heat.

While I recite the next part of the spell, a tiny dot of black is lifted from Vicky's forehead. She moves her head restlessly, and I avert my eyes. If I look at her for too long, I'll forget the words.

"Powers of the moon and sun,
release her from what doesn't belong.
Take the dark that tries to hide,
but leave her powers safe inside."

As soon as the last word leaves my lips, the candles and fire are extinguished. Dylan sucks in air, and the black dot slips into his mouth. He tips his head toward the ceiling and spits it out. Then he bends over Vicky again and breathes in another dot. He blows it up and both specks dissolve.

Vicky blinks several times.

"Did it work?" I ask.

She sits up and cracks her neck. "I think it did."

Jeep backs up to give me some room, and I wrap my arms around my girl.

"Thank you," she whispers. "Thank you both." She turns her head toward Dylan. "I was constantly fighting Beelzebub's powers inside me, but I couldn't tell you. He was trying to turn me against you."

I stroke her hair. "But he didn't."

"Because you noticed in time."

I stare at my feet. "Well, that was actually Charon's doing."

"Thank God you went to see him," D'Maeo says.

Vicky rubs her temples. "What happened after we saw your mother? Did something go wrong?"

I snort. "What happened is that you tried to lift a rock the size of a small elephant with your mind about five minutes after receiving new powers."

Our friends chuckle.

"Talk about a recipe for disaster," Charlie says.

"Not really," Vicky retorts. "It would've been a disaster if I hadn't done it."

"You did save us," I agree. "But you scared the

shit out of me. Please don't do that again."

She tilts her head as if in thought. "I can't promise you anything."

I poke her in her side, and she laughs.

But her laughter turns into a frown. "Wait a minute. I still don't know how to create the circles of Hell."

Taylar finally puts down his bucket. "That doesn't sound good."

I step aside when Vicky flings her legs over the side of the bed. "I asked Charon about that. He said Vicky would know soon."

Her frown deepens. "I have to wait? I thought I'd know what to do instantly."

I shrug. "I guess not."

Taylar lets out a snort. "Sounds like bullshit to me."

"Why?" I ask. "Charon has been straight with us from the beginning."

Jeep rolls his sleeves up to reveal his unmoving tattoos. "And weirder things have happened."

"True," Maël says, stashing her staff somewhere inside her cape.

Taylar throws up his hands in defeat. "I guess you're right."

We go downstairs, and after a high five with Dylan and two cups of coffee, I finally remember to ask what the others did while Vicky and I were gone.

"We found Armando Accardi," D'Maeo says. "The man that accidentally killed Dylan."

The young mage clears his throat. "But we couldn't speak to him because your Shield can't leave this house without you."

I sit back in my chair when Mona's sparks put a plate in front of me. "No problem, we can go see him after dinner."

Dylan nods gratefully. "I would like that. And we know how to find him now."

Mona goes around with the first pan.

"What are we having?" Gisella asks. "It smells good."

The fairy godmother puts a spoonful of rice on my plate. "Rice with chicken and salad, with a fairy godmother twist."

We wait patiently for her and Kessley to finish scooping everything onto our plates before someone dares to ask, "What's the twist?"

"Probably sparkles?" Taylar says. "Aren't you running out of them by now? You've given us so much already."

For a moment, Mona lights up from within. "Don't worry, I've got plenty to spare as long as I get a chance to rest every night. But this time, I've added something else. Something I don't have a lot of, but…" She stares at the ceiling. "Yes, I think it's time to use it."

Several of us slide forward on our chairs, and D'Maeo raises an eyebrow. *Even he doesn't know what's going on.*

Mona gestures to Kessley to sit down and lifts the

last pan from the stove. With a sneaky smile on her lips, she walks over to me first and hands me a ladle. "Go on. It's good, I promise."

My mouth falls open when I scoop something from the pan. It's a sauce of sorts, but it's golden, and it sparkles. I put it over my rice and watch as it pulses. "Are you sure this isn't a sauce made of sparkles?"

She walks around my chair and holds out the pan to Vicky. "I never said that. I only said these aren't *my* sparkles. They do resemble sparkles though."

Vicky scoops up some of the sauce and holds it up to her nose. She sniffs it and dips her finger in it.

Everyone watches her expectantly, but she doesn't say anything. She just closes her eyes and moans in delight. The sound has never been more comforting to me. *She really is okay. Dylan and I did it.*

"What does it taste like?" Kessley asks, bouncing on her chair impatiently.

"Like Heaven."

Mona nods. "Of course it does." She moves on to Dylan, who adds sauce to his rice quickly and picks up his spoon to taste it.

"Wow!" he says.

Unable to hold back my curiosity any longer, I take a big bite.

Immediately, the weirdest feeling washes over me. It's like the tingles you get when someone caresses the hairline on the back of your neck and the feeling of a rollercoaster in one. My taste buds are overloaded. They switch from sweet to salty to sour and back, and I love all of them. Every single thing I enjoy the most passes by, and it's as if something soft touches my lips, just like the feeling you get when you take a mouthful of whipped cream.

I swallow a couple of times, and the feeling spreads through my whole body. My hand has a mind of its own. It scoops up another spoonful, which is just as good.

"Mmm," I say. "This is like all my favorite dishes turned into one perfect meal. But better."

Mona chuckles. "I know."

"What did you mean, of course it tastes like Heaven?" Charlie asks, watching the pan with hawk eyes as Mona moves around the table to serve everyone.

"Well, this is divine light," she says matter-of-factly.

I cough. "What? I'm eating light from God himself?"

The fairy godmother stares into the pan. "Sort of, yes."

Since I'm still not convinced I like the guy so much, I prod my rice aimlessly. My body is screaming at me, pleading for me to take another bite, but I suppress the urge. For now. "Why are you feeding us divine light?"

She holds the pan out to Jeep without meeting his eye. "Because you will be fighting in Heaven soon, so you'll need to be able to see the angels even in their invisible form. Also, you won't be blinded by their light anymore once you've eaten this."

"Really?" I study the glowing stuff on my plate and shake my head. "We sure could've used this sooner."

"There was no need for you to have it before. Now there is." Mona sounds a bit stern as she says it.

"Sorry," I say. "I didn't mean it like that. But I remember my temporary blindness as if it was yesterday. It was no pleasant experience."

"Temporary blindness?" Kess asks as she wipes a bit of sauce from her chin and licks it from her finger.

I take another bite before I answer her. A fuzzy feeling settles in my stomach. "Yes, I went blind for a couple of hours because I opened my eyes when we traveled with Quinn. Normally the human eye can't handle the brightness of an angel's true form."

"But now we can?"

Mona nods and moves on to Taylar. "Yes, once you've eaten this, you will be able to look at the true form of a living angel without going blind."

"Forever?" Dylan asks.

"No, but long enough to do what needs to be done."

"You're so cryptic today, Mona," Jeep comments. "That's not like you."

When she doesn't respond and puts the pan back on the stove, Charlie holds up his spoon. "Aren't you having some yourself?"

She walks around the table and sits down next to Maël with a plate full of rice, chicken and salad, but no golden sauce. "I don't need it. As a fairy godmother, I can already look at an angel's true form."

Kessley leans back in her chair, with her face to the ceiling. "If I could choose what I'd want to be when I grow up, I'd want to be a fairy godmother."

Taylar frowns at her. "You'll never grow up."

"I know that! Thanks for spoiling the dream." She throws him such a deadly stare that he almost chokes on his rice.

The white-haired ghost coughs, walks around the table and wraps both arms around Kess. "I'm sorry. That was a stupid thing to say."

Once he's gone back to his seat, we enjoy the food in silence, all of us absorbed by the blissful taste of the meal.

"I'm a bit surprised to see you eating with us almost every day, Maël," I confess when there's not a single drop of gold or anything else left on my plate. "I know you've come to peace with your past, but the last couple of days, you seem to enjoy food."

The African queen straightens up. The golden headpiece on her tiny curls glows more than usual. "You are almost right. It is not necessarily the food itself I enjoy; it is the act of eating together. It makes me feel like I have been reborn."

Tears prick behind my eyes. "I am glad to be a part of that."

Jeep swallows a mouthful of chicken. "I understand what you're saying, Maël. We never did this with John. And even though we had a good bond with him too, before he was influenced by the Black Horseman, this group feels more like a family than before."

"I agree," Taylar says, wiping his mouth. "And it's as if the more I eat normal meals, like the living, the more I feel like I'm alive again."

A warm feeling washes over me. "I am so happy to hear that, because you all feel like family to me too."

"I wonder though…" Gisella starts. She hesitates. "If it's a good thing that you are all starting to feel like living people again." She turns her head to Mona. "Would that interfere with their powers? Make it harder to turn invisible for instance?"

Mona shakes her head. "I wouldn't worry about that. I've never heard of such a thing, and feelings of happiness will only give someone more strength."

Gisella breathes out. "Well, that's a relief."

Charlie scoops a truckload of chicken and rice on his spoon. "Great, I'm glad that everyone's happy and strong. Can we please continue our meal now?"

The werecat-witch gives him a rough shove and grabs his wrist before he can tumble from his chair.

"You know, if you can't behave, Charlie and Kess can switch seats," Taylar grumbles, leaning back a little to avoid getting hit by Charlie's swinging arm.

Kessley, sitting next to Maël, gives him a bright smile. "That's a good idea!"

"No, it's not," Charlie objects. "I want to sit next to my girl. Even when she punches me."

Taylar opens his mouth to object again, but I hold

up my hand before he can utter a word. "Don't fight about it. There's plenty of room here. Charlie, if you sit on Gisella's other side, Kess can take your place."

Charlie leans forward to check out the empty chair on Gisella's left.

Jeep puts down his spoon and frowns at him. "Come on, don't tell me you're afraid of me. I promise I won't put poison in your food, okay?"

Charlie snorts. "Of course I'm not afraid of you. We're all on the same side here, you know. But…" He lowers his head. His finger follows the line of his almost empty plate over and over.

"Well?" I ask. "Just tell us. If something is bothering you, we should try to change it."

He licks his lips and nods. "Okay. I'll tell you." He coughs and fidgets with his long hair. "I… I'm a bit…" He searches for the right word. "Worried… that more ghosts will pop out of Jeep's tattoos. Since they tend to be rather aggressive, I don't want to be too close."

Gisella rolls her eyes. "Fine. You pussy." She stands up, moves one chair to the left, nods at Jeep and slides her plate in front of her. "Happy now?"

Charlie blushes deeply and moves to her chair. "Yes. Thank you." He glances at Jeep over Gisella's shoulder. "Sorry, Jeep. I didn't mean…"

The tattooed ghost raises his hand to silence him. "It's fine. I know I'm intimidating."

Charlie sits up straight. "That's not what I—" He smirks as Jeep starts laughing. "Never mind."

Taylar is glowing. He pats the free seat on his left. "Kess?"

She apparates into it in a millisecond, and they grab each other's hands.

Dylan, sitting next to Vicky, in what used to be Mom's chair, grabs her plate and slides it over to her.

I exchange a grin with Vicky before turning to D'Maeo. "What about you? If Maël moves one spot to the left, Mona can sit next to you."

"Oh no, that's okay," Mona calls out quickly, standing up to collect the dishes. "Most of the time I'm moving around, and when I'm not, I like to have an excuse to sit on his lap."

D'Maeo chuckles loudly and pulls her close as she passes him, spilling some leftover rice on the floor. "Once again, we agree."

Charlie clears his throat. "I'm sorry to interrupt, but is there more food?"

Mona pushes herself up and hurries over to him with a pan. "Of course there is. But you can't have any more sauce."

"What? Why not?"

"Too much of it will overload your system. You'll start seeing too much."

He looks up at her with a sweet smile. "You mean like things that aren't there? Don't worry about that, I can handle it. I've done it before."

Mona throws some chicken on his plate. "No, you haven't. Trust me on this."

Charlie sighs. "Okay then. It was worth a shot."

Kessley stands up to help Mona with the dishes, even though Mona's sparks could do it too. I guess she likes to help.

I'd like to ask the fairy godmother why she's not telling us everything, but I trust her to have the right reasons, and I'm sure she won't say anything no matter how I press her for answers. All I can think is: our battle in Heaven is drawing near.

CHAPTER 12

"So, Armando Accardi," I say, turning to Dylan. "The man who accidentally killed you. Do you want to go see him now?"

"That would be great. But I understand if there are things you need to do first, and I'd be honored to help."

I throw him a grateful look. "Thanks for the offer, I appreciate that, but I don't think…" I cut off my sentence when a familiar gust of wind hits my neck. This time, however, it is accompanied by a bright light. The others are staring at it, and I whirl around to see what it is, although I already know. Sure, it's been a while since I received a set of cards, but I'd recognize the gust and the rustling anywhere.

When I turn to face the light, I shield my eyes a bit, still afraid of the blinding effects it might have. But nothing happens. It's very bright, with golden spots, but I can see the figure within clearly.

My mouth falls open. I feel it, but I can't stop it. The angel standing behind me with a white envelope in his hand is breathtaking. He looks like a man in his forties, but without any wrinkles. He has a beard made of light, or so it seems, and his long hair is even blonder than Charlie's. I've never seen eyes as light blue as his and… My thoughts come to a halt when I realize something is wrong about him. There's a trail of dark spots on his white robe, and as he steps closer, I can see he's limping.

He drops the envelope and turns his back to us. He spreads his arms, and his wings unfold.

I gasp. There's a tear in the left one, and dark blood trickles out of it.

"Wait," I say, reaching out to him. I want to ask him if he needs help, but the light spreads, the wings move, and the next thing I know, he's gone.

for at least a minute I stare at the spot where he was standing, unable to move. No one else makes as much as a sound either.

Finally, I bend over to pick up the envelope. I meet Mona's eyes across the table and see fear and sadness in them.

"Is this why you gave us the divine light? So we could see this angel?" I ask her.

She swallows several times. "No, it's not. But I think it's a good thing we saw him. Now we know how serious things are up in Heaven. We'll need to come up with a plan to help soon."

I bite my lip and turn to Dylan. "I'm sorry. Armando will have to wait after all. This wounded angel wouldn't have visited us if these cards weren't extremely important. We'll need to find the next soul and save it. And as soon as we do, we need to go and help the angels. Before there are none left to help."

When I turn the envelope over, I find drops of blood on it. My insides turn cold at the thought of angels dying in Heaven right now. Fighting for their lives and ours. I wish I knew of a way to help them. If I did, I'd go up there this instant. But I don't, and I need to remind myself that this angel brought us these Cards of Death for a reason. *If helping them fight was more important than saving the next soul, they wouldn't have brought us the cards.*

I open the envelope and pull the contents out. I'm not surprised to find the symbols on one of the cards being blown in all directions so fiercely it's impossible to see what they are. After all, the punishment in the second circle of Hell is wind. Hence the tornado demons we fought before.

"The back is moving!" Kessley suddenly calls out.

I turn the cards around and study the swirling symbols, this time in shades of gray. "That's normal."

Charlie snorts. "You call that normal?"

With a chuckle, I hold the cards up. "Well, compared to a lot of things I've seen since my veil lifted, yes, I'd call this normal."

Vicky leans closer. "What's on the first card? The one you can already read?"

"Let me see." I lay the one with the wind on the table and take a look at the symbols on the other one. "It's a noose and a strawberry." I show it to everyone.

D'Maeo nods. "Well, this one is easy enough. One of the symbols stands for the sin that will be committed to end up in the second circle of Hell…" He pauses while I try to remember what this sin was.

"Lust," Charlie says.

D'Maeo nods. "Exactly. So that must be the strawberry."

"Which means the noose stands for the way this soul will die," Jeep finishes his train of thought.

Kessley rubs her neck. "By hanging?"

I scratch my head. "That will be difficult to prevent. We'll need to keep an eye on the soul constantly."

Gisella crosses her arms. "We need to find it first. That might be more difficult. What's on the other card?"

I show her the lines that are pulled apart by the wind. "I don't know yet. We need a way to get rid of the wind."

Maël turns to Dylan. "You know of a way to manipulate the wind, do you not?"

Dylan rubs the edge of the table nervously. "I do, but I'm not sure it will work on wind created by magic."

I slide the card over to him. "It can't hurt to try."

He picks it up and slides his finger over it. "If it works the same as normal wind, it should be easy to get rid of it." He gestures at the kitchen cabinets. "Do you have a glass jar, with a lid?"

"I think so." I stand up and open the first cabinet.

"It's in the last one," Mona says.

Heat rises to my cheeks at the thought that she knows her way around my kitchen better than I do. I open the last cupboard and grab the first jar I see. I hand it to Dylan, who removes the lid and places the card inside. "Wind is created by cold and heat currents colliding. If I close the lid, I will prevent the currents from hitting each other, therefore cutting off the wind's power source. In theory, at least."

He puts the lid back on, and both Vicky and I lean closer to check the card.

"It's working!"

Dylan grins at me and slides the jar over.

I hold it up for a better look and describe what I see. "Okay, there's a cross, so this person has something to do with religion."

"Definitely, because there are also two praying hands," Vicky points out.

"And a church or something with two red towers."

"The Monastery of Saint Gertrude," Gisella says immediately. "The roofs of the towers are red."

"And a…" I hesitate and turn the jar toward Vicky and Dylan. "What's this?"

"A boomerang?" Dylan suggests.

Vicky narrows her eyes at it. "Could be."

I show the card to Taylar and point at the curved shape.

"Dog droppings?"

I snort. "Probably not."

"That last one is a candle," he says.

"Yes." I rub my face. "So we're looking for a nun in the Monastery of St. Gertrude, and the only clues we have to which nun we need are a candle and a boomerang."

"How many nuns live there?" D'Maeo asks.

I pull out my phone and open Google.

"About fifty," I say when I've found the website. "So there's no way we can watch all of them."

Jeep places his hat firmly on his head. "We can show them the card and see if it gives them any idea who it's about."

"And what do we tell them about the cards? The truth?"

I bite my lip. "They are Benedictine nuns, right? Catholics? So they believe in Hell?"

D'Maeo nods. "They should. But will they believe us?"

I stand up and grab my keys from the kitchen counter. "Only one way to find out."

The others stay in their seats. "What? We should go as soon as possible, right?"

D'Maeo clears his throat. "You want to knock on the door of a monastery in the middle of the night?"

I shrug. "It's a long drive."

Gisella holds up her phone. "Three hours and forty-two minutes. I'd like to use the rest of the night to get some sleep."

A mumbled 'me too' rises.

"Oh, and I'm not sitting cooped up like we normally do for almost four hours," Taylar adds. He squeezes Kessley's leg. "Not that I mind being so close to Kess."

Charlie taps the edge of the table. "You're right. I'm not looking forward to that either, so I think Gisella and I will take my car. Dylan, you can join us, if you're coming."

I turn my head to the young mage. "You don't have to. If you want, you can go find Armando Accardi on your own. I understand if you don't want to wait any longer."

Dylan's eyebrows go up. "Are you serious? Of course I'm coming. If I can contribute even a little, I will. Besides…" He winks. "You need me if you run into any more of those tornado demons."

I tilt my head. "Really? Are you getting cocky all of a sudden?"

He blushes.

"You could tell us how to fight those demons. It would be much safer for you."

He shakes his head. "No way, I've been safe for decades, inside Jeep's tattoo. I've heard a lot about the Devil's plans, and I could never do anything to stop him. Now that I can, I'm not running away from it. Besides, even if I take care of my unfinished business, where would I move on to? Heaven? Doesn't sound like a great place to be at the moment."

"Good point," I mumble, and I hold my hand out to him. "Well, in that case, we're happy to have you on the team."

He beams at me and shakes my hand. "Thanks!"

I stretch my arms above my head and yawn. "And now it's time for some sleep. I suggest we get up early for the drive to Cottonwood."

Charlie groans. "How early?"

"I want to leave at half past three."

"Are you serious?" He drops his head on the table.

"Very serious. We need to reach this nun before the demons do."

Charlie lifts his head and rubs the red spot on his forehead. "I know, but wouldn't it be better if we got there rested, you know?"

"Better to get there in time and tired, than get there rested but too late," D'Maeo voices my thoughts.

Charlie pushes himself up. "Okay, you're right. I wish you all a good night."

I pat his arm when he passes me. "Don't be so gloomy. We've partied till four in the morning before. You never had problems with that."

He stops and turns back to me. "I have no problem staying up late; it's the getting up early the next day that gets me every time." He smirks at me, waves and walks out of the kitchen and up the stairs, Gisella following close behind.

I rise too and take one last look at the cards. The dots of blood seem to scream at me. *Do something!*

Help them! How can you sleep when Heaven is about to fall?

A hand on my back startles me. "Hey," Vicky says softly. "You're doing the right thing. We can't function without sleep. If we could, we'd have done it already, and we'd always be one step ahead of our enemy."

For a moment, I just gape at her. Then I find my voice back. "But we can, can't we? I could cast a spell to make sure none of us need sleep anymore."

"That won't work," Mona says before Vicky can respond.

My shoulders sag. "Why not?"

"Simply because there are some things you cannot tamper with. The human body needs sleep and food. You might be able to suppress those needs, but no good has ever come of that. A spell like that will either backfire or not work at all."

Reluctantly, I give in. "Fine. Sleep it is."

"Keep the faith, Dante," the fairy godmother calls after me.

"Always!" I call back, and I pull Vicky closer to me as we climb the stairs.

While I prepare for bed, I tell myself things aren't that bad. We're making progress. Yes, things are getting worse in Heaven, but at the same time, *we* are growing stronger. Charon was right, Mom's words did give me more confidence, even if it was only a little. She has faith in me and so should I.

When I snuggle up to Vicky and stare over her shoulder, lost in thought, she presses a kiss on my forehead. "Stop thinking and go to sleep, babe. Everything will be alright."

I close my eyes, and with her warm hand drawing circles on my temple, I fall into a deep sleep.

CHAPTER 14

I'm standing in a big building, my friends behind me, all in solid form. It is dark in here. The main hall is dimly lit by candles. Dark shapes watch us from all sides. Automatically, we all draw closer together. I can feel my friends' arms touching me. They give me courage.

I clear my throat. "We're here to speak to your leader."

At first there's no response. The growing silence around us creeps me out even more than the suffocating atmosphere. I want nothing more than to leave and never come back, but I know I can't.

I decide to focus on the black-clad figure straight ahead and take a step toward it.

"We have no leader," she suddenly says. "We are all equal here." Her voice is low and monotone. "Tell us what you want."

The candle flames around her flicker restlessly. It's as if the light wants to get away from her. I understand the feeling.

Vicky nudges me. "Tell her."

I shove aside my unease. "We are here to save one of you."

Finally, the figure steps forward. At the same time, the others, on all sides of us, do the same. My whole body is screaming at me that something is wrong, but I can't leave without at least trying to save this soul.

The nun chuckles, but it sounds more like she's choking. "Save one of us? Really? From what?"

"From death."

Her eyes bore into mine, and I shiver. "We do not fear death."

I ball my fists in an attempt to remain calm. "That is… good to hear. But there is more at stake than your lives." I look around to see the reaction of the other nuns around us, but they are all standing still like statues, so I continue. "We're talking about the safety of the whole world here." I gesture at the space behind her, thinking that there must be an office of some kind behind it. "Maybe we can sit down to talk about it? We're happy to explain everything to you."

The nun in front of us nods and turns without a word. The others stay where they are, still staring at us silently. I get the fearful feeling that we are being surrounded by a cult, but when Vicky steps forward to follow the nun, I do the same.

Even without checking, I know the other nuns close ranks behind us as we walk through the corridors. I can feel their threatening presence, and I can hear their footsteps, although they are soft and more like dragging.

The nun in front of us comes to a halt at a heavy door. She pulls it open and turns around slowly. "Please step inside." Then she nods at the sisters behind us, and I hear them sliding away, leaving us alone with the nun in the chilly corridor.

With all my muscles on high alert, I peer into the room and step inside. My friends are on my heels.

The nun closes the door behind us and walks around her antique English mahogany pedestal desk. She sits down with the same rigid motion that she uses for walking. "Speak."

I hesitate. I'm not sure I want to share our mission with this woman, who seems to be influenced by evil. But what else can I tell her? How can I find out which nun is the one chosen by the Devil?

"Well?" she asks, impatiently raising an eyebrow.

"I'm sorry," I say with a shy smile. "I was distracted by the beauty of this building for a second."

Her eyebrow stays in place, the rest of her face is stone cold. "Why are you here?"

I wring my hands together and conjure a worried frown on my face. "We are worried about the youth of today."

Her other eyebrow goes up too.

I continue quickly. "Most teenagers don't believe in God anymore, nor do they believe in kindness, respect, honesty and everything else the Bible speaks of. Therefore we…" I gesture at my friends, "… are organizing a benefit and recruitment afternoon. We are visiting several monasteries, convents and churches to ask nuns and priests to come and speak at our event. We want to show teenagers a better way of life. We were hoping to find someone of this monastery to come and speak. That person will have the power to change the world."

I can tell by the cold look in her eyes that she's not convinced. At all.

"You see, our plan goes further than the local teenagers,"

Vicky adds. "Once we've grown our religious community, we want to bring our message to the rest of the state, and after that, to the rest of the country."

I nod as if that thought makes me extremely happy. "And hopefully to the rest of the world."

The nun behind the desk finally lowers her eyebrows. She seems to loosen up a bit. "That is a wonderful idea." Her voice sounds as cold as her face is. "We might be able to help you."

"Really?" I show her a wide smile. "That would be great."

"If possible, we would like someone who can bake," Kessley says sweetly. "Croissants, or something."

When I glance at her over my shoulder, I'm relieved to see she's wearing a different outfit. Instead of her usual—very short—leopard skin dress, she's sporting a neat black suit. Her hair is no longer bleached, but a healthy chestnut brown, pulled up in a tight bun. She's like a completely different person.

"Why?" the nun asks sternly.

Kessley rubs her belly. "Well, because teenagers are always hungry. They tend to listen better to people who offer them food."

The nun taps her desk with her finger. "Yes, that is a good point." Her lips part in a grotesque grin, showing blackened teeth. I lower my gaze before my body responds to it. "How lovely that you have chosen our monastery. We will be delighted to send someone." She stands up, and before I can stop myself, I back up.

She paces up and down behind her desk with her hands together in front of her. "You are an interesting group. I wasn't sure what to think of you at first. Especially since one of the boys is apparently your speaker." She stands still and takes the

147

adults in our group in from head to toe. I wish we had thought of hiding Maël's outfit before we stepped in, but it's too late for that now.

D'Maeo clears his throat. "Yes, we let the youngsters speak because they started this initiative, and they make a great example of how much one can change their life."

The nun shows him her rotten teeth again. "What a great strategy." She walks to the door and opens it. "We would like to help, but I cannot send the sister that cooks for us because she has gone missing."

My whole body goes cold. "Missing?"

She lowers her head in sadness, but I see the glimpse of a grin. "Yes, she disappeared yesterday."

"I'm sorry." I give her a small bow. "We will pray for her safe return."

"Thank you." She holds out her hand. "If you leave your name and phone number, I will call for the details as soon as we've chosen someone for your event."

My brain goes into overdrive as I try to come up with a name and number. But the wheels inside my head are stuck.

Thankfully, Vicky's brain works just fine. She takes a piece of paper and a pen from her pocket, scribbles something down and hands it to the nun. "Thank you so much for your help."

"Any time, my child," the nun says, and for a second, there's a red glint in her eye. "Let me escort you out."

I walk past her and beckon the others. "That's okay, I'm sure we can find our way back."

"I am happy to take you," she says, not sounding happy at all. "After all, we wouldn't want you to get lost."

Once again, cold creeps up my ankles and onto my neck. Something is very wrong here, and I can't wait to get out of this building. But I know we'll have no choice but to come back. The way this woman speaks about the building and the missing sister tells me enough. The soul we need to save is still in here, and if we don't find her soon, she'll be lost.

We all let out a relieved sigh when the nun closes the front door behind us. It takes us all some time to recover. Meanwhile, I study the outside of the monastery and try to think of a way to get back in without anyone noticing. This might be hard, because all of the sisters appeared to be under some kind of evil spell or something.

I'm about to suggest googling a floorplan of the building when there's a frightened shriek, followed by the slamming of a door.

My eyes move over our group, praying that I heard it wrong. That the shriek only sounded like someone I know.

When I see we're one person short, I curse under my breath.

"That was Dylan," Jeep remarks redundantly.

I turn and raise my hand to open the door.

"Don't," D'Maeo says, grabbing my arm. "We can't go back in unprepared. You saw her eyes. All of their eyes. They are possessed."

I grit my teeth. "All the more reason to go in now. If we don't, they'll possess Dylan too. Or worse…"

There's no need to finish my sentence. D'Maeo lets go. "I see your point but going in without a plan would be foolish. Harsh as it may sound, if we lose Dylan, we can still win. If, however, we lose one of us…"

"That might be true, but I'm still not leaving a friend

behind."

"I'm not saying we should. But we need a plan."

I throw my hands up in desperation. "Thinking of a plan will take too long!"

Jeep steps up between us. "Bickering about it will take even longer, guys."

Kess raises her hand as if she's in school. "I might have an idea."

D'Maeo and I nod at the same time.

"I can disguise myself as one of them. While I distract them, you guys can try to find Dylan and get him out."

I slam my hands together. "Works for me."

D'Maeo frowns at Kessley. "Have you thought of a way to get out again? And a way to escape in case you're exposed?"

"Yes, and no."

I lower my hands. "I'm not trading you in for Dylan."

She smiles brightly. "I'm glad." She tilts her head. "How about I just holler if I need help? You can be my distraction then. If it comes to a fight, at least we'll all be together."

I glance at the old ghost for approval, and he scratches his beard. "I guess that's the best we can do in such a short time."

Kessley steps forward. "Okay, wish me luck."

"Good l—"

Suddenly the front door swings open. The next thing I know, I'm lifted off my feet and pulled inside by an unseen force. The others are flying next to me, equally helpless. Maël clutches her staff tightly and opens her mouth to work her magic, but before she can utter a single syllable, we're all turned upside down so abruptly that my breakfast rises to my lips. We spin several times before coming to a halt outside a closed door near the ceiling. I expect everyone to pull out their weapons or activate their powers, but no one moves. When I try to lift my hand and conjure a lightning ball, I understand why. We're paralyzed. I can't even blink anymore. But even if I could, the chilling scream that comes from the other side of the door would make me freeze now. I can tell by the muffled moans of my friends around me that I'm not the only one who recognizes Dylan's desperate voice.

"No, please! I'm telling you the truth! I don't know anything about a plan! I didn't even know about… ouch! Please, stop! I don't know what you're talking about. I just met them!" His words are followed by a loud scream and sobbing.

Anger rises inside me. I can use my powers without moving, and I will.

I focus on the door, take in every detail of it, every carving made into it. My eyes follow the outline of each carved-in flower and branch. Inch by inch I imagine them filling up with ice. More and more ice until they burst apart. The wood groans in protest, and in my mind, it's torn to pieces.

"You found her," a raspy voice says from behind the door when Dylan finally stops crying. "You found the soul you were searching for. But she will be the last thing you see. As you will be the last thing she sees."

I start to shake, and my concentration is broken. I'm hit by a roaring tornado and slam into a wall. The sound of breaking bones reaches my ears before my brain registers the pain. Then everything goes dark.

CHAPTER 15

"What is it?" Vicky sits up when my hands frantically check every bone in my body. I know I'm still in one piece, I know that it was a premonition, but my brain keeps sending pain signals to my limbs.

Vicky rubs my back and waits patiently for me to calm down.

After about a minute, I lean back against the head rest of the bed and take a couple of deep breaths. "That was intense."

Vicky shoots me a worried look. "I can tell. What did you see?"

I pull her closer to me to comfort my shaken body. "We were at the monastery. The nuns were all possessed. The soul we were searching for was missing, according to them. I guess Dylan didn't believe them, because he snuck off when we left the building. He went through a door, found the nun there and got caught. We heard them torturing him." My voice trembles at the thought. "We were pulled back inside, immobilized, and then…" I move my hand back to indicate my flight. "We were thrown against the wall by a tornado demon. Or several, I'm not sure, it happened so fast. The impact with the wall broke most of my bones."

I shiver, and Vicky rubs both my arms.

"It's okay, you got the premonition in time. Now we know what to expect *and* we know where to find the soul."

"And we know we should listen to D'Maeo when he tells us we need a plan," I mumble.

We sit still like this for a while, and slowly my heart and body settle down. Then I remember my plan to leave early and shoot upright. "What time is it?"

"It's half past two."

"Good… good." I turn back to kiss her before jumping out of bed. "That leaves us an hour to come up with a plan."

Vicky slides out of bed too. "I'll wake the others while you get dressed."

"Thanks, babe."

I'm surprised at how alert my brain is when I go downstairs and join my Shield at the kitchen table.

"Sorry to wake you all so early, but I had a premonition."

I wait for Mona, Dylan, Charlie and Gisella to join

us before telling them the whole story.

"Are you sure it wasn't a dream?" Dylan asks as soon as I finish.

"Yes, I'm sure. Premonitions feel different than dreams; not just more real, but also more haunting. Besides, in dreams, things often don't make sense. One minute it can be the middle of the night, and the next it's dinnertime. Or I'm talking to Mona, but she has Mom's face. Things like that. In my premonitions, everything fits."

He shakes his head. "Not everything. I can't imagine sneaking into a room in a monastery run by possessed nuns."

"Maybe not, but you were going to do it anyway."

Vicky slaps him on his back. "You must be braver than you think!"

"That's unlikely," he mumbles.

I lean onto the table, closer to him. "I've done some things I wouldn't have considered possible myself lately. Fighting the Devil changes you. Trust me, you *are* brave."

"He's right," D'Maeo says from the other side of the table. "You probably heard something behind that door, had to make a split decision and decided to check it out."

"And that didn't end well," Dylan finishes gloomily.

I smile at him. "No, but thanks to my premonition, we can change that. We now know what to expect and where to look." I slam my fist onto the table. "So let's make a plan to save these sisters and ourselves."

To my surprise, we manage to come up with one fast. Maybe it's because we've seen so many battles already. We're getting better at this. If only my nerves would get used to it too. The dark eyes of the nun keep swimming in front of me, and Dylan's screams are on repeat in my head. Every time I move, the pain of all my broken bones shoots through me again.

I feel a bit better when I've devoured another one of Mona's legendary breakfasts. Eggs and bacon on toast with a pinch of sparkles. I add two cups of coffee to wake myself up completely and get to my feet. "Right, everyone in the cars in five minutes."

"Aye, aye, sir," Charlie says, saluting before stuffing the leftovers into his mouth.

While Mona's sparkles clear the table, the fairy godmother herself pulls herbs and snacks from the cupboards and hands them to Vicky.

She winks at me when I watch her with wide eyes. "I did some shopping. With a new soul to save, I knew you'd need new supplies."

"Thanks, Mona." I smile at her. "What would we do without you?"

"It's nothing, really. I'm glad I can help."

Jeep is frowning at the card we put in the jar. "If only we knew what that boomerang meant."

I slap my forehead. "I forgot to tell you! In my premonition, we knew what it was. Kessley mentioned it to the nun."

155

Kessley looks up from the dishes. "I did?"

"Yes, it's not a boomerang. It's a croissant. We need to save a nun that bakes croissants."

"I like her already," Charlie mumbles with his mouth full.

"She's a nun," I say, emphasizing the last word.

He stops munching for a second. "So?"

"So, you're not exactly a model citizen."

He wipes his mouth with the back of his hand. "What do you mean? I'm spending my whole summer break fighting demons to help save the world!"

I roll my eyes. "Yes, but before that."

He lowers his voice. "Before that, I tried several things to find enlightenment."

I punch him on the arm. "You're so full of shit."

He pats his belly contently. "Full of eggs, bacon and toast actually. Thanks to Mona."

Jeep stands up and places his hat on his head in a graceful motion. "The five minutes are almost up."

Charlie pushes the last of his second breakfast into his cheeks and rises too. "Mm dun."

Gisella shakes her head at him. "You should've been done ten mouthfuls ago."

Taylar snorts, but Kessley defends my best friend. "It's not his fault he needs so much fuel for his power."

"I know, I still love him." Gisella kisses him on the cheek so enthusiastically he spits pieces of egg.

Jeep pushes past them. "Can we please stop the smooching and get going?"

I follow him to the front door with a smile on my face. "Great idea."

We file into the two cars and wave goodbye to Mona. Charlie follows me out of the forest and then out of Blackford. As soon as my hometown is nothing but a speck in the rearview mirror, I repeat the plan to my Shield.

"Do you think it will work?" Vicky asks, resting one arm on each seat in front of her.

"I think it's a good plan, but…" I hesitate.

"Tell us," Jeep urges me.

"I'm a bit worried about the tornado demons."

Jeep adjusts his hat, but half of it still merges with the roof of my car. "You don't think Dylan's idea is a good one?"

I shrug. "He said himself that he wasn't sure it would work. How did he explain it again?"

D'Maeo repeats Dylan's words. "Wind is caused by air flowing from high pressure to low pressure. Areas of high and low pressure are caused by ascending and descending air. If the pressure is the same everywhere, there will no longer be any wind."

"Right…" I say slowly.

"As air warms, it ascends, leading to low pressure at the surface," he continues. "As air cools, it descends, leading to high pressure at the surface."

I groan. This is like being in school again. And although I'm a meteokinetic, meteorology is obviously not my strong suit.

Jeep fumbles with his hat again. "Which means

157

you need to cool down the lower part of the demons to the same temperature of the upper part."

"Okay, okay, I got that." I rub the steering wheel, trying to envision how that cooling down would work. "The thing is… how do I know up to which height I need to cool them? And how much?"

Vicky squeezes my shoulder. "Try not to worry about the details too much. Just start from the lowest part and work your way up. You'll know when you've reached the spot where the air is already cool because the tornado will cease to exist."

Briefly, I turn my head to her. "You understand this stuff?"

Her eyes sparkle. "I'm smarter than I look."

"Then you must be ridiculously smart," Kessley comments from the back seat.

Vicky blows her a kiss over her shoulder.

Phoenix roars contently as I put my foot a little firmer on the gas. John Hiatt sings to me on the radio to have a little faith. And I decide that I will. After all, Dylan came into our lives with a reason. Even if I can't defeat these demons with my powers, we'll find another way. We always do.

Since I don't feel like worrying for the rest of the way, I turn up the radio and let the music take me back to the fifties, sixties and seventies.

CHAPTER 16

When we arrive in Cottonwood, the streets are starting to fill up with morning traffic, and my stomach is rumbling. I guess all the singing we did on the way here made me hungry again. We stop at a diner for some pancakes, and Charlie walks up to us with a big smile after parking his car behind mine. "Are we having second breakfast?"

"More like third for you," Taylar jokes.

I put my arm around him as we walk to the door. "I need some more coffee. Let my eyes adjust to something else than the road. Besides…" I glance at the others following close behind. "I want to go through the plan one last time."

Dylan and my Shield turn solid, and we sit down at a large table in the corner. Suddenly it feels like a day out with the family, and that feeling is strengthened when the waiter brings us two giant plates of pancakes.

Of course, it doesn't taste nearly as good as something with fairy godmother sparkles in it, but it's still a treat. While we all enjoy this feast, we quietly go over our plan again.

When the waiter comes to pick up our empty plates, I feel a lot better. *I actually have a good feeling about this. We're well-prepared for once.* I wipe some sugar from my mouth and stand up. "Okay, let's go do this."

Charlie refuses to let me pay and walks to the cash register. When he steps outside, he holds up a cupcake with a broad smile.

Kessley's mouth falls open. "Where does he leave all of that? There can't be any room left."

I grin. "I have no idea, but at least he's prepared for a fight."

"True."

We all get into the two cars, and I lead the way to the monastery.

The closer we get, the darker the sky becomes. With each street we drive through, the newly built houses all around the monastery seem older and more neglected, even though I know they aren't. We found some pictures of the neighborhood, and it showed light houses and a beautiful monastery with flowers blooming all around it and bright green trees. Now it looks even worse than it did in my premonition. It's as if a shadow has fallen over the building. Even over the whole street. All traffic goes around this block.

We're the only ones driving on the street, and there are no pedestrians, even though it's been busy all along the way from the diner. I'd think the street was invisible if it wasn't for the many parents urging their children to hurry past the dark place to the new school. The houses here all have their front windows covered, and their cars must be parked out back because there's not a single one in sight. Two blocks back, the plants weren't too healthy, and the colors of the flowers were dull, but here, everything green has died. All color has been drained from flowers and houses, and the trees are nothing more than dry sticks.

I slowly drive past the monastery to check it out. It looks the same as it did in my premonition, except darker. I park at the end of the street, and Charlie stops behind me. Without a word, we all get out and sneak up to the gloomy building.

I turn to Jeep. "Are you ready?"

He nods and cracks his fingers.

"Good luck."

He, Maël and Kessley slip between the outer wall and the dead trees.

We wait quietly for the tattooed ghost to attract the attention of the nuns inside.

Soon, the ground between the dry plants starts to move. Small zombie animals crawl out of the earth and make their way to the back of the monastery.

I can't help but let out a relieved sigh. Jeep's powers are at full strength again.

Taylar moves to the front door, but I stop him. "Not yet."

Sounds start to trickle in from the back of the building. An exclamation of surprise followed by barked orders, doors that fly open, footsteps behind the closed front door.

Taylar sends me a questioning look, and I nod.

Carefully, he opens one of the high front doors and peers inside. Then he slips through the gap. The others follow quickly, and I take one last look around before closing the door behind us.

It sounds like our distraction worked beautifully. There's a lot of commotion at the back of the building, and everyone inside seems to be drawn to it. The hallway is empty, and we tiptoe to the door that Dylan was screaming behind in my premonition. To make sure this doesn't come true, Dylan will stay here with me and Charlie to prevent anyone from sneaking up on the others, who will go get the nun.

I'm here to kick the asses of the tornado demons that will show up soon, or so I think. Then we'll find out if Dylan's theory about cooling down the lower part will work.

"Is this it?" Vicky whispers, pointing at the door.

I take in the decorations on it and nod.

She beckons D'Maeo, Gisella and Taylar and wraps her hand around the door handle. It squeaks a little, and we all freeze. I concentrate on ice and focus it on the floor, where snow flowers appear.

Charlie grabs my shoulder. "Not yet. Try to stay

calm."

I take a couple of deep breaths and nod at him. *I guess my confidence only needs the squeak of a door to evaporate.*

But no one comes running to check out the sound. Jeep's skeletons must make enough noise to hide our presence.

Vicky opens the door a crack and peers through. She holds up two fingers to us, then goes inside with her sword drawn. D'Maeo, Gisella and Taylar follow close behind. The sound of metal on metal echoes through the hallway before the door closes, and Dylan, Charlie and I take our places next to each other to defend the door and keep our escape route open.

I can hear the whistling of wind before the first demon rounds the corner.

Charlie nudges me. "This would be a great time to focus on ice again."

My gaze moves to the floor, and I freeze it bit by bit. The cold moves further away from us as I envision cold sweeping over the lower part of the demon.

"Not too cold," Dylan warns me. "The trick is to let the funnels of the demons take on the same temperature as the upper part."

Sure, it sounds so simple when he says it, but try realizing it!

"You can do it, Dante. I know you can," Charlie says calmly.

Blobs of grease soar through the air as soon as the first arm becomes visible.

I picture cold air instead of ice crawling up the funnel that forms the lower part of the demon. It starts to turn slower and looks down in surprise.

"Yes!" Charlie yells. "Keep going!"

"A little colder," Dylan advises, and I turn down the temperature a bit more.

The tornado demon stops turning, lets out a fearful moan, and goes up in black smoke.

Dylan jumps up and down in a solid imitation of Kessley when she's excited. "You did it!"

"There are more of them," Charlie warns, throwing more grease away from him.

In a short moment of silence, I can hear yelling and groaning behind the door to our right. I hope our friends and the soul are safe.

Charlie gives me a quick nudge. "Focus, Dante!"

I shake my head and drown out the sounds coming from my right. "Yes, I'm focused!"

A second tornado demon has stepped out. This time, it doesn't take me long to envision his lower body getting colder and colder. Gradually, his movements come to a halt, and he too goes up in smoke.

"This is going better than I expected," Dylan says.

Of course, there's no better way to jinx something. On cue, a demon, bigger than the ones we've seen so far, whirls around the corner.

"The head demon," Charlie whispers. He showers

it with grease, but the monster evades all of it easily, changing shape several times in seconds.

I concentrate on cooling its funnel, but it's not working. It isn't slowing down. In fact, it's speeding up. The howling from the wind is so loud now that I feel the urge to cover my ears.

Don't let it distract you. No matter how big it is, you can defeat it by cooling the lower air down.

"Can you build a bigger ball?" I ask Charlie.

He nods without answering.

My eyes zoom in on the funnel of the demon, and I will it to get colder. I envision the cold spreading quickly.

Still, nothing happens.

Maybe this demon is colder than the others.

I try ice. It crackles around the vortex as the monster slides closer to us. Finally, it turns a bit slower, and I double my efforts.

But then the demon raises its arms and throws them forward.

We're hit by a blast of wind and knocked over. I fly back so far that I slam against the front doors. Charlie slams into them next to me, and Dylan goes through the wood.

The demon roars triumphantly. Behind it, a nun appears.

We're running out of time. We need to take it out before all of the nuns come running back inside.

Dylan seems to have come to the same conclusion. He dives back into the hallway and sprints past us.

"I'll distract it!"

"What? No!" I yell, but he's already halfway there.

He performs a jump that an acrobat would be proud of, with his feet forward to kick the demon in the stomach.

With a roar, it brings its arms forward to squash the young mage. I cover my eyes. I can't bear to watch this.

Charlie yanks at my arm. "Cool it while it's distracted!"

I lower my hands. "Right."

When I aim the ice at the demon again, I see that Dylan is hanging on to its neck. How he managed to get there, I have no idea, but it gives my hopes a boost.

Instead of building up the cold slowly, I send out a blast of ice myself. Charlie picks up the big ball of gel that he created and throws it when the demon's whirling slows down a bit.

The nun behind the monster doesn't lift a finger when the demon stumbles. *What is she waiting for?*

I ignore her as much as I can and bring the temperature of the ice down some more.

The demon bucks and hisses in an attempt to get rid of the ice as well as Dylan, who is hammering its head with his fists non-stop. But the young ghost is clinging on tight with his legs, and I'm still sending the ice up, making the monster lose more and more speed. He's barely twisting at all anymore.

As it comes to a halt, Dylan raises his hands above

his head and brings them down with force.

In a last near-death twitch, the demon rises to its full height, flattening Dylan against the ceiling. Then the monster falls apart, and the mage lands face first on the floor.

Charlie and I immediately bombard the waiting nun with balls of ice and grease, drawing nearer to help our friend up at the same time.

Dylan is unconscious, so we both grab an arm and start dragging him back with us.

After a couple of steps, he comes to, and I ask him if he's okay.

"Fine. Just some old-fashioned bad luck. Wrong place, wrong time."

"That was pretty brave and pretty stupid," I say. "But I think you saved our asses with it."

"Really?"

I don't get the chance to answer him, because suddenly, the spot where he hit the ceiling cracks, and debris rains down. The nun finally wakes from her almost hypnotized state of staring at us.

CHAPTER 17

The nun blinks, and a flicker of worry crosses her face.

"I think you were in the exact right spot, Dylan, at the exact right time," I whisper to our new friend.

Charlie nods. "Something important is hidden there. We should find out what it is."

I hold out my arm, in case he means to check it out this instant. "We can't. The soul is what we're here for. She's our most important mission."

"But if we can, we should free these nuns," he insists.

I bite my lip. *He's right. We can't leave them possessed like this, for their sakes and for the sake of everyone around them. Who knows what they will do to the people of this town if we leave them here.*

"As soon as the soul is safe, we'll come back to kill the demons that possess these nuns, and we'll check out that ceiling." I gesture for Charlie to move toward the decorated door. I wonder what's taking our friends so long. But going inside will leave the hallway unprotected, so we have no other choice but to wait here, fight off the sisters, and hope that our friends will come out soon.

Another nun rounds the corner and comes to a halt beside the first. She whispers something in her ear, and a grin appears on both faces simultaneously, sending chills down my spine. Still, they don't move; they just stand there, staring at us with eyes that glow red.

I knock on the door next to me. "Come on, hurry up," I mumble.

The calmness of the two nuns is making me nervous. *They're not worried about losing the soul at all. Does that mean that our friends behind the door have already lost their battle? Are they being trapped or killed as we wait for them to come out?*

"We should go check it out," I say softly to Charlie.

My best friend shakes his head. "No, it's a trick. They want us to go inside, and as soon as we do, they'll block all the exits."

I lower my hand, which was moving to the door handle already. "What's taking them so long?"

"You go check it out, Dante," a voice says from behind me. When I look over my shoulder, Jeep, Maël and Kessley step through the front doors. Jeep opens one of them to let a bunch of zombies in, which he

169

directs into a line between us and the two sisters. "Go on, Dante, we'll keep them at bay."

"Why aren't you out back?" I ask.

He shrugs. "We could only fool them for so long. As soon as a couple of them went back inside, we decided to join you here. After all, we're stronger together, don't you think?"

I grit my teeth when a third nun appears. "Okay. I'll go inside to see what's going on. I'll be back as soon as possible."

Kessley splits herself in two. "Don't worry, we've got this."

After a curt nod at the others, I tentatively push open the door. It's quiet in the room that lies behind it, and only a weak light comes from about six paces away.

I gather up all of my courage and step inside, closing the door behind me. "Vicky?" I whisper.

No answer.

I conjure a lightning ball in my hand and prepare to throw it at the first thing that jumps me, but nothing happens. With a quick flip of my hand, I send the lightning to the ceiling. When it lights up the whole room, I can see that there's no one here. There is, however, a door next to the tiny light in the corner. I walk over to it and put my ear against the wood. There are voices behind it, urgent, but not panicked. No sounds of a fight.

With a simple hand gesture, I extinguish the lightning. I grab the handle and pull the door open inch by inch. It doesn't make a sound, but nevertheless, I find myself staring at the sharp tip of a blade.

"Don't move," Gisella says.

"It's me," I squeak.

The blade changes into a hand. "Dante? Why are you here? Is everyone okay?"

She opens the door further, and I rub the spot between my eyes where her blade touched my skin. "Everyone is fine. For now. I came to see what's taking you guys so long. The nuns are gathering in the hallway. We need to get out of here."

When Gisella steps aside, I get a full view of the situation. The soul we need to save, the nun that bakes croissants so it seems, is sitting with her back against the wall of the room. It's a storage room, filled with carton boxes. D'Maeo and Taylar are standing on each side of her, and Vicky has crouched down in front of the nun. She's talking to her softly. The nun herself is in tears. But at least she's alive and all of my friends are okay.

I turn back to Gisella. "What's wrong with her?"

"The possessed nuns have gotten to her. They made her lust for a man, apparently. I'm not sure how they managed it. But now, she says she needs to be punished for this sin."

"You're kidding," I say.

She gives me a stern look and gestures at the weeping nun.

"You're not kidding," I conclude.

171

"I wish I was. She refuses to come with us."

I rub the stubble on my chin that I forgot to shave off. "Did you tell her why we're here?"

"Of course."

I glance back at the closed door. The pressure of getting out of here feels like a real weight on my shoulders. I roll them back and forth a couple of times, trying to come up with a solution. Then my gaze falls upon Vicky again.

"Babe, did you try your powers on her yet?" I ask.

She nods without turning around. "They blocked them somehow. I can't influence her."

I curse under my breath, and the nun looks up. Anger flashes across her face, and she makes the sign of a cross.

"Sorry," I say, "but we really need to get you out of here. If we don't, the Devil will win. Do you understand?"

"I do, but I need to punish myself for my sin."

"Okay, but can you do that later? Time is running out for all of us here."

She pushes herself to her feet abruptly and takes a thick rope from her pocket. "I can't come with you. I need to die!" she screams. "I felt lust!"

My heart pounds loudly at the sight of the rope. I remember the noose on the Card of Death and realize I need to stay calm. "That wasn't your fault," I explain. "You were manipulated. Magic was used to influence your feelings."

She shakes her head fervently. "It doesn't matter. I

172

was susceptible to it. I need to be punished."

I hold up my hand when she moves the rope up to her neck. "Wait. Please. There are other ways to punish yourself. If you die, you will only bring Satan closer to his plans. Is that what you want? Is that what God would want?"

Finally, a glimpse of hesitation crosses her face.

Carefully, I take a step forward and place my hand on the rope. "Besides, what kind of people would *we* be if we stood by while you killed yourself?"

She stares at me for a moment, and I'm convinced that she'll come with us. But then she jerks the rope back and pushes me away. "You would be good people, for letting me punish myself for my sin."

I purse my lips. *Why isn't she cooperating? Why can't she see that her life is important?*

Gisella pushes me aside. She throws down her hands, that change into blades. She presses the sharp tips against the nun's neck. "You're coming with us now, or else…" she hisses.

The nun doesn't even blink. "Or else what? You'll kill me? Go ahead, I deserve it."

Gisella's blades change back into hands, and she steps back. Her jaws are set tight. "Fine. Then I'll let the shadows carry you away from here."

She stretches her arms sideways and calls the shadows to her. They circle above us and block the light from the lamp on the ceiling. They whirl around Taylar and darken his face so much that my heart almost stops for a second. *Is he turning evil again?* I

173

haven't seen any signs of evil in him for a while, so I pushed my concerns to a corner of my mind. *Was I wrong to do that? Should I ask Dylan to cure him? If he even can… what if this is not the result of a curse or spell?*

The shadows wrap around his hand, but he shakes them off, and they continue their path to the nun. The darkness that lingers in his eyes vanishes when he blinks several times. I breathe out slowly.

"Wait," Vicky suddenly says.

The shadows come to a halt.

"I was wondering…" Vicky tilts her head in thought. "Isn't suicide also a sin?"

The nun's eyes grow wide. Her lips move, but no sound comes out.

Vicky holds out her hand. "Please come with us. God will be grateful if you help us in our battle against the Devil. You can always punish yourself after that."

With clenched teeth, she places the rope on the ground and takes Vicky's hand. "Okay, I will come with you."

My fingers unclench, and I flex them several times. I hadn't even noticed my hands balling into fists.

Taylar moves to the door and opens it slowly, holding his shield high to protect his face. My worries about him evaporate again. *Maybe I'm imagining things. No one else seems to think anything is wrong.*

"The coast is clear," he says, "but there's a lot of noise coming from the hallway."

I run over to him and conjure a lightning ball.

"Let's go then. This has taken way too long already."

Taylar and I leave the room first, and the others escort the nun to make sure she doesn't go anywhere and that she's safe from any surprise attacks.

"D'Maeo and Gisella, can you protect her? The rest of us will join the fight."

They all nod. At the door to the hallway, I count down from three. On zero, I pull the door open as wide as it will go, and we spill out of the room.

The noise in the hallway is deafening. There's shouting and huffing plus the sound of bones hitting the walls and ground as Jeep's skeletons attack the two lines of nuns that have formed. There are nine of them, all dressed in the black robes I saw in my premonition, and with red flaring eyes. The five in front twist and bend to avoid the incoming skeletons and grease bombs. They keep the other four sisters behind them safe from the attacks. Every couple of seconds, one or two of them move in slow motion, but it's clear that Maël isn't able to freeze them in time completely. That gives the four nuns in the back line the opportunity to hit our friends with some sort of invisible force by simply moving their hands.

Without hesitation, I throw four lightning balls in their direction. Then I focus on hail stones raining down on them. Some of them miss, but with a jerk of her head, Vicky sends them sideways.

The nuns are hit. Their psychic pushes stop for a moment, and I gesture for my friends to get out of here.

175

"I'll stay here to help you," Charlie says, moving closer to me when the others start to walk backwards and open the front doors.

I envision the hail stones getting bigger and hitting all of the sisters, but suddenly I'm flying through the air. I connect with the wall to my right with unpleasant speed, and everything spins. I see Charlie collapsing against the wall opposite me. I expect him to push himself up immediately, like I do, but he lays still.

There's a shrill scream from behind me, and Gisella slides over to my best friend. She shakes him, but he doesn't move.

I try to get the hail falling again, but I can't concentrate. Charlie's still form is etched into my vision.

An invisible hand lifts me and pushes me against the wall. I try to grab it as it goes for my throat, but I can't move my arms anymore. A pathetic whine escapes my lips as I try to call for help.

Gisella glances over her shoulder at me. She stands up to help me, but as she does, Charlie is lifted from the ground. He hovers at waist height for a second, his head tilted back, before suddenly rising higher and slamming against the ceiling. I can hear some of his bones breaking, but the harder I fight to free myself, the harder the invisible hand squeezes. Everything around me is getting hazy as I fight for oxygen.

The last thing I see before my brain shuts down is the werecat-witch slamming her hands together.

There's a loud whoosh, followed by… nothing.

CHAPTER 18

"Babe?" Someone is shaking my shoulder. It must be Vicky, because no one else calls me babe. But her voice sounds contorted, dark and far away.

"Come on, breathe." She slaps my cheek, and I open my eyes.

My lungs scream for air, and I suck it in with big gulps.

"You're okay. You're okay." She strokes my hair and kisses my forehead.

When my breathing returns to normal, she takes my hand and pulls me up. "Come on, we need to get out of here. Gisella can handle this."

I blink several times, but my vision is not playing tricks on me. The hallway has grown darker. The sisters are all facing the werecat-witch with their arms outstretched. Shadows circle around Gisella as she stands there, her legs spread, her arms wide and her jaw clenched in anger.

One by one, the nuns start to sway on their feet. One falls down, clutching her chest. This only makes the others more determined to take Gisella out. Their red irises glow brighter as they double their efforts. As one, they take a step forward.

While Gisella brings her arms to her chest, Vicky and I hurry over to Charlie. He's still out cold, and I place my finger on his neck to check his pulse. Tears boil to the surface when I feel his heartbeat. "He's alive."

We lift his arms over our shoulders and make for the doors that have closed behind our friends. When we move through the left door sideways, I glance back and see Gisella bringing her hands forward in a pushing motion. I can feel the air move even from where I'm standing. Vicky pulls at Charlie, but I stay put as the force field that Gisella created hits the nuns. They are thrown back and land in a heap on the floor.

"Gisella! Time to leave!" I yell at her.

When she turns, her face is a mask of hate and anger. Dark, pulsing lines are etched into her skin, and her pupils are gone. It's as if I'm staring into two gaping holes.

"Pull yourself together, please," I beg her. "We don't want to lose you."

Her lips part, and she smirks at me. "You won't lose me." She shakes her head, and her red hair turns a shade lighter. The dark lines leave her skin, and her eyes return to normal. "I'm fine."

She catches up with us in what seems to be one stride, turns back one more time and sends all of the shadows to the fallen sisters.

We step outside, and Gisella closes the door behind us. Charlie mumbles something incoherent when she gently touches his cheek.

"He'll be okay," I tell her, and I gesture at our cars. "If we get out of here now."

Behind us, the doors of the monastery open.

Gisella turns back around. "Go!" she urges us.

The nuns file out of the building, and immediately, the whole street darkens even further. We push a half-conscious Charlie in the back seat of his car. Vicky slides in beside him and Dylan on his other side. When I see Jeep has already started Phoenix, I jump behind the wheel of Charlie's car. I prepare to back up the car to pick up Gisella, but Jeep is already steering Phoenix toward her.

Dark clouds gather above the battling women. Even though I can barely see them, I can tell they are throwing force fields at each other. Gisella is constantly bracing herself against the pressure, and the nuns keep swaying on their feet.

The werecat-witch really looks like a witch now, with her red hair blowing in an unseen, strong breeze and shadows soaring above her. When the clouds part for a millisecond, I can tell that the look on her face is murderous.

Charlie groans behind me, and my gaze shifts to

him. "Are you okay, mate?"

His hand goes to his head and then to his ribs. "I've been better, you know. What happened?"

Dylan chuckles. "Your girlfriend is kicking their asses."

Charlie works himself up on his elbow to peer through the rear window. "Really?"

Gisella throws her hands forward again, creating a blast that knocks over the sisters. A couple of them fly through the open front door. The rest scramble to their feet quickly, but Gisella hops inside my car, and Jeep hits the gas. I do the same to make sure we don't collide.

Something I can't see shakes the car. The doors and windows rattle, and the vehicle sways. I grab the steering wheel tighter and push my foot down as far as it will go. The corner of the street comes closer at frightening speed. But so does the darkness behind us.

A glance in my rearview mirror tells me Jeep isn't the only one following us. The nuns have started their pursuit. They remind me of bad guys in superhero movies with their robes billowing behind them.

"Make the turn!" Vicky suddenly yells.

My attention flies back to the road in front of me. I turn just in time to avoid the lamppost and thunder on into the garden behind it. "Sorry!"

"It's okay, we understand," Dylan says.

"It still makes me nauseous," Charlie responds.

"Sorry," I repeat. Then I point at the sky. "Look.

It's getting brighter above us."

Vicky turns in her seat. "They're giving up."

I risk another glance in my mirror and let out a sigh of relief. The others have gotten away too. And Phoenix is still in one piece.

I drive back to the highway and stop on the corner of the last street before it. Jeep comes to a halt behind us.

"What are you doing?" Vicky asks. "Jeep can drive your car home. She'll be fine."

I smile when she refers to Phoenix as a she, since everyone usually refuses to do that. "I know that, but I want to check on the nun, and we need to discuss our options. Plus, Gisella has to heal Charlie."

Vicky raises an eyebrow. "It would be better to do those things at Darkwood Manor. And if something was wrong with the nun, the others would've let us know already, don't you think? We should get her to safety, at home. What if those possessed nuns come after us again?"

I point my finger at her. "Exactly! That's what worries me. Why did they possess those sisters instead of killing them and taking the soul with them? And what was in that hole on that ceiling?" I suppress a shiver. "They're up to something. We need to find out what that is, and how to stop them."

Vicky's mouth nearly falls open. "And risk the nun falling back into their hands?"

"Of course not, Charlie and Dylan will take her to Darkwood Manor. The rest of us will go back to the monastery." I tilt my head. "And do you really want to save one nun and leave the rest in the claws of those demons?"

She grits her teeth. "Not really." She rubs her face with a guilty expression. "I guess I was a bit too focused on our mission."

"That's not a bad thing." I blow her a kiss. "I know you would've suggested to go back later. I just think it would be better to stop them as soon as possible."

Charlie moves closer to the car door with a groan. "I'd like to help. I feel better. Maybe Dylan can take the nun back to the mansion on his own?"

I ponder that for a second while Jeep gets out of my car. "No, I'm sorry, but I think it's better that at least two of us go with the nun. She's unpredictable, so we need two people who can keep her calm and make sure she stays at Darkwood Manor until the coast is clear. And we need Gisella to fight the demons."

He bows his head. "I understand. You don't need me to fight anymore."

"Actually, I need all of us, but as you know, you three are the only ones capable of driving home without me."

He grins at me. "I know, I was just playing with you. Keeping the nun safe is an important task, and I'll be happy to do it." His hand flies to his side. "As soon as Gis has put my ribs back together."

"Great." I gesture at the driver's seat. "Can you

drive?"

He looks at Dylan. "My head still hurts, and I'm a bit dizzy, so maybe you can take us home?"

Dylan starts to laugh. "Are you kidding me? I'm too young to drive, and I don't know how."

Charlie lets Vicky pull him out of the car while Jeep comes to a halt next to me. "You've been old enough in ghost years for quite some time, you know."

"I guess you're right, but I still don't know how to drive, so that doesn't help us. And neither would getting pulled over by the cops."

"What's the plan?" Jeep enquires.

I nod at Charlie's car. "Charlie and Dylan take the nun to the mansion while we come up with a plan to get those demons out of the other nuns."

"Good idea."

Charlie takes a step forward and nearly keels over. He grabs the car door for support. "Maybe we need a new plan."

Gisella comes strolling over too. I want to ask her where she got all of that power, but we have other priorities at this moment. So instead, I ask, "Can you heal Charlie?"

She takes Charlie's head between her hands and looks into his eyes. "I can only heal broken bones and such, but I'll see what else I can do."

I leave him in her competent hands and walk over to my car, followed by Vicky. The nun nearly gets squashed between the ghosts in the back seat.

Although not literally, of course, since they blend together to give her some room. Her arms are folded across her chest. I'm not sure who she's mad at: us or herself.

I pull the car door open. "We're changing teams." I bend over to meet the nun's eyes. "Two of us will take you to a safe place while the rest of us go back to the monastery to save your sisters."

I give Taylar and Kessley some room to get out of the car. When I hold out my hand to help the nun out, she takes it reluctantly. "My name is Dante, by the way. I am glad you decided to help." Without letting go of her hand, I walk back to Charlie's car.

Gisella has worked her magic. Charlie is doing a lot better. I open the back door and gesture at the back seat. "Charlie and Dylan will protect you. I hope we can talk later."

She lifts her foot to get in but changes her mind and turns back to me. She holds out her hand, and I take it. "My name is Sister Carol. Thank you, Dante, to you and your friends. I may be a sinner, but I still know good when I see it. I was wrong to leave my sisters, but I know they will be okay now. Please let me know if there is anything I can do to help you save them."

I nod gratefully. "Maybe there is. Is there another way into the monastery? A way through which I may be able to slip inside unnoticed?"

She frowns but soon starts to nod feverishly. "We recently installed a garbage chute in the kitchen. Since

I'm usually the one who does all the cooking and baking, hardly anyone else ever uses it. You may be able to climb in through it."

She explains how to approach the kitchen without being seen, and we quickly say goodbye.

I slap Dylan on the back. "Stay safe. I'll see you soon."

"I will light a candle for you," Sister Carol says before she steps into the car, and I give her a small bow.

Charlie hugs me as soon as he lets go of Gisella. Then he gets behind the wheel and drives off. I watch the car until it's swallowed by traffic. Then I turn my head toward Gisella, who's still standing next to me. "Are you okay? How did you do that?"

There's no need for more words; she knows what I mean. "It started as a reflex. I got so angry about what they did to Charlie that the power simply rose to the surface. But I could control it. I could direct it at them, and my mind remained clear."

"The evil inside didn't overwhelm you? Not even for a second?"

She tosses her hair over her shoulder with a flick of her head. "Not even for a millisecond."

Hope flows through me, warming my chest. "Do you think you can do it again, without the anger?"

Briefly, she closes her eyes. "Yes," she says. "I can control it. But…" She opens her eyes and meets mine. "It won't be enough. I can slow them down, but I can't stop them. I don't know enough about my powers to do that yet. There might be more I can do, but not now. And I certainly don't know how to get the demons out of the sisters. I'm afraid we'll need a priest for that."

I beckon her to follow me back to my car. "Let's ask the others if they know anything about exorcism."

CHAPTER 19

As expected, Vicky and D'Maeo know a thing or two about exorcisms.

I rub my hands when they've finished their stories. "Great. I suggest we try that. It'll be faster than locating a priest who can do an exorcism for us. And one priest for nine nuns probably won't be enough anyway."

"Good point," Jeep says. He walks around the car and opens the door on the passenger side. "Let's go get supplies and hurry back to that monastery."

He doesn't seem concerned about another confrontation with the nuns at all, and that gives me more confidence. We saved Sister Carol, defeated the demons and held back the other sisters. And now we have a new plan: to free the nuns of their possessions. We can do this.

A quick search on the internet tells me where we

can find the nearest DIY-shop and supermarket. Since my Shield will flash home if we get separated, we can't split up, so we all file into the supermarket to get everything we need, and then drive to the DIY-shop to get some wood.

Maël takes it and sits down on the back seat, with her legs outside, covered by an old towel that I found in the trunk. I hand her my athame, and she starts to carve.

Meanwhile, mostly hidden from view by Phoenix, we prepare the ingredients for our exorcism. I'm about to ask Vicky to hand me her necklace, which is a cross, to create holy water, when I think of something. "Hey, wouldn't it be much more effective if we asked Quinn for help? He is an angel after all."

Vicky frowns at me. "Sure, if he has the time. Which he probably doesn't."

"Easy enough to find out." I check for passerby, and when the coast is clear, I call out to Quinn in my head.

With a whoosh and a bright flash, he lands next to me. His dark face is covered in red lines, and I cover my mouth with my hand. "Are you okay?"

His hand touches his cheeks and forehead, and he examines the red that sticks to his fingertips. "Oh. Yes, that's not mine." With a shake of his hands and head, he gets rid of it.

"Did you find the missing angels?" I ask.

"Not yet," he grumbles. "What do you need?"

I raise the bottle of water in my hand. "Can you

189

turn this into holy water?"

"Sure." He takes the bottle from me, lifts it to his mouth and breathes out. A tiny light jumps from his lips into the bottle. It illuminates the water for a second, spreading from the surface to the bottom, before vanishing.

Quinn hands me the bottle. "There you go. Anything else?"

"Yes, do you have some kind of angelic object that we can use for an exorcism?"

"And the exact lines we need to recite?" Vicky adds quickly.

Quinn's hand goes through his short curls. "I can get you an angelic object, no problem." He turns to Vicky. "And you don't need to recite anything specific. That's just something they do in the movies, but demons are not affected by them. All you have to do is be confident and tell them exactly what you want. The only specific word that truly affects them is their true name, but I'm guessing you don't have that."

I scratch my head. "Not unless they're called Tornado Demon 1, Tornado Demon 2 and so on."

His lips curl up a bit. "I don't think so."

Kessley giggles. "We can always try."

With a smile, I shake my head. "Sure. But seriously. Quinn, what kind of angelic object can you lend us? And is there anything else that could help us exorcise nine demons?"

His eyebrows move up. "Nine demons?" He

breathes out loudly. "That's a lot. Give me a sec."

He vanishes into thin air with only a soft whoosh.

D'Maeo is pacing up and down beside the car, mumbling to himself. "If the bible citations and such won't do us any good, does that mean the other things won't work either?"

I put a hand on his arm to stop him when he passes me. "Don't worry about it. Quinn would've told us if the holy water was useless. We can ask him about the cross when he comes back."

As soon as the last word leaves my lips, Quinn lands beside us.

"Will the wooden cross work?" Kessley asks immediately, as if she's afraid we'll forget otherwise.

"Yes, but only if you dip it in holy water," the angel answers.

He hands me a thick stick about half my height, with white flowers sprouting from the end. "This is the rod of Aaron. He used it to correct and guide his flock. It has divine power, but there is not much left of it. You can only use it once, and I am not sure for how long. But it will make the demons move wherever you want them to."

Vicky holds out her hand and gently touches the wood. "I remember the stories. Is this the real thing?"

"Of course it is. Would I bring you a fake one that doesn't work?"

Her cheeks go red. "No, you wouldn't."

He smiles. "I've got more." He shows us a large bottle filled with glowing red liquid.

"What's that?"

"Angel blood."

I gulp. I don't even want to think about how he got a hold of that much blood.

Sorrow falls over his face when he looks at the liquid. "At least these angels didn't die in vain." He presses the bottle into my hand. "Demons can't handle angel blood very well. Use it wisely."

I press the bottle against my chest. "I will. Thank you so much, Quinn. I owe you one."

He tilts his head to the sky. "Don't worry about that. You'll pay me back your debt soon."

"What does that mean?" I ask, but there's nothing but air between me and my Shield. Quinn has gone back to Heaven.

I examine the rod and bottle in my hands. "Well, I guess we're ready to rock and roll."

Maël walks around the car and holds up the wooden cross she's carved. Vicky takes the bottle of holy water from under my arm and trickles some of the contents onto the cross. A glow wraps all around it and makes the intricate carvings more visible. Maël created little crosses and stars with flames around them.

Taylar looks over her shoulder. "What do those stars mean?"

Maël's finger follows the small lines on the cross. "These are anti-possession symbols. They will help us to drive the demons out of the nuns' bodies."

"How do you know them?"

She wipes some wood splinters from her dress. "My grandfather drew one for me once. I forgot about it, but while I was carving, it is as if my hand remembered the shape of it."

A tear falls down her cheek, and D'Maeo wipes it away. "This is a good sign. Even our ancestors get through to us to help us in this battle."

Maël rests her head against his, and that shows so much love and respect, from both sides, that I have to swallow a couple of tears myself.

I turn away from them and hand the rod and bottle to Vicky. "Can you hold on to this while I drive?"

She takes it but doesn't move. "Shouldn't we think of a way to use this blood one drop at a time instead of the whole bottle at once?"

I slap my forehead. "Right. Sorry, I was so excited that I overlooked that. Do you have any ideas?"

She holds out the rod to me with a wide grin. "I sure do."

When I grab the stick, she digs into her endless pocket and pulls out a spray bottle. "I've got two of these. Put them in not too long ago. Thought I might need them to spray holy water. But this is even better."

I could hug her, but I don't want to risk her dropping the bottle of blood. So instead, I blow her a kiss with my free hand. "I love how well you always anticipate."

Her grin widens, and she pours the blood into the

first spray bottle. D'Maeo takes the full one from her, and she pulls out another, which fills up completely too.

The old ghost holds them both up. "We've got two great weapons here. But we shouldn't assume this will do the job."

"Right," I agree. "It's never as easy as it seems."

Jeep snorts. "When did it ever seem easy?"

"Good point." I nod at the spray bottles in D'Maeo's hands. "Can you try them, please? I want to make sure they work."

He sprays them both, and two small fountains of red come to life.

"Great, let's go," I say, and I get behind the wheel.

Jeep holds the rod for me while I drive back to the monastery.

I'm relieved to see that the darkness hasn't spread more, even though the impenetrable gray clouds above the street seem more threatening than before.

I park Phoenix in the driveway of the first house, hidden behind a hedgerow.

I take in my small army and try to decide who gets which weapon. Someone needs to use the rod to try and keep the sisters in place while we perform the exorcism.

Eventually, I realize there only one choice. "Vicky, are you willing to take the rod and use it on the nuns?"

It's as if the request alone makes her glow from head to toe. "You think I can do that?"

"Not only that, I think you're the most suitable person for the task. You already have the power to control people's feelings, and you're able to remain calm enough to use it under stressful circumstances."

She blushes. "I hope you're right. But…" She glances at the ghost queen standing behind her. "I think Maël would be even better at it. She's probably the calmest of us all."

I smile. "True, but Maël can help you by slowing the nuns down in time."

D'Maeo nods contently. "Sounds like a good plan."

Jeep hands the rod to Vicky, who handles it as if it's as fragile and valuable as an antique vase.

The old ghost holds up the spray bottles. "What about these two?"

"I think you and Taylar should take those. Jeep can resurrect the skeletons again, Kessley can multiply or change into something big in case we need extra strength to hold them back, Gisella is probably the only one who can actually take them out if anything goes wrong, and I need to perform the exorcism. We'll all have our hands full."

Taylar moves his shield to his back and exchanges it for a sword. "I like to have my hands full. I fight better with a weapon than without."

"Great. So it's settled then?"

After a unanimous 'yes', I walk to the end of the hedge and peer around it. "I think the coast is clear."

We cross the street quickly and make our way to

the monastery one garden at a time. I'd rather get there three minutes later than be seen. There's probably a nun on the look-out.

"Maël," I whisper, when there's only one more house between us and the monastery. "Can you stop time for anyone outside the monastery or looking out of the window?"

The African queen pushes her cape down before the wind can lift it above her head. "No, I need to see my target."

"I can provide some cover," Gisella says, and she lifts her head to the sky. Some of the dark clouds above us are torn apart, and the pieces slowly descend, surrounding the church on all sides. I'm surprised at how natural it looks, as if it's nothing more than a normal shift in the weather. The difference in the sky can't even be seen with the amount of clouds that still hover above the street.

The werecat-witch stands up in full sight of the monastery. "We're good to go."

We follow her to the entrance that Sister Carol told us about. The garbage chute ends above a transportable steel container. It hasn't been emptied for a while, by the looks of it, and the smell is so bad that I almost throw up.

"Do you think there's a dead body in there?" I ask D'Maeo in a hushed tone.

He covers his nose with his free hand. "No, I think this is just the smell of rotting food."

Taylar and Kessley roll the container aside quietly.

The wheels squeak a bit, but not loud enough to be noticed inside. Or so I hope.

"I'll go first," Gisella says. She steps up under the chute, calls a couple of shadows to her, and they push her up through the steel tunnel. There's another squeak when she opens the door at the top, followed by silence. A couple of seconds later, the shadows shoot out of the chute and wrap around me. I try to relax as they drag me toward the tunnel and pull me inside. It's not that big, and I have to push my shoulders forward to squeeze through. The shadows go faster and faster, and I squeeze my eyes shut, expecting to collide with the door at the top. But at the last second, we slow down, and I'm eased through the opening. Gisella is waiting for me on the other side, with a smug expression on her face.

"Great job," I whisper when the shadows put me down.

The corner of her lips twitches up, and she nods before directing the shadows into the chute again.

I take in the deserted kitchen, walk to the door and put my ear against it. There are no sounds coming from the other side, and for the first time, I'm starting to worry that the sisters are no longer here. *What if they didn't go back inside at all? What if they are tracking down Sister Carol or killing the locals?*

I want to tell Gisella to wait, but then I hear a faint voice in the distance, low and threatening. *It sounds like the nun in my premonition. Is she giving the others instructions?*

Taylar arrives and joins me at the door. He listens for a while before asking the question that goes through my mind too. "What are they doing?"

"I think they're working out their next step," I whisper back. "They must be up to something, or they wouldn't have possessed those nuns. And I don't think they've given up on getting Sister Carol's soul yet."

He places his hand on the door, and his face turns dark. "They have infected the whole building."

He tilts his head unnaturally far, and a deep frown appears in his forehead.

I take a step back, dread filling up my chest. "Taylar, are you okay?"

His eyes stare past me, a shade darker than usual. "Fine," he says, but it comes out as a low growl.

Ignoring the voice in my head that tells me to get away from him, I reach out and grab him by the shoulders. "Are you turning evil again? Fight it, Taylar! We need you on our side."

I squeeze his shoulders hard when he doesn't respond. "Please!"

His gaze shifts to me. His frown deepens, and I feel him stiffening under my touch. Then he shakes his head fervently, and his face returns to its normal pale see-through state.

I smile at him. "Glad to have you back." I scratch my head in thought. "Maybe you should stay outside?"

His mouth forms a determined line. "No, I can

handle it. Don't worry about me."

I nod slowly, trying to decide if it's worth the risk. But we're short-handed already, so I guess we don't have much choice. "Okay, but be careful. If something feels wrong, tell me."

He chuckles. "Really? Something feels wrong all the time. Satan is close to escaping Hell, and Heaven is under attack. Let me tell you, lots of things feel wrong right now."

My fist hits his shoulder playfully. "You know what I mean. If you feel like evil is getting a hold on you, give me a heads-up. I can't deal with friends turning against me when I'm fighting those nuns."

He raises his thumb. "Deal."

Meanwhile, Gisella is lifting the last member of the Shield into the kitchen. There's no need to ask them if they're ready. Their faces speak volumes. Each of them is as scared as I am but determined to get this done. The only one who doesn't seem the least bothered by the task that lies ahead is Gisella. She's always been confident, but her recently added powers must have shredded the last of her fears.

I like it. It boosts my confidence a bit too.

The werecat-witch releases the shadows, that slip back into their corners. She gestures for us to get out of the way. "I'll go first, to hold them back."

Vicky holds the rod out in front of her. "Wait. I think I should go first. I can keep them in place with this stick. It's better if you save your energy for when we really need it."

Gisella comes to a halt. "Fair enough. Let's go together, in case the rod doesn't work."

Vicky places her hand on the doorknob and waits for Gisella to join her at the door. Their eyes meet, and when they nod in unison, Vicky opens the door. They step out into the hallway with their hands high and all of their muscles tensed, ready for any kind of attack. When all remains calm, I follow them out, with the others on my heels.

The nun's low voice is coming from the room across the kitchen. The door is closed, so they haven't noticed us yet.

"What do you want to do?" Vicky asks me in a whisper. "Go inside or lure them into the hallway?"

I turn to D'Maeo and Maël for advice, and they reach a conclusion at the same time. "The hallway."

"We don't know what's behind that door. There might be weapons in there they can use. Here, we know what we've got," D'Maeo explains.

Before anyone can respond, the low voice of the nun rings out loud and clear. "We go after them. Now!"

The last word is like thunder, and we back up as one.

I make a beeline for the wall next to the door and press myself against it, hoping to be invisible to anyone leaving that room. The others follow my example just before the door opens, and the nuns spill out into the hallway.

CHAPTER 20

The lanterns on the walls flicker as the sisters walk by. I can feel the atmosphere changing, even though I could already sense the evil as soon as we left the kitchen. With the possessed nuns so close, the air is thicker. It's as if the darkness sucks the oxygen from the air, and an invisible weight presses down onto me, making it almost impossible for me to stay upright.

I don't feel ready at all when the last nun turns around to close the door behind her and spots us.

She opens her mouth to warn the others, and I expect Vicky or Gisella to stop her. Or even Maël to slow her down in time. But they let her utter a scream that makes all the other nuns turn around.

Then I understand Vicky's plan. The two sisters that were about to turn the corner at the end of the hall are walking back. Or sliding is more like it. The demons have obviously strengthened their hold on their hosts while we were gone. The 'head nun' even starts to spin like the tornado demons do.

I want to yell for someone to stop her, before she knocks us all over, but before the first consonant leaves my lips, Vicky holds out the rod, and the nuns all come to an abrupt halt.

Maël, who must have had the same fears as me, lowers her staff.

D'Maeo, Taylar and I step in front of our friends. Seemingly without any trouble, Vicky steers the nuns closer together so we can reach them all with the angel blood easily.

I take the wooden cross that Maël carved from my pocket and hold it out in front of me. Despite their frozen state, the expression on the sisters' faces changes from menacing to fearful. They know what's coming.

"I expel you from these innocent bodies," I say, my voice clear and steady. I make the sign of a cross on myself and step forward to repeat the gesture for each of the nuns, holding the cross out with my other hand.

The nuns hiss and recoil as one, and I glance over my shoulder. "Are you losing them, Vicky?"

"I think I can hang on for a couple more minutes," she grunts.

Maël raises her staff. "I will help her."

"Great." I nod at Taylar and D'Maeo. "Let's continue."

I lift the cross again and step closer to the sisters. I can see them struggling to pull themselves free from the power of the rod and Maël's words. My eyes bore into those of the leader, and I make the sign of a cross, starting with a careful touch of her forehead.

"I compel you to leave this body and this world," I say forcefully.

When I bring the cross forward, to press it against her forehead, D'Maeo sprays angel blood at her. Tiny drops hit her face, neck and hands, and a growl rises from her throat. My body tells me to back up, but I stay put and keep going.

I take a step sideways to face the next nun, make the sign of a cross and repeat my words. "I compel you to leave this body and this world."

The nun opens her mouth and spits at me. Black stuff lands on my shirt, just beneath the collar, and rapidly burns a hole in the fabric. Instead of ripping the shirt from my body, like I want to, I calmly reach for Taylar's bottle and spray blood over the acid-like stuff. It falls apart in the same pitch-black ash that remains when a demon is killed. Although relief and hope burn inside me, I hide them when I look the nun in the eye again and press the wooden cross against her forehead. After all, the best way to face a demon inside a host is without emotion. Since it is impossible to drown out all of your feelings, unless you use a spell, this means you should make sure your face and body language don't show anything.

All I do is give the nun a cold stare before moving on, as if the poison she spit at me didn't affect me at all.

We've reached the last of the nuns when I sense something shifting in the air.

"Spray them, quickly!" I urge the two ghosts with the bottles.

Meanwhile, I back away from the group of nuns. D'Maeo and Taylar follow, and I shout out the words now, not caring about the emotions I'm showing. "Demons of Hell, I expel you from these bodies. I command you to leave and never come back to this world!"

The sisters simultaneously open their mouths and let out a deafening shriek that makes the walls tremble. The lights around us flicker, and some of them die.

"Don't use it all," I tell Taylar, who keeps spraying.

"But it's working," he calls back, without turning around. "Check out their skin!"

D'Maeo places a hand on the young ghost's arm and pushes it down. "We will continue the exorcism as soon as we have them trapped again."

Taylar nods reluctantly and falls in line with us.

I stop next to Vicky, whose face is contorted with concentration. The rod in her hand trembles worse than the walls, and her teeth chatter a bit. The flowers at the end of the stick are withering so fast I can barely tell what color they were.

With the cross stretched out in front of me, I lean closer to Vicky. "It's not working anymore. Save your strength for the fight."

She drops it, panting heavily and leaning on me for

support.

The nuns break free of their invisible prison and lunge as one. Maël's muttering grows louder, and their movement stutters and stops completely. But not before six of them spit a mouthful of muck at us. It's too late to duck, and my mind whirs as I try to come up with a way to evade the blobs of acid soaring straight at me.

At the last moment, D'Maeo moves in front of me and stretches his arms out in front of him. The poison comes to a halt mid-air, stopped by his power of deflection, hovers there for a second and falls down. It leaves holes in the floor, and the old ghost sprays some blood over them.

I breathe out slowly. "Thanks."

When I check on the others, they all seem fine. Jeep has pulled Vicky to him, and I can tell by her small smile that she is recovering.

My gaze rests on Maël a little longer.

"I think she can hold them long enough for us to finish the exorcism," D'Maeo says.

A small nod from the ghost queen confirms this.

When I step up to the sisters again, their faces are twisted in anger. Their skin is cracking, and an oozing black is starting to seep through. One of them was frozen just as she released some acid from her mouth. I need a couple of breaths to steady my emotions. Hate pulses through me, which makes it difficult to focus. And also difficult to see the real women trapped inside the minds that the demons have taken over. *I need to remember that these nuns are not evil. They are victims that need to be saved.*

I study the faces one by one until I find the nun I haven't spoken to yet.

I make the sign of a cross on myself before walking over to her. Her eyes follow my every move, but Maël's powers make it impossible for her to even lift a finger. Which makes me wonder about something.

My hand freezes halfway to her forehead, and I turn my head. "We forgot something important."

"Like what?" Vicky asks, looking energetic again.

"We can't hurt someone who's frozen in time."

Taylar lowers the spray bottle he was holding at the ready. "You're right."

D'Maeo rubs his beard with his free hand. "I hadn't thought of that."

"What do we do now?" Jeep asks.

I sigh. "There's no time for a spell, so I guess I'll have to continue this while we fight them." I hold out the cross and my hand, ready to touch the nun's forehead. "Maël, release them on one. Three... two..."

"Wait!" Gisella's voice rings out so loud I nearly drop the cross.

She hurries over to Maël. "Keep them frozen until I'm ready."

The stone at the tip of Maël's staff glows brighter, and with a satisfied nod, Gisella turns her attention to the nuns. She calls the shadows from the corners and steers them toward the sisters, who are almost steaming with anger now. I imagine the demons inside them didn't count on us being able to immobilize them.

More and more shadows untangle themselves from the ceiling, walls and floor, and several even slide around the corner and from under the doors to the adjoining rooms. They wrap themselves around the frozen women, pressing their black robes tightly around their bodies, which makes them look more like a weird rock band than the residents of a monastery.

"Okay, I've got them," Gisella says, her jaw clenched with the effort of keeping the shadows under control.

Maël stops her mumbling and lowers her staff. Immediately, the nuns start to curse and wriggle, trying to free themselves. But the shadows are strong, and even when one of the sisters starts to turn as fast as a tornado, she's not able to get rid of the shadow holding her in place.

D'Maeo, Taylar and I raise our make-shift weapons at the same time. I press the cross against the nun's forehead. "I compel you to leave this body and this world."

She shows me her teeth but flinches when the angel blood hits her.

I walk backwards until I can face the whole group. "I command all of you demons to leave these innocent bodies and return to where you came from.

I order you never to set foot in this world again." I hold out the cross and move it from left to right slowly. "By the power vested in me by the angels in Heaven and our father watching over us, I command you to leave." With every word, my voice grows louder, and the nuns start to shake uncontrollably. D'Maeo and Taylar spray so much blood over them that my whole vision grows red. Rage shoots up from my toes when parts of the women underneath the demonic masks become visible. I can see the fear behind their eyes and the pain as their fingers cramp into claws. They bend at impossible angles, their angry curses cut off by shrieks of despair.

"Leave this world!" I shout, stepping closer to the sisters in front and touching them again with the cross. "You are not welcome here! Your time on Earth is up!"

A horrendous coughing rises from their throats, and they all throw their heads back. They convulse so violently that I fear their necks will break, but then, nine slivers of dark ash slither from their mouths, up to the ceiling and straight through it. The nuns stop moving. They hang limply in the shadows until Gisella lets them down gently.

With the cross still in my hand, I kneel next to the nearest sister. I touch her forehead with the wood, and when there's no response, I feel for a pulse. "She's okay," I tell the others.

I quickly check them all, and Gisella frees them of the shadows. Kessley multiplies herself and rushes into the kitchen to grab a glass of water for each of the nuns. One by one, they wake up. My Shield does a great job calming them down and explaining what happened.

I help the 'head nun' to her feet and grab her arm to make sure she doesn't fall over again.

"Thank you so much," she says breathlessly. "We fought with everything we had, but they were too strong. I don't know what we would've done without you."

"I do," one of the other sisters says, wiping the dust from her robe. "We would've killed Sister Carol and cloaked the whole town in darkness."

The other women cover their mouths in horror. Tears burn in their eyes, and they put their arms around each other in search of comfort.

"Wait…" The nun that's leaning on me shoots upright, her head swiveling from left to right in search of something. "Where *is* Sister Carol? Did they take her?" Her voice rises in panic, and I quickly grab her arm again.

"Don't worry about her. Our friends took her to a safe place."

She presses her hand against her heart. "Thank the Lord. We're finally safe again. For a moment there, I thought we were all lost."

The Kessleys collect all the empty glasses, and only one of her returns. Some of the sisters raise an eyebrow at her, but no one comments. I can't blame them for being a little suspicious of magic. After all, their first encounter with it wasn't very colorful.

I put the wooden cross on the floor and carefully let go of the nun. "I'm sorry, but we should go. We have a lot to do. Now that the demons have returned to their circle of Hell, we can send Sister Carol back to you."

The nuns bow as one and thank us over and over.

"Those demons wanted to use us to get into Heaven," the head nun says, her voice so much softer than the one she used before. "So it is not just us you saved."

I swallow a curse. "I knew they were up to something. But... are you sure?"

She taps the side of her head. "Absolutely. I could hear that beast's thoughts inside my head while my mind was trapped." Her eyes go wide, and she clasps my hand in hers. "Which reminds me. I searched for useful information in its mind and found something interesting." She turns and pulls me along as she makes her way down the hallway. "Come, I'll show you."

She's in so much of a hurry that I don't have time to tell the others to follow, but their footsteps tell me they are right behind us.

After several turns and a stairway, we reach the hallway where we fought the demons and sisters, close to the front doors. The nun lets go and points to the ceiling.

Only now do I remember the weird hole we saw before, the one we wanted to check out, because we felt something wrong with it.

"There's a secret space there," the woman says. "And in that space, there is something, or rather some*one*, that I think you would love to see."

My throat goes dry, and I lick my lips. "What do you mean?"

She smiles. "Your mother, son. They locked your mother up there."

CHAPTER 21

My heart starts to beat twice as fast, and sweat prickles on my neck. I listen for any sound coming from the ceiling, but everything is quiet. "Mom? Can you hear me? Are you in there?"

"She can't hear you, dear," the nun says. "She's locked inside a vacuum."

I jump to reach the ceiling, but it's too high, so I search for something to stand on. "We need to free her."

"Of course," the sister says calmly. "I will fetch you a chair."

While I continue my efforts to touch the hole in the ceiling, and occasionally call out to Mom, in case she *can* hear me, Vicky joins me and tries to comfort me.

I ignore her, because the last couple of times I saw Mom, she was far from fine, no matter how hard my

Shield tries to convince me that she was.

"She's strong, Dante," Vicky says.

I shake my head and pause my jumping for a second. "That doesn't matter, Vick!" My voice is shrill. "Yes, she'll survive. But in what state? She's marked for life! She might not be happy ever again after all she's been through, because how could anyone ever get over that?" I shake off her hand when she tries to grab it. "She was tortured in Hell, forced to fall in love with one of Satan's helpers, dragged into Purgatory only to fall into a pit that led back to Hell. Locked up time and again…" I gasp for breath. Summing it up only makes me feel worse.

Vicky reaches out for me again, and I push her hand away, but this time, she doesn't take no for an answer. She shoves my hands out of the way and pulls me into a tight hug.

Tears sting behind my eyes, but I'm too angry to cry.

"I know she's been through a lot," Vicky whispers. "And she probably won't be the same ever again. But neither will you. You've both seen enough for ten lifetimes, but that is the way it is. My point was, she'll get through it. She'll have good moments again, just like you. She's got an amazing son and a wonderful best friend to lean on and think of how strong she must be to have survived everything you mentioned." She wipes away the tear that has disobediently fallen down my cheek and kisses the wet spot. "Have faith. She'll be okay."

I kiss her on the lips and try to smile, but the corners of my mouth refuse to obey me. Anger still pumps through my blood.

"Thanks," I manage.

The nun returns with a chair, which she places under the hole.

"Thank you, sister…"

"Mary," she says with a small bow.

"Dante." I give her a bow back, climb onto the chair, and reach for the hole. A groan escapes my throat when my hands touch nothing but air.

Two Kessleys hurry over, carrying a small ladder. "Take this."

I blow her a kiss and wait for her to set it down. Then I push the chair aside and climb the ladder. Vicky holds it in place.

Now I can reach the ceiling, and without hesitation, I shove my hands inside the hole. Immediately, a sharp pain shoots from my fingers all the way down my spine and into my heels. My whole body shuts down and falls backwards like a cut down tree.

I expect to hit the floor hard, but someone catches me and puts me down gently. Red spots dance in my vision, and my head shakes without my permission. It hits the floor painfully over and over until Vicky kneels down and places her hands underneath. "Babe? Can you hear me?"

I blink rapidly, because my eyelids are the only muscles I'm able to move.

"Are you okay?" Vicky asks.

I blink a bit slower, hoping she'll understand that the pain has subsided, but that I can't move.

"I'm sure it will pass soon," she says, and she clasps my hand in hers. It feels weirdly warm and solid.

She knows what I'm trying to tell her. Of course she does, she can read my emotions.

My skin starts to tingle, and limb by limb, sensation seeps back into my body. I sit up slowly, supported by Vicky, and crack my neck. "Ouch."

I look up at the hole, and Vicky follows my gaze. "It must be protected."

"No shit," I answer.

Taylar climbs the ladder, holds up his spray bottle and releases a shower of angel blood.

I scoot out of the way of the falling drops as fast as I can. My muscles protest, and I clench my teeth against the pain.

Vicky throws me a concerned look. "Does it still hurt?"

Gisella squats down on my other side. "Let me see if I can help."

She wraps her hands around my right leg, and I can feel her power trickling into me. It's not like the other times she healed me. No sensation of tiny ants biting me. Instead, it's as if my skin bursts into flames. I yell in pain and fear and double over, but the feeling dies before I can push her away.

Panting heavily, I sit up straight and carefully flex

215

my legs and arms. "Wow."

"Did it work?" Gisella throws me an almost shy smile. A sliver of black slithers from her pupil to the back of her eye.

I swallow. "Yes, it did." I frown at her. "It was different though."

She wipes her hands on her hips and stands up. "Yes, the powers inside me are blending together. I wasn't sure that would be a good thing, but…" she gestures at my leg, "I guess it was."

Taylar turns around and sprays blood all over the werecat-witch.

"Hey!" she yells, jumping out of the way. "What the heck, man?"

Taylar raises his hands defensively. "Sorry, just wanted to make sure the evil hadn't taken over."

Gisella shakes the red liquid from her hands. Lines of blood make their way down her face, like an imitation of *Carrie*. "Thanks a lot."

Sister Mary clears her throat. "You can't blame the boy. It was smart of him to check, since you used evil powers to help Dante."

Gisella licks the blood from her lips. "You're right. And…" she looks down and studies her body, "… I'm actually grateful for his decision." She taps her chest where her heart lies. "I can feel the darkness retreating."

I push myself to my feet. "Was it taking over?"

She tilts her head and strokes her chest, lost in thought.

"No, not yet," she says eventually. "But I probably shouldn't do that again."

I stand up and test my leg. No pain. "I agree, but…" I point at the hole in the ceiling, "maybe the shadows will be able to break through the protection? Are you ready to try, or do you need a moment to recover?"

Gisella cracks her knuckles. "Nope, I'm fine." She pushes the ladder out of the way and gestures for us to step back. "Give me some room."

She closes her eyes and raises her head. The shadows untie themselves from the walls and corners and eagerly join her under the hole. As soon as she points up, the shadows shoot past her and into the ceiling. A loud banging reverberates through the hallway as they hit the barrier between us and Mom. Then, a hissing sound drowns out the banging, and smoke twirls down in thick columns.

Vicky and I back up at the same time, and we both reach for our weapons.

Taylar jumps forward and raises his shield to protect Gisella. D'Maeo joins them and holds up his hands in an attempt to stop the smoke with his deflecting powers. But it keeps pouring down, and when it comes closer, I realize it's not smoke at all. It's a line of tiny beige creatures, like lice or bed bugs. I can't make out their wings, but they must have them. And now that they're close, I can hear the soft buzzing rising from them. Not like the buzzing of bees; there's another sound underneath it which reminds me of my Dad's old computer; the sound that it made when he connected it with the internet, as if the machine was choking. Crackling, that's the word. Only... angrier. More threatening.

On impulse, I lash out to the stream of bugs with my athame and hit them with a ball of lightning at the same time. The crackling and buzzing get louder, and the whole stream of creatures goes berserk. They form into a giant ball of wriggling fury that attacks so fast I don't have time to duck. I do stumble sideways, but the killer ball is agile. It follows my every move as if it's my mirror image. When I raise my hand to conjure more lightning, the ball shoots forward and knocks me over. Before anyone can intervene, the whole army of cracklers slides into my mouth and down my throat. I gurgle and thrash, falling onto my knees and bending over in pain as the creatures make their way into my organs.

My mind is screaming at me. *It was a trap! How could we fall for this? They put Mom in there to lure me. They knew I would come to save the nun, and they knew I would find Mom hidden in the ceiling.*

My breathing is ragged, and I hear several voices yelling, but I can't make out who they belong to. Everything around me is a blur; it's as if the world is fading, and all that's left is the pain of the wriggling inside me, and the buzzing and crackling that spreads through my body like wildfire. When I feel them making their way to my arms and legs, I scream. That's when several shadows dive down my throat.

My scream turns into more gurgling, and someone presses me flat onto the floor.

"Hold him steady!" someone yells. The sound is muffled, so I can't make out who says it.

I don't care either. All I want is for this agony to come to an end.

The shadows are fighting with the cracklers. I can feel bumping against my intestines. My skin is being stretched as the bugs try to escape the shadows. The buzzing changes into shrieks of fear while the crackling gets more vicious.

I wriggle on the floor, even though several people are now on top of me, trying to hold me down.

Tears slide down my cheeks non-stop, and my voice is hoarse from all the screaming.

Something rips inside me, and I gasp as a sharp pain hits me. I blink and try to look at my stomach. Someone must have driven a hot poker inside me. The excruciating pain spreads through my belly, and everything turns red.

CHAPTER 22

Someone presses a wet cloth against my lips. Cool liquid seeps through them, and I swallow. My throat burns. I cough. Something itches at the back of my head, and reality hits me like a bulldozer. I sit up straight, head-butt someone—who curses—and cry out hysterically while I wipe the itchy stuff from my head.

"Babe, take it easy." Vicky's voice trickles into my ears, but I can't stop wiping. And the more I wipe, the more the itching spreads.

"Make it stop!"

Vicky raises her voice. "There's nothing to stop! They're gone!"

I shake my head and blink the tears from my eyes. "No, I can feel them. They're tearing me apart."

My breath comes in shallow gasps, and dizziness hits me.

"Take it easy." Gisella squats down next to me and places both hands on my chest. "Lie still."

I obey, although it's not easy to stop moving with all the wriggling and itching going on inside me. "They're eating me alive."

"No, they're not," she says gently. "Take a deep breath."

I close my eyes for a second and try to block the rising feeling of despair. The pain is gone, but there's still something inside me; I can feel it.

Suddenly a wave of nausea hits me. I turn onto my side and puke my guts out. Or so it feels. But thankfully, no organs come out, only a slivery shadow carrying a small string of cracklers. With the movement of a single finger, Gisella sends two more shadows down to take care of the little bastards.

I wipe my mouth and swallow several times. No more itching. No more buzzing and crackling.

"That was the last of it," Gisella says, and she pats my arm. "You'll live."

I let Vicky help me into a sitting position. Before I say anything, I lift my shirt to check my stomach. Then I roll up my pant sleeves and touch my legs.

Vicky kisses my temple. "You're okay. The shadows saved you. Gisella saved you."

I throw my arm around her neck and pull her against me. When she strokes my back, I close my eyes. Her new-found body heat warms the coldness inside me. "I thought I was done for, that that was it."

She rubs my back more fervently. "It sure looked

scary."

I let go and smile at Gisella. "Who would've thought your dark powers would help us so much?"

The werecat-witch shrugs. "I didn't."

Supported by Vicky, I get to my feet and look up at the ceiling. "Now that those creepy little bastards are gone, can we get to my mom?"

Gisella flexes her fingers. "Let me try."

It's as if the shadows have been waiting for new orders. They rush toward her, almost fighting to be the first. One by one, they dive through the hole in the ceiling. I cringe and almost crush Vicky's hand.

But this time, everything remains silent... until a familiar voice makes my heart skip a beat.

I rush forward and almost knock Gisella out of the way. "Mom!" I yell up to the ceiling.

"Dante?" She sounds panicked, and I can't blame her. The first time I saw those swirling shadows, they creeped me out too.

"Something is attacking me!" she calls down.

"Don't fight them, Mom, they are on our side!" I yell back, ignoring the fact that it's completely insane to talk about shadows as if they are living beings. But they seem to be, and I'm grateful that they obey Gisella.

"I'll make them carry her down," the werecat-witch says. "Tell her to relax."

"Mom," I call up again, "the shadows are going to carry you safely down, okay? Try to relax."

"To relax?" Her voice is shrill. "How can I—?" She

shrieks in fright, and I can hear her thrashing around.

"Stop fighting them! They want to help you!"

There's a soft sob, followed by a short silence. The first sliver of shadow frees itself from the hole. The rest follow quickly. They all move slower now, carrying Mom gently down. They only unwrap when she's got both feet firmly on the floor.

The fear on her face is replaced by joy and relief when she spots me. It takes me a millisecond to see that she is no longer under a spell.

She opens her arms wide, and I dive straight into them.

"Are you okay?" I ask her.

The force of her embrace almost breaks my diaphragm, but I don't care. I've experienced worse pain than this, and even if I hadn't, I wouldn't mind. I want nothing more than to hold her right now, just as tightly as she's holding me.

"I've missed you so much," I say, tears trickling down my face.

"I've missed you too." She wipes her eyes with one hand while the other one is still squeezing me. "I'm not sure what happened. I remember being with Trevor, but everything is vague, and parts of my memory are blank."

"I know." I rest my head against her shoulder. I'm surprised at how delicate she is. *Was she always this skinny?*

She loosens her grip and holds me at arm's length. "Look at you. You've become a man, Dante. You're so…" She gives me a once-over, "… muscular."

A blush creeps up from my neck, and I grin. "That's what you get when you fight demons and evil mages every day."

"Speaking of which," Gisella interrupts, her finger pointing behind us to send the last of the shadows back to their rightful place. "We need your help in our fight against Lucifer."

I shoot the werecat-witch a reproachful look.

"I'm sorry," she says, glancing at me briefly before turning her attention back to Mom, "but Susan needs to start her training as soon as possible."

"Training?" Mom's eyes nearly pop out of her head. "Are you saying I have powers too?"

"Not yet." Gisella winks at her, as if the fight is something to look forward to.

Mom shakes her head. "I don't understand."

I rake my hand through my hair. "We've got a long drive ahead of us. We'll fill you in on the way."

I'm about to say goodbye to the sisters, when Taylar, suddenly standing behind me, clears his throat. "Excuse me, but do you mind if I spray your mother, just to be safe?"

I step aside. "Not at all. I don't want to fall for another trick."

The white-haired ghost holds up his spray bottle and grimaces at Mom. "Better safe than sorry."

I hold my breath when the angel blood hits Mom's skin. Nothing happens.

On impulse I grab the bottle from him and cover

Taylar in a layer of red. He wipes a small red river from his eyes, but stays where he is, a resigned look on his face. "I should've seen that coming."

I hand the bottle back to him. "Sorry. I had to be sure."

"Reassured?"

I slap him on the back. "Completely."

D'Maeo slams his hands together. "Great. We should get going. We've got a lot to do."

Mom frowns at Kessley over my shoulder. "And people to introduce, I see."

While Kess talks to Mom, I turn to the nuns. "Will you be alright?"

The head sister bows. "We'll be fine. Thank you, Dante, thank all of you, for saving us, and for fighting to keep this world safe."

"You're welcome. Stay safe."

All of the nuns walk us to the front doors to wave goodbye. With Mom by my side, I feel so much lighter. Knowing she's okay gives me energy like nothing else can. Well… except a kiss from Vicky.

When we open the front doors, sunlight blinds us. I suck in the fresh summer air and lift my face to the sky. The dark clouds are gone. The heaviness that pressed down upon this street has been lifted. The threat has been taken care of.

When I turn to say my last goodbyes to the sisters, they are all smiling. The monastery seems to light up around them, the stones several shades lighter than when we first came here. The cold has been replaced by a comforting warmth.

"You will win this," the head nun says to me as she takes my hand. And when a beam of sunlight hits our hands, I feel, for the first time, that luck is on our side.

I smile. "Yes, we will."

CHAPTER 23

The drive home is filled with laughter, even though not everything that Mom missed is cheerful. But now that we've freed everyone, we all feel a lot better. Maybe even a bit invincible.

Once we've told Mom everything that's happened though, we need to tell her the bad news. That we want to transfer the powers of Jeep's wife into her and use them for our final battle with Satan.

I expect her to freak out and tell us there's no way she'll be able to do such a thing, but she just nods, stays silent for a couple of seconds and says, "Okay."

The car swerves right when I turn my head abruptly to face her. "What?"

"Watch out," she says calmly. "There's no need to crash."

I focus on the road again and search for words. "You... why... you're okay with this plan?"

"Well…" She hesitates. "Okay is a big word, but it's not as if I can ignore what's going on." She throws up her hands in surrender. "Lucifer has a back-up plan to escape Hell, so the odds of you having to face him are tremendous. I think there's no avoiding it, and although I'm terrified, I hate the idea of watching helplessly from the sideline, like I did before. If you and your father are in this fight, I want to contribute to it too. That will be difficult without magical powers, so I'm glad you found a way to give me some."

I glance at her sideways to see if she's serious. She is.

"You make it sound so easy."

She places a hand on my leg. "I know it's not easy, but I want to help. And frankly…" She balls her hands into fists. "I'm sick of being the helpless mother who needs saving. It will be nice to finally be able to defend myself. Also, I know you guys can use all the extra power you can get."

I take her hand in mine and squeeze softly. "You're so brave and strong. I couldn't be prouder, Mom."

She gives me a push with her free hand. "Hey, those are my lines!"

I chuckle. "I guess we're both awesome."

She raises her hand, and I give her a high five.

Vicky, merged with more than one other ghost because of the lack of space in the back seat, clears her throat explicitly. "Excuse me, aren't you forgetting a couple of people?"

I send her a guilty grin in the rearview mirror. "Oh, sorry. I meant we're all awesome."

"That's better," she mumbles grumpily, but I can see the twinkle in her eyes.

We spend another hour discussing our next step, but the rest of the way home is filled with jokes and songs. Time flies, and I consider making a detour. I want to hold on to this care-free, elated feeling. I don't think I've ever felt so whole in my life, not even when Dad was still with us. Everything is falling into place, and I have to believe that this means we have a good chance of beating the Devil.

In the end, I opt for the fastest way home. We're all tired, and Mom can't wait to see Mona. Also, Phoenix is starting to groan and squeak. She's not used to long drives; she needs a rest too.

As soon as the house comes into view, the front door flies open, and Mona comes running. She is uncharacteristically imperfect, with a wide smile but puffed-up eyes and tears streaking her cheeks. Even some blonde locks have come loose, but she doesn't care. She hurries over to the car so fast that I have to hit the brakes early to keep from running her over. Mom gets out before we've come to a halt, and the two almost knock each other over.

Tears well up in my eyes when I watch them. I get out, lock the car and walk over to them while the others file into the mansion.

"Oh, Dante, I'm so glad you decided to go back to

check out that hole in the ceiling and to save those nuns."

I frown. "How did you...? Oh, I get it, you were watching me."

She ruffles my hair. "Watching over you. Yes, of course I was. And I can't tell you how relieved and happy I was when Susan came out of that hole. She was out of my reach for so long, I thought I'd never find her again."

I hug her and pull Mom closer too. "You really thought that?"

"Well, I had hope," our fairy godmother says. "But I'd never experienced something like that before, so I was scared. I used to be able to check in on the both of you whenever I wanted. Honestly, I was even starting to doubt myself a little. Thought I might have lost my touch." She throws some sparks into the air, and they form into a heart above our heads.

Mona grins. "No, I've still got it."

Since we skipped lunch, Mona is happy to fix us all something to eat. She goes a little crazy with it, juggling five pans at a time and sliding things into the oven in between.

Charlie's grin has never been wider. Not just because of all the delicious food Mona's making, but also because Gisella has grown so powerful and because we found Mom. He even hugged her when she stepped into the kitchen. I don't think I've ever seen him do that before.

Dylan surprised us all with a bow and a sweet comment when I introduced him to Mom. "This is your mother? She's even more beautiful than I imagined."

Mom blushed at that and thanked him.

Sister Carol was already gone by the time we arrived. After I called Charlie with the good news, she was fine with taking the train back, and Charlie dropped her off at the station. Mona told us she used her sparks to get rid of the feelings of guilt inside Carol. After a long talk, she and Charlie convinced the nun that her feelings of lust were not hers at all. Therefore, there was no need for punishment. When she finally agreed, they figured it would be safe to let her go back home.

Which means I am finally in the company of the full 'gang' again, plus one. And like Charlie, I can't stop smiling. The only one missing is Quinn, but I have good hopes of seeing him soon too. Hopefully with all of his good looks and his wings still intact. I smile when I realize that if Quinn joins us, all the chairs around the kitchen table will be occupied. *Does that mean I've got everyone I need for the final battle? Does it mean that Dylan will stay with us until the end?*

I have to say, despite his rocky start—with us almost killing him—he blends in well with the rest. It's almost as if he's a part of my Shield too. He's so eager to help. But I wonder what will happen if we take care of his unfinished business. *Will he move on? If we don't do anything about it—*

"What's wrong?"

Dylan is frowning at me, and I realize I've been staring at him for a while.

I grimace. "Sorry, I was just wondering what to do about your situation."

He pulls a disgusted face. "My situation? Ugh, that sounds nasty."

I can't help but grin. "It *is* kind of disgusting. If we don't take care of your unfinished business, you will crumble to pieces that rot." I wave my hand in front of my nose. "I'm not looking forward to that smell."

Dylan's eyes grow wide. "Are you serious?" He pushes his chair back and stands up. "Then I should go find Armando Accardi before it's too late!"

Vicky, sitting next to him, grabs his wrist and pulls him back down. "Relax. He's kidding."

Dylan's gaze flicks between her and me. "He is?"

I point at my mouth. "Would I grin if I wasn't?"

With a heavy sigh, he sits down again. Mom, on his other side, pats his back. "You'll be fine."

"Not for long, if we don't do something," I say. When Dylan snorts, I hold up my hands. "For real this time. We told you before what happens if you fail to deal with that stuff."

Taylar nods solemnly. "He's right. I went through it. Trust me, you don't want to sit around and pretend it's not there. You might not crumble to dust, but you'll get weaker and weaker, until you disappear." His gaze goes distant. "And it doesn't feel all that great either."

Kessley rests her head against his shoulder. "But you're fine now, right?"

The young ghost kisses her on her temple. "Yes, I killed the pixie that murdered my brother, and Shelton Banks, who ordered the murder, is facing jail time."

"Speaking of which," Vicky says, turning to Mona. "Did you find out anything about that?"

Mona shakes her head. "He's still at home. But I also paid a visit to the detective handling the case, and he was looking into the evidence we gave him."

"Thank goodness," I say wholeheartedly. "And now it's time to help Dylan, like we helped Taylar."

Jeep twirls his hat on his finger. "That is, if the next set of cards isn't delivered before we can."

"Speaking of which." Charlie slides forward in his chair. "Are we sure Sister Carol is safe now?"

"Oh, right." I slip my hand into my back pocket and take out the cards. They crumble to dust before I can even hold them up. I smile. "Yes, she's safe."

Dylan watches in amazement as a sudden gust of wind carries the remains of the Cards of Death through the small crack under the back door.

I wipe my hands on my pants. "So, only one more set of cards to go. One more soul to save."

Gisella snorts. "Sure. Unless Satan plans to go for a second round, to get all the souls he needs."

"He won't," D'Maeo says, stroking his gray beard. "He's going for that back-up plan. He'll use what he's already got, because he's growing impatient. Starting over will take more time, and he knows that it's nearly impossible to get us out of the way."

Maël nods. "I agree. Lucifer does not know that we are aware of his other plan. He will think that he has the element of surprise. That he will be able to take us by surprise. But we will be ready for his arrival after we have saved the final soul."

I want to counter with a 'we will?' but manage to swallow it at the last moment.

Maël seems to pick up my doubts, because she continues by saying, "If we want to make certain that we are ready in time, we should split up."

I take in the hesitant faces around the table. My brain is working overtime, trying to figure out our best move.

I can tell by D'Maeo's face that he agrees with Maël, but he appears to be just as unhappy about it as I am.

He waits patiently for me to make a decision, though. While I go through all of our options in my head, the only sound in the room is that of the old oven whirring and spoons clanking in pans as Mona finishes her feast.

The sudden tension hanging in the air is palpable. I meet Mom's eyes, and she nods encouragingly.

I take a deep breath. "As much as I hate to admit it, I think it's best if we split up. Two of us should go with Dylan, to solve his unfinished business, while the rest of us stays here to transfer Charlotte's powers to Mom and train."

"Then there's no question about who is going with Dylan," Taylar says. "Charlie and Gisella are the only ones who can leave the house without you."

When I don't answer, his left eyebrow moves up. "Unless you want to go with him yourself?"

As fear suddenly washes over me, I place my elbows on the table and hide my face in my hands. "I don't know. I hate that we need to split up again." I press my hands against my face. "Three of us got lost before, and we've only been reunited for a couple of hours. I'm afraid to lose someone again if I let one of you out of my sight for even a minute." I push myself up and start pacing, the tension inside me too heavy to sit still. Mona raises a hand when I pass her, ready to sprinkle me with her soothing sparkles, but I shake my head. "No, please let me finish."

She nods and turns back to her pots and pans.

"I know it's irrational to worry about all of you constantly. I know that we're all in danger and that some of us, or maybe even all of us, will get hurt whether we're together or not. But I am…" I bite my lip, wondering whether I should say this out loud or not, being the leader and all that. Eventually I decide to be honest. "I am scared of losing you guys. Sometimes I'm afraid I'll lose you no matter what we do."

Vicky reaches out to me, and I smile at her. "But I can't let that get in our way. That's what Satan wants, for us to get so scared we'll do stupid things. And the stupidest thing we can do is lose faith in our abilities.

So we will split up, because there's not much time left to prepare for the battle that's coming. The demons have been chasing down the souls faster with each circle, so I expect the last Cards of Death to arrive soon. And Dylan needs to get rid of his unfinished business before it bites him in the ass." I grin when Kessley lets out an involuntary chuckle. "I just want you all to know that it's okay to be scared, but that we need to do what's best. And splitting up for a little while is what's best now."

I nod and sit down, suddenly tired. I guess pouring your heart out can do that to a person. But I also feel better. I think I needed to hear these words myself the most. I knew deep inside that it was fine to be afraid. Logical, inevitable even. But that feeling won't stop any of us. We'll keep fighting until Satan is back in Hell, covered by nine layers of sinners, or until we can't fight anymore. Which I guess is never, because even from Heaven, we'll be able to continue our fight. Or from the Shadow World or wherever we will end up if we die or move on. We'll keep going until the threat is gone.

Jeep places his hat on the table and rests his hands on it. "That was a great speech, Dante. I don't admit this often, but I am afraid too. Being trapped inside that empty world, with those ghost mages escaping from my tattoos, was one of the worst and scariest moments of my life, yet I'm sure facing Lucifer will be worse. But you are right, it's fine to feel fear, because it means we have something to lose. It means we care about ourselves, each other and the outcome of our fight. Remember that the demons only care about themselves, and the Devil only cares about himself and the outcome. None of them will shed a tear if any of their 'friends'..." he makes quotation marks in the air, "get killed. Which is why they have less fear."

"But also less love," Maël adds.

He points at her. "Exactly! We have much more to fight for! Lucifer fights only for himself."

Dylan sits up straight, nodding vigorously. "Thanks, guys. I feel much better. Just as frightened, but much better nevertheless."

Vicky slaps him on the back. "Join the club."

Charlie leans closer to him across the table. "You'll feel even better soon."

Dylan blinks at him. "Why?"

Charlie points his thumb over his shoulder. "Because Mona's treats are almost finished."

Dylan stares at him without moving. Then, slowly, the corners of his mouth turn up. "You're right," he says, and then he starts laughing.

I've never heard a laugh like his before. It's much lower than his speaking voice, but when he laughs harder, it changes to a higher 'hee-hee-hee', which reminds me of a donkey. It's super weird, but very contagious, and soon we're all laughing, some of us more hysterically than others. Kessley bends over so far that she hits her head on the table, which only makes her laugh more.

Even Maël is laughing, although she doesn't make a sound. Once a queen, always a queen.

Mom looks happy and relaxed too, and once again, I'm grateful that she doesn't remember much of what happened to her.

Since Mona is laughing as much as we are, she sends her sparks to take the pans from the stove. They also hand out plates, that almost smack some of us in the face because they are affected by Mona's laughing. They tremble almost as much as she does, which sends them off-balance. Of course, their erratic motions cause even more laughter. Eventually, Mona gives up and calls back her sparks. I catch my plate before they drop it on the ground and try to suck in air between my hiccups.

Dylan is still imitating a donkey, and Vicky places a hand on his arm. "Please stop, you're killing the people in the room who aren't dead yet. They can't breathe."

My gaze shifts to Mom, who has covered her mouth, as if she can stop laughing that way. Charlie, on the other side of the table, is nearly choking. Gisella slaps him on the back forcefully, with a wide grin on her face.

Dylan turns around in his chair, and the high-pitched sounds are soon replaced by the low chuckling again.

I wipe the sweat from my forehead and take a couple of deep breaths. "What a great way to end the day, guys."

Taylar regains his cool too and says, rather seriously, "The day isn't over yet. We've got plenty of time to mess it up. It's not even dinner time yet, even though it sure smells like it!"

Everyone stops laughing, and Kessley nudges Taylar in the side. "Way to spoil the mood."

"It's fine," I say, swatting her words away. "We can't laugh all day." I nod at Dylan, who's still hiccupping. "At least, most of us can't."

The tension evaporates again. Mona wipes her blonde locks back in place and straightens her dress. "The food is ready!"

We take our time trying each of the dishes she cooked. They're all beyond delicious.

When we're finally done—and more than satisfied—we all lean back in our seats.

"When this is over," Kessley says, rubbing her belly, "you should start a restaurant, Mona. You could make tons of money."

The fairy godmother shrugs. "I could, but I don't need money. The Magical Government pays me."

Mom stands up suddenly, swaying on her feet. "I'm sorry, if I could, I would stay here for hours to talk, but I'm exhausted. I think I'll go lie down for an hour or so, if you don't mind."

Charlie opens his mouth to object, but D'Maeo is faster. "I think that's an excellent idea. You've been through a lot, and you'll need all the energy you can get for when we're transferring Charlotte's powers to you."

Mom shoots him a weak smile that makes my heart shrink. *She's not okay with this plan. I can't let her go through with it.*

"I'll come with you for a second," I say, rising to my feet as well.

She seems surprised, but she merely nods and says goodbye to the others.

I follow her to the top floor.

"What's up?" she asks, while she closes the curtains.

I have a feeling she doesn't really want Charlotte's powers, but when I tell her that, she repeats that it is the best option and that she does want it.

She walks over to me and gives me a hug. "We'll be okay, Dante." She holds me at arm's length. "Remember how this all started? First with the fits. We had no idea what they were or why they were happening, but we dealt with them, didn't we?"

I nod, unable to answer her because of the big clump of emotions suddenly stuck in my throat.

"And then John left. We were both devastated. Angry, somber, bitter. But we kept going."

"Yes," I whisper.

"And then you found out you were the chosen one. You didn't want to be. You knew nothing of the magical world. You didn't know how to fight; you didn't even know what your powers were. But you kept going. You know why?"

I wet my lips. "Because I had no other choice?"

She squeezes my shoulders. "Because you knew

deep down that you could do it. Because you are stronger than you thought you were. We both are."

I let her words sink in and realize she's right. I didn't always believe I was strong enough, but I kept going anyway, which probably means that I *am* strong enough to pull this off.

Mom moves her hand to my chest. "Besides that, you've got a good heart, Dante. You don't give up, because you know people will die if you do, and you can't stand the thought of that."

With every word she says, my doubts and longing for the old days get weaker.

I put my arms around her again. "You know, I inherited that good heart from you and Dad."

I can feel her smiling against my shoulder.

"You're the best mom in the world. I love you so much."

"I love you too, Dante. Let's do this together, okay?"

I let her go and hold out my hand. "Deal."

She shakes my hand and smiles.

Then I turn and walk to the door. "I'll let you rest now. We've got a lot of preparations to take care of."

She blows me a kiss. I catch it and close the door, only to hear her calling my name a second later.

I stick my head back inside. "Yes?"

"Look what I found in my pocket." She shows me a piece of paper. Confusion paints her face, and a small blush creeps up from her neck.

"What does it say?"

At a loss for words, she holds the note out to me. I walk over to her and take it. My eyes flick over the words fast, but it takes me two reads to believe what it says.

My dear Susan,

I am sorry for what I did to you. All I wanted was for you to love me back. I see now that this was not the right way.

Lucifer wants me to use you to get to Dante. I could never do that. Therefore, I must let you go, for now. I will lock you in a protected space in the Monastery of Saint Gertrude. I know Dante will find you there. He might be a pain in the ass, but he is also smart and perceptive.

I can't let him take you easily though. Lucifer would know. And Dante is still my enemy.

Which is why I will set up a trap. If the trap works and none of his friends survives to take you home safely, I will come and get you myself. But I suspect there will be someone left to take care of you.

Oh, Susan, I wish you could stay with me. I already miss you.

I hope you will love me, some day.

Forever yours,
Trevor

My mouth is still open when I finally look up at Mom. "Trevor put you there to make sure you were safe?"

Her cheeks are a bright red now. "I guess so."

"Well," I hand the note back, suddenly shivering at the thought of Trevor almost crying over it, "there must be a tiny bit of good left inside him, after all."

Mom stares at the piece of paper in her hand. "Yes, I guess there is."

I narrow my eyes. "Mom?" My voice is sharp, and she looks up.

"What?"

"Don't let this fool you. He is still evil."

Her shoulders sag a little. "I know."

A cold hand wraps around my heart. "Don't tell me you've got feelings for him."

She shakes her head vigorously. "I don't! I think there's a bit of the love potion left in my blood. And to be honest..." she clears her throat, "I *am* flattered."

I grin. "Well, it's obvious how awesome you are, so I can't really blame him."

She grins back and crumples up the note. "I guess not."

CHAPTER 24

When I get back down, the others are all hyped up about something.

They're all talking at once and gesturing like mad.

I stop in the doorway and wait for someone to notice me, but no one does.

Eventually, I clear my throat. The only one who hears me is Mona, who is standing beside Vicky. She turns to me with a wide smile. "Oh, great, you're back! We've got some good news."

The buzz in the room dies down, and all eyes are on Vicky, who looks at me with glistening eyes. "I know how to create the circles of Hell."

It's as if electricity flows through me, but in a good way. It propels me forward, and instead of hugging her, it's more like crashing into her. The back of her chair bores into my chest, but I don't mind.

When I finally let go, I beam at her. "See? I knew

Charon was telling the truth."

One corner of her mouth goes up further. "No, you didn't. I sensed your doubts."

I swat her words away. "That was just a tiny bit." I slap my hands together. "So, that's it? You know what to do? Or do you need to practice?"

Charlie swallows the last home-made brownie in one bite and wipes the crumbs from the table onto his hand. "That's what we were discussing when you walked in. It's not as if she can create a whole new structure of circles while the existing ones are still intact."

"And even if she can," Jeep says, tossing his hat in the air and catching it on the tip of his finger, "Satan is bound to notice. He will send his troops to take her out, for sure."

I tap my chin in thought. "True…" I turn back to Vicky. "But if you're confident that you'll be able to do it, we'll need to trust in that."

She averts her eyes and plays with the fork that's still lying in front of her. "Well… I'm not completely sure I'll do it right the first time. That's why I was thinking…" She wets her lips before she continues. "Maybe I could practice on a smaller scale on… a demon."

There's no sound in the room as I process her words. I try not to freak out. *She wants to risk our lives and that of countless others by luring a demon to us? If we would do that, which I doubt is smart, we're definitely not doing it here. This place is impossible to find for our enemies, and I'd*

245

like to keep it that way. So… "Where did you want to do this exactly?"

She exhales slowly, relieved that I didn't brush the whole idea off immediately. "Well, obviously far away from people, and preferably at a place that we know well." She seems to weigh her next words before she says them out loud. "I was thinking: the silver mine."

She hasn't even finished her sentence, and I'm already shaking my head. "No way. We can't do anything that dangerous close to the portal that Beelzebub came through. They will notice. And what if something goes wrong and the mine caves in?"

She adjusts her leather jacket. "What other choice do we have? We can't do it here, and we can't do it with people nearby."

D'Maeo starts pacing. "I was thinking… you could cast a spell to make sure neither of those things happen. Practicing on solid ground will be better than on something soft like grass or forest soil."

"I agree, that's bound to be more challenging," Taylar says.

"Plus," Maël interrupts. "She will only create circles big enough to trap a small demon."

I cross my arms over my chest. "I see you have already decided this together. No need for me to give my opinion."

Vicky reaches for my hand. "That's not true. We want to know what you think. This was the best we could come up with, but maybe you have other ideas. I know this isn't ideal, but I don't want to go into the

246

final battle blind. I need to know for sure that I'll be able to create the circles."

I sigh. "Of course."

Mona starts clearing the table. She does it by hand instead of sending her sparks to do it. When she sees me staring, she shrugs. "It helps me think."

Everyone is lost in thought for a moment. The fairy godmother is the first one to break the uncomfortable silence. "I think it will work. After all, the invisibility I put on the house works on Lucifer, so why shouldn't your spells work?"

Maël stands up and throws back her cape. "She is right, Dante. I think you underestimate yourself. We should do this now."

The others nod, and I rub my face hard. *If so many people believe in me, how can I refuse? Should I trust them or my own instinct? Is this even instinct I'm feeling, or is it only self-doubt?*

Vicky pulls my hands away from my face. "Look at me."

I do, and for a moment, I'm lost in a deep blue ocean. The moment ends with a kiss on my lips. "Stop doubting yourself. You can do this."

I lean forward for another kiss when she pulls back. "What would I do without you?"

She places a finger against her lips in mock-thought. "Eh… Probably something stupid."

I shove her playfully. "Thanks a lot."

Charlie stands up and rubs his hands together. "Does this mean we're going to do it?"

247

With my hands on my hips, I stare at him. "Don't tell me you're looking forward to this."

He flips his hair over his shoulder. "Of course I am, Dante. This is our strongest weapon! The Devil can do whatever he wants; escape Hell, throw more demons at us, kidnap the people we love… but in the end, he will always lose. Because…" he swings his hips with every word he utters, "we've… got… Vicky!"

Kessley giggles, but I suppress my snort. Because frankly… Charlie is right.

"Come on, come on," Charlie sings cheerfully. "Say it, say it!"

I exchange a quick look with Vicky before I give in. "Alright, alright, you can stop the dancing, or whatever you want to call it. You're right."

He performs a pirouette and nearly topples over. "I knew it!"

Gisella catches him. "You're right, okay? But please stop acting like a five-year-old. You're embarrassing me."

He stands still immediately, as if someone has frozen him. His mouth hangs open, as if he wanted to respond but forgot what to say.

At first, I think he's messing around, but after several seconds, he still hasn't blinked. Besides, I don't believe he's able to stand still for this long.

I frown at Maël, whose staff is pointing in Charlie's direction. She smiles apologetically. "Sorry, he was driving me crazy. I needed a second to think."

Gisella doubles up with laughter and even D'Maeo grins. Jeep stands up and places his hat on Charlie's head. "What a great imitation of Charlie Chaplin!"

"What's a Chaplin?" Kess asks, which makes everyone laugh.

"You don't know Charlie Chaplin?" Jeep seems offended. "He is one of the greatest comedians that ever lived. He was famous for his silent movies. Movies in which he didn't say a word."

Kessley rolls her eyes at him. "Yes, I know what a silent movie is, thanks."

"Can I borrow your staff sometime?" Gisella asks Maël, ignoring the bickering people next to her. "I'd love to be able to shut him up once in a while."

Before the ghost queen can answer, I hold up my hand. "Okay, guys, enough fooling around. This still doesn't give Maël the chance to think."

"That's okay, I am already done." The ghost queen taps her staff, and Charlie starts moving again.

He shakes his body like a wet dog. "That was weird."

I lean on the table in front of me. "Tell us what you were thinking, Maël."

"Charlie made a good point and…" She stops talking when my best friend moves his hips again.

As soon as she points her staff at him, he holds up his hands. "No, don't! I'll be quiet."

He sits down, and Maël continues. "I think our focus should not only be on Vicky's practicing, but also on the rest of us protecting her. Vicky can end our battle on her own, which means she is the most important of us all. We need to make sure nothing happens to her."

I grab Vicky's hand when she starts to protest. "I think this is a good idea. But it will be difficult to keep you safe when we're fighting who knows how many demons, Trevor *and* the Devil himself."

"You could put a protection spell on her," D'Maeo suggests.

I frown. "If something like that worked, we could've used it a long time ago."

The old ghost turns to Mona, who has her back to us and her hands in the dishwater. "Can it be done, Mona?"

She shakes the soap from her hands and turns around. "It can, but it will drain power from the spell caster constantly."

I drop back into my chair. "Great, so our only option is to find someone else to cast it."

"What about you, Mona?" Taylar asks. "Is there anything you can do with your sparks? You were born to protect people, after all."

Mona nods thoughtfully. "Our most powerful tool is to whisper a warning into our protégée's minds when something bad is about to happen."

I scratch my head. "You never did that to me, did you?"

"Sure I did. But you won't know. You can't hear me when I do it. Sometimes it comes through as a sound, disguised as a thought."

"You mean an inner voice," Gisella says.

"Exactly. That voice that tells you something is wrong, or that you should think about something before you do it."

Kessley has turned around in her seat. She rests her arms on the back of her chair, absorbed by Mona's story. "And if it doesn't sound like a voice?"

The fairy godmother wipes a bit of soap from her dress. "Then it's more like a feeling. Like your gut raising the alarm." She narrows her eyes, searching for a better description. "It's like having an extra set of intuition."

"And you can use that on Vicky too?" I ask hopefully.

"I can, but I think we need more than that."

My shoulders sag. "Well, we don't have more than that."

"Sure we do," she says with a meaningful smile. "Don't tell me you have forgotten about my friends."

"You mean the other fairy godmothers?"

She nods excitedly. "I can't believe I haven't thought of this before, but we can all help in the final battle. We can be Vicky's guide. Her extra intuition and eyes."

D'Maeo clears his throat. "I'm sorry to burst the bubble, but won't that be too overwhelming? Vicky won't be able to listen to seven voices at once. It will only confuse her."

"No, I don't think so." Mona shakes her head while she paces in front of the kitchen counter. "You see, if a protégée is in real trouble, we can intervene directly. Which means we can…" She waves her hand in the air as if the right word hovers there somewhere, "… steer her. Take over control of her body for a second."

Jeep takes back his hat when Charlie hands it over. "Would that work on Vicky, though? She's a ghost. Technically speaking, she doesn't have a body anymore."

Mona tilts her head. "That's a good question. We'd have to test that."

I get to my feet and slam my hand down onto the table. "Okay then, we'd better get started. We've got a lot of training and testing to do and not much time left to do it in. Mona, can you go talk to your friends, see if they're willing to help?"

She nods. "I know they are, but sure, I'll arrange a meeting."

I take my Book of Spells from behind my waistband and tear out a page. "I'll write Mom a note to let her know we're okay."

Mona, who was already half gone, becomes clearer again. "Speaking of your mother. It's probably wise to assign one or two fairy godmothers to her too, since we're giving her lots of power. She will be a target."

"So will Dante," Vicky adds. "I'm guessing he's the chosen one for a reason. Without him, we can't win."

Mona closes her eyes for a second. "You're right. But your powers are the most important in this battle, so we'll focus on you for now. And if I can find more friends to help, we'll divide them over all of you."

Vicky gets no time for more protests because Mona turns back to the dishes. "I'll talk to my friends as soon as I'm done here."

I squeeze Vicky's hand. "Don't worry, I think it's a great plan. You can do your thing while we fight the demons off."

She throws her head back, laughing loud but joylessly. "If only it was that easy."

"Pretend that it is, for now. Worrying about it will do us no good." I wink. "Trust me, I've tried it many times."

"Okay, I'll try." She kisses me and stands up. "Can we go to the mine now?"

I tap my notebook. "I should write a spell first, to summon a demon and to keep us invisible."

"Oh, right." She starts pacing behind me. *I don't think I've ever seen her this nervous. I know how she feels, though. I remember what it felt like to have someone put the weight of the whole world on my shoulders.*

I turn around and wait until I can catch her eye. "It will get better."

She nods and continues her pacing.

Gisella stands up and nudges Charlie, who's munching on some leftovers. "We should go."

He looks up with a frown, grease smeared around his mouth. "Go?"

"With Dylan, remember?"

"Oh!" He licks his lips. "Shouldn't you scry for

253

Armando again first?"

She glances at me. "Yes. Let's do that in the annex. Give Dante a moment of peace so he can think."

I bend over my Book of Spells and let the words flow into my mind. I've jotted down five of them when there's a knock at the door. The moment I hear the sound, I somehow know... *trouble.*

CHAPTER 25

When Mona heads for the front door, I stop her.

"What is it?" she asks. "You know evil can't find us here."

True… so why does it feel as if a brick has landed in my stomach?

I make for the door and steady my breathing before I open it.

As soon as I see the three figures hovering on the doorstep, I know why I got that sudden cold feeling inside. The low whistling at the front of the mansion should've given me a clue.

"Hello, Dante," the gorgeous woman in the middle says with a sweet smile. "It's so nice to see you again."

"Yeah…" I say, my voice barely audible. "You too."

All three fairies giggle. They're even more

255

mesmerizing than I remembered, with the white gowns that cover their feet and the white hair that flows up and down lazily in a warm current.

The one in the middle gestures lightly with her head to the hallway behind me. "Mind if we come in for a minute?" she asks in a tingly tone.

I realize I've been staring for too long and step aside quickly, a blush creeping up to my cheeks. "Of course."

When I want to lead them into the kitchen, I find Mona blocking my way. She must have followed me to the door.

"You belong to the iele folk, don't you?" she asks, bowing deeply. "It's such an honor to meet you."

The middle one drifts forward and opens her arms. "Another fairy! How lovely."

They hug, and the other two iele bow to Mona. I stand and watch, a little stunned. This greeting is a lot friendlier than the last time we met. I won't forget the way the iele grew and got darker when we saw them at the church, and how they threatened to kill us if we didn't give them their bell back.

"I'll fix us some herbal tea," Mona says, and she hurries back into the kitchen.

I'm grateful that she's taking the lead, because I haven't recovered from the shock of finding the fairies on my doorstep. But the iele wait patiently for me to invite them into the kitchen. Following Mona's example, I bow before beckoning them to follow me.

When we pass the annex, Charlie walks out of it.

"Hey, who was at the…" He cuts his question off abruptly when his gaze falls upon the iele. Instinctively, he takes two steps back and bumps into Gisella.

The three floating women simply smile at him. "Hello."

"Hi," he says carefully.

The leader peers over his shoulder. Her smile grows wider. "Oh my, there's so much power in this house!"

I clear my throat. "Yes, we've made some new friends since we last saw you. May I introduce our new friend, Dylan."

"Another young mage," the leader says. "How lovely."

I beckon everyone into the kitchen.

"And this is my sixth ghost, Kessley," I continue.

Kess stands up, takes the hems of her leopard dress and bows. "It's an honor."

The iele give a small bow back.

"Do you want us to stay?" Charlie whispers in my ear.

"No, we'll be fine. I can always call if I need your help."

"Are you sure?" he asks, never taking his eyes off the fairies.

"Yes, go and free Dylan of his unfinished business."

I can tell by the nervous fiddling with his hair that he's not too keen on leaving us with the iele, but he says goodbye anyway, and Gisella and Dylan follow his example.

The iele sit down facing the kitchen counter, where Mona's sparks are preparing the tea.

When Mona serves the tea, we all watch in awe as strings of white hair pick up the cups and lift them to the fairies' lips.

"So," I say after a long silence. "What can we do for you?"

Once again, it's the leader who speaks. The women on her left and right remain silent. "We've come to claim our payment, for lending you the Bell of Izme." She taps a long, slender finger on the table. "Our bell is still in one piece, isn't it?"

I nod. "Yes, of course."

"Good. I'll tell you what we need then."

I hold my breath and hope for the best. Their timing isn't bad, although I would've preferred them to have waited until we've defeated Satan. But I don't have a clue what sort of help they might need. I can only hope that we can give it to them. If not, I'm sure they'll turn into their monstrous selves again.

The leader of the three fairies rises a couple of inches from her chair. "The three of us have been working on restoring the bond between iele and humans that once existed. We used to work together to keep the peace and spread love. But humans turned out to be unreliable, and often cruel."

Jeep leans back in his chair with a sigh. "Tell me about it."

"We believed in our alliance until one of us was kidnapped, as you might know."

I nod solemnly. "Yes, we heard about that. I'm so sorry that happened."

She pushes her flowing gray locks back and smiles. "I know. I could feel the good in you, in all of you, when we first met. It made me think." Her gaze goes distant, as if she's reliving our first meeting.

I can't imagine I made such a loving impression. More like a stubborn and slightly desperate one. But her smile only grows wider as she turns her eyes back on me. "You have restored our faith in humankind. You made us realize that not every human is evil. But... our sisters are not convinced so easily. They have grown bitter. This affects not only them, but the whole world." She opens her arms wide, and I can feel warmth emanating from her hands. "We need to break the downward spiral, and we need love to do it. Therefore, we must move all of the iele to the town of Affection, Idaho."

I frown. "I've never heard of that town."

She floats back into her seat and lowers her head. "That's because it has been occupied by the marodium, a hateful species that feeds on nightmares and shapes hatred. The town is invisible to everyone, except the people they lure into it with the plants that grow there."

"Wait, wait," Kessley interrupts. "Slow down. I don't mean to be rude, but I don't understand a thing you're saying." She rubs her forehead. "They lure people with plants?"

The iele leader shoots her a smile. "Yes, the town of Affection is filled with plants that stimulate love and relieve stress. There are microbes in the soil, called Mycobacterium vaccae, that have an antidepressant effect on the brain. Bamboo was planted in the east to increase the flow of positive energy. And benign creatures have lived there for centuries, spreading love and understanding. The air is still filled with it. Walking into the town will still make you feel good. But it has become a trap."

"And you want us to stop the marodium," I deduce.

"Yes. We cannot fight them on our own. There are only three of us. But once the marodium have been banished, we can take the rest of our folk to Affection and make them see that we have strayed from our path of love and peace. Without Affection, we cannot do it."

Maël stands up and grabs her staff tightly. "I will gladly fight for this."

Kessley stands up too, her fists held triumphantly in the air. "Me too!"

The others throw me a questioning look. I clear my throat and gather up the courage I need to say what I must say. "If this is all true—and I'm inclined to believe you—we will be happy to do this as payment for lending the Bell of Izme."

Before I can finish, the fairy interrupts me. "But you need to be sure. I understand."

I nod at Vicky to walk over to the iele leader. She does, and the fairy stands up and faces her.

"Would you mind repeating your intentions and reasons to Vicky?"

"Not at all."

She gives Vicky a summary of what she just told us. Vicky never breaks eye contact, and when the iele finishes, she turns back to me and nods.

I rise to my feet, feeling relieved and hopeful, even though we've probably got a dangerous fight ahead of us. "That's settled then. We will help you defeat the marodium in return for using the bell."

D'Maeo places his hands flat on the table. "And if we do this, can we keep the bell until our final battle with Satan is over?"

The three iele bow as one. "You can."

I hold out my hand, and the leader bends forward to shake it. "What a human way to seal the deal." She giggles, and it sounds so lovely that I can barely believe she's the same creature that threatened us at the church. The one that changed into some sort of evil spirit. But she means well, and I'm glad to help. The marodium sound like a species that should be wiped out.

"How would you like to seal the deal?" I ask her with a smile of my own.

She walks up to me and holds out her hands. "Cross them," she says when I want to take them. I do, and she crosses her arms too. Now our arms form an infinity symbol. Warmth floods through them, chasing away the last of my worries.

"Now, close your eyes and lean closer."

I do, and after several silent seconds, our foreheads touch. I'm locked in place, but it feels good, as if this was meant to be. Images spill from her mind to mine. I see cobblestone paths decorated by flowers in bright colors. Palm trees that sway lazily in a warm breeze. A warm sun shining down on playing children dressed in long white dresses, with white hair that seems to play as much as they do. They giggle and chase each other, sometimes jumping higher in the air than humanly possible. These must be memories of the iele leader from when she was young and living in Affection. Everything is so peaceful, and when the images suddenly fade, I keep my eyes closed, hoping they will return.

"Now you know how it is supposed to be," the fairy says. "And I have seen the love in your memories. Together, we can make this world a better place."

When I smile back at her, the words flow out of my mouth on their own. "And we will."

Before we discuss our plan to take on the marodium, the iele want to see their bell. I lead them upstairs and show them the hidden room. I'm surprised myself that I don't even hesitate. It hasn't been easy for me to trust people since two of my so-called best friends betrayed me, but we've also met a lot of great people, like Ginda and Chloe and Dylan. So maybe I'm thawing a bit again. Besides, these iele can't be bad, or they would never have found Darkwood Manor or have been able to cross the salt lines.

Vicky apparates into the secret room with a ball of herbs in her hands. She gives it to me and sets up four candles, one in each corner. The iele watch her with interest, floating an inch above the floorboards.

For once, there's no need to check Dad's notebook for the instructions. I've cast this spell so many times that I know it by heart.

I draw a circle on the ceiling with a pentagram inside it.

Vicky hands me another candle which I use to melt the circle above our heads. Soon, the substance starts dripping. It forms a second circle on the floor. When it's complete, I lower the candle and say the words.

"Shadows high and shadows low,
show me what I do not know.
Bring in sight what's hidden here.
Let the unseen reappear."

Slowly, the darkness inside the room disappears. The shadows stretch and get lighter. They pull away the ivy that covers the small window. Dust vanishes, and as the shadows disappear, they reveal the porthole that leads to the silver mine.

The candles in the corners are blown out, and Vicky lights them again.

The iele float closer, and I shake my head. "Not yet. There's a double protection on the bell."

They nod approvingly and float back to the doorway.

I repeat the spell, and a large doll is revealed in the middle of the room. A *matryoshka*. The yellow 'laser beam' scans me and Vicky and explodes into harmless dots of light when it senses our good intentions. More beams follow as I take smaller dolls out of the biggest one. When I open the last one, I look over my shoulder. The yellow beam scans the three fairies in the doorway. They are frozen in place, just like we were when it scanned us. There's surprise on their faces.

The light moves over them, once, twice. I'm starting to wonder if they will pass this 'test'. *Was I wrong to trust them?* Beside me, I see Vicky reaching for the knife in her boot. But then, the beam goes up in sparkles, and the iele can move again.

Vicky straightens up, and the iele shake the weird feeling off. The leader draws closer when I lift the Bell of Izme from the doll. "You have protected it well."

"Actually, my father did that before he was killed. I just kept it in place."

The leader's face goes dark when I mention Dad. I can't blame her. He stole the bell from them, after all. But when I hold it up, to show her that it's intact, the darkness trickles from her cheeks. She holds out her hands. "Can I hold it for a second?"

"Of course." I hand it to her gently, and she studies it from all sides. My gaze is drawn to it too. The mesmerizing effects of it never cease to amaze me: the sparkling white marble the outside is made of, the beautiful branches, moons and stars carved into it that seem so real. I could describe every detail of it, and you still wouldn't be able to grasp the beauty of it.

With a nod, the iele leader gives it back. "Very well. I see that it's in good hands here."

"It is." I gesture at the porthole, and they follow me there. "I need to make sure the portal remains closed. You can watch, if you want."

Vicky has joined us at the porthole, and the others gather around us, weapons drawn.

Vicky and I peer through the round window. The secret tunnel is open, as always these days, and the birdcage that opens it hangs still. There's no one in sight.

"I think we're good," Vicky says, and she unlocks the porthole.

I step through first and scan the secret tunnel again. The blackness at the end of it pulses wildly.

When Vicky joins me, she places a hand on my arm. "That doesn't look good."

I wrap my fingers around the bell tighter. "But it's not open."

When she takes a step closer to the portal, I grab her and pull her back. "Don't."

She frees her hand gently. "It's closed, babe."

"It could be a trick," I say, tilting my head to study every inch of the black mass. "I nearly lost you when Beelzebub came through. I'm not taking any more risks."

"You saw Beelzebub?" The voice that speaks up is sweet, but there's a hint of anger and panic underneath it.

When I turn toward the sound, I find one of the other two iele staring at me. It's the first time since they arrived that she has spoken, and I can tell this surprises the leader as much as me.

"You defeated him?" she asks now, her gray hair floating up behind her.

"Not yet, but we drove him away," I answer.

Her eyes grow wide, and she drifts toward me. Her hand goes up to my cheek, and warmth floods through it. Her gaze grows soft. "I owe you an apology."

I frown. "What for?"

"For not believing in you." She lowers her chin and floats a bit further down. "To be honest, I envied you. I never understood why the chosen one was a human. Why God hadn't chosen one of us. But now I see it. You are special, Dante. You can change the world without help, if you need to."

I give her a small bow. "I'm not sure about that, but thank you for your kind words."

"Is this why you didn't speak before?" Vicky asks.

The iele goes a bit paler than she already was. "It is. And I am sorry. It was childish of me. Please forgive me."

"You are forgiven," Vicky and I say at the same time, and we exchange a small smile.

"Thank you." She retreats to the side of her leader.

The iele on the right bows too. "I apologize too. I did not want to ask for your assistance. But I see now that there is no shame in seeking help."

"There certainly isn't," I confirm.

Now that the air has been cleared, I turn back to the portal and start ringing the bell.

Then I stop and nearly drop it. I inch closer to the black void, narrowing my eyes. I turn my head left and right, but that doesn't change what I'm seeing. I press the bell into Vicky's hands and take another step. I wet my lips before saying the name that keeps swimming through my head. "Dad?"

CHAPTER 26

"Dante?" The voice is distant and hoarse, but it's definitely Dad's. "I can't see. I got lost."

"Don't worry, we'll get you out."

"Where am I? Dante, can you hear me?" He sounds on the verge of a panic.

Instinctively, I reach out to the vague face. "I'm right here, Dad. Give me your hand."

He blinks and turns his head in all directions. "I'm stuck. I can barely move."

My own hand is inches from the pulsing void. I know I shouldn't stick it in, but the urge to do so grows stronger every second. "Keep trying. Hold out your hand, and I will pull you out."

An arm bursts through the portal. It's covered in scratches and bruises, and dark mud crawls over it.

I jump back and hold out my arm to stop Taylar, who hurries to my side to help. Slowly, I step further back until the hand can no longer touch us.

"What is it?" Taylar asks. "Don't you want to free John?"

I shake my head and take the bell back from Vicky. "*That*… is not my father."

The young ghost lowers his shield a bit and leans forward. "Are you sure?"

I point at the hand sticking out of the darkness. "Look at all the injuries." I turn to the others behind us and lower my voice. "Remember when we saw him recently? He looked bad, sure, fragile and pale, because he starved to death, but he wasn't beaten up. His arms were thin, but there were no cuts or bruises on them. Even if someone beat him up now, the injuries wouldn't stick because he's dead. His body will always return to the state it was in when he died, like yours do."

Anger falls over Jeep's face. "It's a trick."

I hold up the bell. "Let's get rid of it."

Maël points her staff at the portal. "I could try to freeze it in time. You can pull it out, find out who or what it is."

"No," I say without hesitation. "We're not wasting our time on this thing. There's no need for us to know what it is. We already know what it wants and whom it was sent by. That's enough. Pulling it into the tunnel will only make it more difficult to defeat."

D'Maeo gives me his fatherly smile. "That's a good decision."

The iele remain silent while Jeep and Kessley hold

269

up their thumbs.

It's when I turn back to the portal that everything suddenly goes haywire.

A shriek of horror echoes through the secret tunnel. A figure, moving so fast it's no more than a blur, shoots past all of us before we realize what's happening. It dives straight for the hand sticking out of the portal, letting out a sort of howl of sorrow. It's not until it stands still that I recognize it.

"NO!" I stagger forward. "Mom, don't! It's not him!"

"John!" she wails, deaf to my warning. "John!"

She reaches out to him, and no matter how big my strides are, I know I'll be too late. And I can't help but think that by now her luck will have run out. Trevor no longer watches over her, and Satan has given the order to use Mom to get to me.

My Shield, however, reacts fast as lightning. Before I've even put one foot in front of the other, my six ghosts apparate next to her. Some of them land in the same place, but that doesn't slow them down one bit. They all grab Mom and pull her back. Or, they try to. But she has grabbed onto the hand. And what's worse, the hand has grabbed onto her too.

D'Maeo tears the fingers loose one by one while Vicky tries to catch Mom's eyes. "Listen to me, Susan," she says, raising her voice to be heard above Mom's yelling and 'Dad's' pleas to free him. "This is not John."

When she doesn't respond, Vicky shoots me a

worried look over her shoulder.

"Maybe we can try holy water again," Jeep suggests.

"We can't," Taylar answers, using his shield to try and push the imitation of Dad further back. "I used the last of it on Beelzebub."

"Can't you apparate out of here and take Mom with you?" I yell.

D'Maeo shakes his head. "We might accidentally take the creature inside the portal with us too, since it's holding on to her."

I curse and lift my hands in desperation. *What are we going to do?*

A warm breeze hits my neck, and the leader of the iele gently pushes me aside. "Let us help you."

I can only nod.

The last of the iele to pass me points at the bell. "Start ringing it."

"Okay," I mumble, a little intimidated by their slowly growing forms.

My hands starts moving again. The sound that the Bell of Izme makes does not reach my ears, but I know it is working, because the darkness around 'Dad's' face starts to close. I see his hand wrapping tighter around Mom's and pray for her safety. *Please don't take her away from me again. Please, please, please.*

The iele come to a halt behind my Shield. They've grown so much that their heads touch the ceiling. But this time, they have not gone dark. They are still light and beautiful, and I can feel their comfortable warmth spreading through the tunnel. Their long, white dresses move as much as their gray hair does. They reach out to each other to form a line. Then they tilt back their heads and close their eyes. A sort of low humming rises from their lips. It's a mesmerizing melody that reverberates through every bone in my body. Everyone is affected by it. Movements are growing softer, sounds fainter. The fear and anger inside me are dialed down.

All heads turn to the three fairies, even Mom's. The humming gets louder. Any other sound would be deafening, but this... it's wonderful. It's like floating on your back in a babbling brook with the sun shining on your face and no cares in the world.

I blink when something shifts in the air. An energy field detaches itself from the three women and sweeps toward the portal. When it hits its target, the dark void wobbles. It turns lighter, and the hand opens.

Immediately, my Shield pulls Mom out of its reach.

That wakes her from her daze. She kicks and fights like a cornered cat. "Let me go! John, hold on!"

I step aside as they pull her back to the entrance of the tunnel. "Take her back to the mansion and try to calm her down. In the meantime, I'll close the portal."

Automatically, my hand starts to shake more aggressively. The iele push out another burst of energy. The hand shudders, the fingers curl up as if the creature is in pain. Slowly, it starts to pull back.

The face is completely covered in black mud again, although it looks more like normal mud now. It still pulses, but slower.

The iele's long locks float forward as if to touch the hand, and it pulls back quickly.

When the gap closes, my arm stops moving, and the iele cease their humming. The silence that follows is heavy, and for a moment, I can't move. I'm not sure what happened.

When the iele shrink back to their normal size and turn to face me, a question rolls from my tongue. "What did you hit it with?"

All three of them smile at me sweetly. "With positive energy," the leader says.

"Or love, if you want to be specific," the one to her right adds.

I clutch the bell to my chest and bow. "Thank you so much for your help... eh..." I suddenly realize we've never been properly introduced, "... I don't even know your names."

The leader gestures to the entrance of the tunnel and only responds when we're all back in the secret room with the porthole closed firmly behind us. "We cannot give you our true names, we never do, but you can call us Soimane, Sfinte and Mandre."

I bow again, which seems to please them.

"Give me a minute to hide the bell again. I'll see you downstairs."

They leave, and I take my time casting the spell to hide the porthole and the bell. I can barely wrap my head around what just happened. *I almost lost Mom again. If the iele hadn't been here, I probably would have. And I can't believe she would survive another kidnapping or curse. She's been so lucky up till now, and that luck has to run out sometime. We need to take matters into our own hands, and soon.*

When I close the cupboard that leads to the secret room, a hand on my shoulder startles me.

"It's just me," Mom says when I whirl around with a lightning bolt in my hand.

I breathe out slowly to calm down my heartbeat. "You scared the shit out of me."

"Sorry." She doesn't even scold me for cursing. "I…" She hesitates. Her eyes flit from my face to the secret door. "I wanted to apologize."

"What? Why?"

"For getting myself into trouble. Again." She breathes out heavily. "I should've thought twice before throwing myself at that… abomination."

"You couldn't have—"

"No," she interrupts me, "I could have known. I should know better. I should think before I act. Isn't that what I always taught you?"

"It is, but I understand. Everyone does."

"Really?" Her shoulders sag. "Because we can't afford to make mistakes like this."

"Everyone makes mistakes, Mom. Even the Devil himself."

She looks so small and sad that I wrap my arms around her and pull her close.

She sobs, and I rub her back.

"I've blamed John for our troubles for so long. I was so angry. And then it turned out that it wasn't his fault. He was sucked into this horrible battle, just like you were, and all he wanted was to protect us. Now I feel guilty for ever doubting him. He was my tower of strength, and I dropped him like a rock. And when I saw him again, all of my feelings for him came rushing back. I couldn't think straight anymore."

"I understand, Mom. Anyone would've done the same."

She frees herself to look at me. "You didn't run to him."

I shrug. "It's different for me. I saw him recently, and I've had a piece of him with me since this all started." I pull out Dad's notebook and stroke the cover.

Mom places her hand on mine. "You are so much like him, you know that?"

"I am?"

"You have his eyes, his strong will, and his urge to protect others." She follows the side of my hand with her finger. "Even your hands are the same. Strong, but soft." She moves her hand to my chest. "Like your heart."

"Thanks, Mom, but I didn't inherit all of that just from him. You have the same traits."

She encompasses my face with her hands. "I'm proud of you both. Now, let's go put those wonderful traits of ours to good use."

CHAPTER 27

When we get back to the kitchen, there's no trace of the iele.

"They went home," D'Maeo answers my stunned stare. "Said they would be back tomorrow."

I slide onto my chair and lean back. Only now do I feel the fatigue that has settled inside my muscles. A day with so much fighting and emotions tends to wear you out like that.

"Time to work out a plan?" Taylar asks.

I rub my eyes and try to concentrate. "I'm not sure how much help I will be, because I'm beat, but I guess it's a good idea to make a plan now so we can start early tomorrow."

"We should start by transferring Charlotte's powers to Susan," Maël says.

"I agree. But not now. We need a clear mind and a fit body for that."

"I'm fit," Mom says, sitting up straight to prove it.

With a grunt, I rest my head in my hands. "I know, but I'm not. And I'll be the one doing the spell."

"Okay, you're right. We should wait."

The disappointment in her voice makes me look up. "You really want this, don't you?"

She places her hands on the table with force. "Yes, I do. The more I think about it, the more I like the idea. I'm tired of feeling helpless, of *being* helpless, Dante. And after my foolish behavior in the silver mine, I'm positive that this is the best choice."

"It wasn't that foolish," several of the ghosts mumble at the same time.

Mom blushes. "Thanks, but I know it was. I should've known better, after all I've been through."

Mona rubs her back before sitting down on D'Maeo's lap. "It seems we agree on the plan to give Susan Charlotte's powers. We'll do that first thing tomorrow, and after some training, maybe she can even come with you to take out the marodium."

"Absolutely not," I say, lowering my hands again. "We give her those powers to help in the final battle. It's best to keep them quiet, just like the power Maël got from the black tree in the Shadow World. Mom will stay here and train with you."

Mona nods slowly. "I suppose you have a point there."

Mom opens her mouth to object, but a stern look from me makes her swallow her words. She folds her hands in front of her. "Okay, whatever you say, Dante. You're the boss."

I raise my eyebrows.

"In this case," she adds quickly.

I chuckle. "And here I thought the days of you shouting at me to tidy my room were over."

She glares at me. "They are. You're off the hook until you beat the Devil."

Charlie slams his fist down onto the table. "Damn, your freedom is about to come to an end, mate."

I rub my hands to get rid of the cold that seeps into them as images of the battle that's drawing close flood my brain. "I can't wait for Mom's shouting and my grades to be my biggest concerns."

"Hey!" Mom wags a finger at me. "I hardly ever shout at you."

"I know, Mom." I blow her a kiss. Then I plant my butt firmer into my chair. "So, what we need now, is a plan to take out the marodium. What do we know about them?"

Vicky shakes her head. "Only what the iele told us, I guess. That they live in Affection—a town we've never even heard of—and that they feed on nightmares and shape hatred."

D'Maeo takes on a more comfortable position and moves Mona to his other leg. "We should find out *how* they feed on nightmares."

"Maybe they scare people and then make them fall asleep," Taylar suggests.

I shiver at the thought of monsters creating nightmares like that and then sucking them from your brain somehow. "That's possible. Is there a way to find out for sure?" I poke my sleepy brain for a solution. "What about that place you guys always go to when you need to talk to other ghosts? What is that place called?"

Jeep clears his throat loudly. "We can't tell you, Dante. Only ghosts can enter there, and we've all made a blood vow not to tell anyone else."

Kessley is bouncing in her chair. "I'm a ghost! I'm a ghost! Can I come?"

Taylar reaches out to hold her down. "It's fine with me if Dante has no other plans for us."

"I don't think you all need to go, right?" I ask. "It would be nice if some of you could stay behind to think out at least the start of a plan. And we also need to talk about how to let Vicky practice the creation of the nine circles safely."

"I will stay here," Maël offers.

D'Maeo nods. "Me too."

Kessley pushes her chair back so fast that it topples over. "Great, I'm ready to go!"

Taylar shakes his head at her. "There's nothing exciting about it, Kess. Just a bunch of ghosts exchanging information."

She doesn't miss a bounce. "It's in another world, right? That's exciting!"

I grin. "She has a point. If I could, I would come too."

Jeep stands up too. "Let's go then. It will take longer, since Kessley will have to make the blood vow first."

Kess finally stands still. "But how can I make a blood vow? I'm dead; I don't have any blood left."

Vicky walks around the table and takes her hand. "Don't worry about that. We'll guide you through it."

"Be careful!" I call out a second before the four of them vanish into thin air.

"They'll be fine," D'Maeo says. "It's not a dangerous place."

"Good," I answer with a sigh. "We could use more places like that."

Mona gets up and starts to unload all kinds of cooking supplies from the cupboards. "Does anyone want dinner? I know we've had a late lunch, but..." She turns away when I scrutinize her.

What is she so restless about? D'Maeo said the others are safe, so... My thoughts come to a halt when Mom stands up and pulls Mona into a hug. The fairy godmother drops the pans she's holding, and when the loud clattering subsides, I can hear her sobbing.

Mom pats her back. "It's okay, let it all out. You can't be strong all the time."

"Sure... I can," Mona hiccups. "I need... to be. I'm a... fairy godmother, for crying... out loud."

"Yes, and you worry way too much about me and Dante." She rocks her gently. "And about D'Maeo."

Mona takes a deep, shaky breath. "I'm worried about all of you. I try to hold on to my natural optimism, but with everything that's happened, it's becoming a bit... too much."

Mom lets go of her and wipes the tears from her

280

cheeks. "We all have our limits, Mona. Even fairy godmothers."

"No," Mona says with a determined expression. "I admit I got overwhelmed there for a second. But I'm fine now." She shakes her head, and the red around her eyes disappears. "Thank you for the hug, I needed that. I should go talk to my friends now."

After a quick wave, she vanishes in a cloud of sparks that seem duller than usual. Mom stands frozen in place, with a baffled look on her face and her arms still at waist height.

D'Maeo shakes his head as if to say, 'let it go', and she does. She sits down, and soon, we're neck-deep in a discussion about how to approach the town of Affection without being spotted.

An hour later, the front door opens.

"We're back!" Charlie calls out.

When he, Gisella and Dylan walk into the kitchen, there's no need to ask how it went.

"So, you found him?" I ask Dylan when he drops down into the chair next to Vicky's empty one. "You look much better."

His hand flies up to his see-through face. "Really?"

"Yes, you've got a bit more color," Mona agrees, appearing next to D'Maeo. She slides a packet of crisps in Charlie's direction and smiles as if nothing happened.

Charlie picks it up with a grateful nod and rips it open. "Welcome back. How did your meeting go?"

Mona sits down on D'Maeo's lap. "I'll tell you later. First tell me what happened with you."

"We found Armando, but it didn't go the way we expected at all."

He stuffs five crisps into his mouth at once, and when he doesn't continue his story, Dylan picks up where he left off. "Yeah, it turned out I wasn't his unfinished business at all." When I frown, he scratches his head. "I mean, I *was*, once, but not anymore."

"Then what is he still doing on Earth?" I ask. "And why are you still here too?"

He points his finger at me. "That's exactly what we asked him. He said he went to a psychic, who showed him his past. He saw what happened."

"And so much more," Charlie adds cryptically.

Dylan nods vigorously and does a pretty good imitation of an excited Kessley. His chair nearly topples over. "Yes, it turns out my bad luck is actually good luck."

I bring my head closer, thinking I must have misheard. "What?"

"All this time I wasn't in the wrong place at the wrong time at all!"

I stare at him with what must be the most vacant expression ever. "You lost me."

He tries to sit still, but his feet still tap the legs of his chair, and he can't keep his hands in one place. "You remember I told you guys about my bad luck?"

"Of course. That's how you died too, by stepping

through the only hole in the fence around a military training camp. Armando shot you by accident." I raise an eyebrow. "That doesn't sound like good luck for either of you."

"I know!" Dylan cries out. "But we both saved a lot of people because of it."

Charlie swallows the last of the crisps and licks the salt from his lips. "It turns out our Dylan here is a lucky charm."

Mom takes the cup of tea that Mona's sparks hand her and wraps her hands around it. "How did your death save other people?"

"That hole in the fence was made by someone who was working for a terrorist organization. When the army combed the whole vicinity, they found some equipment. They were able to take fingerprints from a tool that wasn't wiped. Traced it and followed the guy they found. He led them straight to a terrorist cell consisting of two hundred people. They brought them all in and found detailed plans to bomb the military base *and* several other targets." His smile stretches from ear to ear. "They saved thousands of people."

I sit back and rub my face. "Wow. That is something, Dylan."

Charlie picks up his crumpled-up packet of crisps and starts to flatten it. "And that's not all. We did some digging into other moments of extreme bad luck in Dylan's life. Found out he saved a lot of people each time."

Dylan spreads his hands. "Without even knowing it."

"But what about the soldier who shot you?" Mom asks. "Armando… what was his name?"

"Armando Accardi."

"How was this good for him? He killed himself, and now he's roaming the earth? Why?"

Dylan's smile doesn't waver for a second. "Well, my story wasn't the only thing he found. It turns out there is—"

"Wait!" Charlie holds up his hands.

Dylan gives him an irritated sideways glance. "What?"

"We need a drum roll for this." My best friend throws his hair over his shoulder with a shake of his head and starts drumming his fingers on the table.

With a grunt, I roll my eyes and turn back to Dylan. "Okay, there is what?"

"There is a place between Earth and Heaven where soldiers with unfinished business go."

Charlie's drumroll ends with a bang when he slams his fists down.

Since I don't understand what the big deal is, I ignore him.

Dylan continues, the excitement in his voice rising. "As you can imagine, this place, called Salvatorum, is filled with soldiers who died fighting for peace and to save the lives of others. They can have a peaceful afterlife there, but most of them chose to travel to Earth on a regular basis to save people in need." He clears his throat. "You know, people who don't have a fairy godmother to watch over them."

He cringes when Mona turns around. But her reaction is a positive one. "I've never heard of that place, but it sounds like a beautiful thing."

Dylan slowly lets out his breath. "It is. And Armando is one of the leaders now."

"And…" Charlie says, a twinkle in his eye.

Dylan coughs loudly, and Charlie's mouth slams shut.

"And what?" I ask.

Charlie shifts uncomfortably in his chair. "And…"

I raise my eyebrows at him.

"… the others are back," he finishes quickly when the four ghosts drop into their seats out of thin air.

"We've got the info," Kessley says cheerfully. Then she spots Dylan, Charlie and Gisella. "Oh hey, you're back! How did it go?"

Dylan gives them a quick recap of his story.

"So you're a good luck charm!" Kessley gives him a high five across the table.

He chuckles. "I guess I am. Although it doesn't always work. I can't turn it on or anything."

"Well, some extra luck is always welcome," I say. "Although our friend Ginda gave me a golden flower for luck already." I search my pockets, not sure where I put it. When I find it, I hold it up, surprised that it's not squashed.

Dylan gasps. "I've got one just like that! I don't remember Ginda giving it to you."

He reaches inside his pocket and shows me a copy of the peony I'm holding. As soon as we both lean closer to take a better look, the layers of petals of both roses slowly unfold, and the gold starts to shine.

Charlie's hand, on its way to take another packet of crisps from Mona, freezes midair. "They react to each other."

Warmth spreads from the peony into my fingers and up my arm to my neck while the flower keeps unfolding. It's as if it has an endless amount of petals. More and more are unfolded until the warmth touches my toes.

"Wow!" Kessley breathes. "You guys are glowing!"

I look at Dylan and then down at my own body. Kess is right, a glowing line has appeared around us both. Their brightness almost blinds me, and I narrow my eyes. Dylan and I watch each other. His line starts to pulse, like a sound wave. A soft crackle rises from both of us, and then the light lines shoot into the flowers. They encompass both peonies before shooting into the air in an arched line, meeting each other halfway.

In the corner of my vision, I see Kessley leaning forward with her hand outstretched to touch the light. I want to tell her to stand back, but Jeep is faster. He pulls her back and shoves her into Taylar's arms. "Be careful, leopard girl, we don't know what it is yet."

"But it's beautiful…" she breathes.

I'm about to agree when everything explodes in a blinding flash. I shield my face with my free hand. An energy blast hits me in the chest, and I'm thrown backwards. My chair topples over, and the back of my head connects painfully with the floor. Grunts of surprise and pain echo through the kitchen.

When I hold my hand up to my face, the rose is gone. So are the light and the warmth.

I reach out to Vicky, lying next to me. "Are you okay?"

She nods. "I went through the floor."

We both reach for the table and pull ourselves up. "Is everyone al…" The rest of my question dies on my lips. Vaguely, I can hear the others getting to their feet, but their mumbling and grumbling fades too. We're all hypnotized by the thing that's floating above the kitchen table.

CHAPTER 28

Everything inside me is pulled toward the hovering glowing ball, even though I'm not moving. I try to speak or take my eyes off it, but I can't. The ball is the size of a marble, except… it isn't. It keeps changing. It rotates lazily, and different colors shine through the white light, as if there's a rainbow inside, trying to escape. A soft sound comes from within. Sort of a buzzing song, very high and clear. I've never heard anything like it, and I don't want it to stop. Ever.

The marble—or is it a pearl?—comes to a sudden halt. A ring of yellow light pops up around it, making it look like a tiny planet. The buzz-humming stops. It's waiting…

But what is it waiting for?

"What is that… mesmerizing ball?" Dylan voices my thoughts.

Mona is only now pulling herself up. "Oh my

goodness," she says in a hushed tone when her gaze locks onto the white marble. She's completely out of balance, her hair a mess, her eyes big, the color drained from her face and her arms outstretched, searching for support.

I swallow and cough to find back my own voice. "Do you know what it is?" I manage to ask.

"Yes…" Mona's head goes up and down in slow motion, and D'Maeo grabs her to prevent her from falling down again. "Yes… it's… the Pearl of Arcadia."

The ball glows brighter in response, as if it can hear her.

"What is it?" Taylar asks, pulling Kessley closer to him.

"It is the recording of a message…" she licks her lips, "… from God."

Vicky leans closer to it. "What kind of message?"

"The original message he gave to the angels when he created them." Mona lets D'Maeo pull her onto his lap. She's still pale, and her hands are shaking. "The one that tells them why they were created. Only the angels know what it says exactly, although some seem to have forgotten."

I stare at the pearl. Now I understand why it's so mesmerizing. It was created by God himself.

It takes a couple of seconds for Mona's last words to reach me. "Wait, is that why it found its way to us? Because more and more angels are betraying Heaven?"

She wipes a stray blonde lock from her forehead. "To you, Dante. You're the one chosen to save Heaven."

Maël squints at the ball of light. "We will save Heaven together, just like Earth. You will not stand alone in this, Dante."

I smile at her. "I know, and I don't think that's what Mona meant to say."

"I didn't," the fairy godmother quickly assures us. "What I meant to say was that Dante is probably the only one who can touch it. The rest of us could get hurt if we try."

Dylan immediately steps back with his hands raised. "I wasn't going to touch it."

Jeep wipes the dust from his hat. "Do you know what the message says? Roughly?"

"Of course. Most magical people do." She throws up some sparkles, and they rain down on her, pulling her hair into her usual perfect hairdo and putting the color back into her face. "They are the guides of humans and protectors of Heaven and Earth. They were created to keep the peace."

Maël points her staff at the floating pearl. "And that will remind them of their task, their responsibilities."

Only now do I understand what this could mean for us. "We can use it to get the traitors back on our side. The angels that sided with Lucifer."

Taylar lets go of Kessley and carefully sits down again. "We're not sure that those missing angels have defected, are we?"

Jeep places his hat back on his head and nods in the direction of the pearl. "I think we can assume that they have."

"Yes, this can't be a coincidence. So, why is it called the Pearl of Arcadia? Is Arcadia a place?"

Mona shakes her head. "Not that I'm aware. Arcadian means 'idyllically innocent, simple, and untroubled'. I guess it's a fitting name, since it contains a message from God to the angels."

While she's been explaining, the urge to touch the pearl has grown. It wants to be held. So I take a deep breath and reach out to the glowing marble.

"Be careful," Vicky whispers beside me.

The closer I get to it, the warmer it becomes. It's like sticking my hand into an oven, but the heat is pleasant.

Everyone in the room holds their breath. I take the pearl between my index finger and my thumb and clench my jaws.

Nothing happens.

Except that the pearl stops glowing and cools down until it reaches body temperature.

I bring it closer to my face and turn it around and around. "How does it work? How do I start it?"

"Maybe it is already playing," Mona offers. "We won't know because we're not angels. Only they can hear it."

Charlie sits down and opens his packet of crisps. "We can ask Quinn."

"No, he's too busy." I lower myself into my chair too and study the pearl again.

Once everyone is seated again, Vicky speaks up. "I think Quinn would be happy to see what we've got here. And maybe it's him that has to use it, not us. He might know how to reach the rogue angels."

"Okay…" I lift my eyes to the ceiling and clear my throat. "Quinn? I'm sorry to call you again. If you have the time, could you come over for a minute? We found something that might help take care of your missing angels."

We wait for Quinn's bright form to appear, but he doesn't show.

I sigh. "See, too busy."

"He'w c'me soonazy can," Charlie says with his mouth full.

"Okay, so where do I put it in the meantime?"

Vicky points at her butt. "In my endless pocket? Nothing can fall out of that."

I look at Mona. "Is that safe?"

The fairy godmother scratches her cheek. "I think so. As long as you don't actually touch it."

Vicky turns her back to me, and I drop the pearl into her pocket. Then I slam my hands together and make eye-contact with Jeep, Taylar, Kessley and Vicky one by one. "Okay, tell us what you found out about the marodium. Is it enough to form a solid plan?"

They nod in unison. Jeep seems to be the only one with doubts. "It is, but it won't be easy. These monsters are dangerous. If they get a hold of you…"

He doesn't finish, but his eyes speak volumes.

"You're toast," I summarize.

"I like toast," Kessley says. "Can we have some?"

Charlie raises his crisps. "I second that idea!"

I hide my face in my hands. "We're talking about a plan that could kill us, and you two are thinking about food again?"

Charlie shrugs. "We can get killed every day, what else is new? Besides…" he empties the packet into his hand, "some of us need fuel to keep going. Without fuel, we can't defend ourselves, you know."

I won't argue with that. We can discuss our strategies over dinner.

Mona must agree, because she's turning on the stove.

"So tell us, Mona. How did your meeting with your friends go?" I ask.

"I couldn't reach them all. But the ones I spoke to are happy to help. They are going to contact the other fairy godmothers they know." She throws us a small smile over her shoulder. "I think most of them will agree to help."

"Good."

Dylan and I put away the peonies, that have folded their petals back in. When Vicky starts to fill us in on what they've discovered about the marodium, I see Dylan exchanging a furtive glance with Charlie. I grit my teeth when I realize there's no doubt about it: they're hiding something.

After dinner, we finalize our plans for the following day. Afterwards, we do some training in the protective circle, and we go to bed early. I fall asleep before Vicky's head touches my chest.

I'm standing in the protective circle outside Darkwood Manor. My shield is standing next to me and so are Mom, Mona, Charlie and Gisella. We've formed a circle ourselves, our feet touching the border of the space that protects us.

An arm-length away, Lucifer is pacing in front of rows of his servants. Demons, mages, angels and all kinds of other monsters. "I never thought it would come to this." He waves his hand in my direction. "I mean, sure, I knew we'd come face to face one day, but you never struck me as a coward." He comes to a halt in front of me and tilts his head to scrutinize me. I glare at him. But the more his head tilts, the harder it gets to keep my eyes on him. "You can't stay in that circle forever." His head keeps tilting until it's in a position that's way beyond natural.

I swallow and clench my jaws. Instinctively, my hand moves to my pocket.

The corners of Lucifer's mouth stretch. His head snaps up with a loud crack, and he chuckles. "I get it. You've got something up your sleeve." He opens his arms wide. "Well, show me! I can't wait to see it."

He seems so confident, but there's a hint of fear in his voice, and that gives me the push I need.

Without taking my eyes off him, I reach into my pocket and pull out a small cloth. Satan's eyes are drawn to it. I can tell he's getting nervous.

Slowly, I unfold the cloth and hold up the Pearl of Arcadia.

Without looking, I know that Mona, standing between Mom and Taylar on my right, stretches out her arm in my direction. Out of the corner of my peripheral vision, I can see sparks shooting from her fingertips. They whirl around Mom's head and hit the pearl with a soft crackle.

The pearl rises from the cloth, but I still don't look at it. My gaze is fixated on Satan. His grin hasn't wavered, but his hands are trembling slightly.

The pearl starts to turn as if it has gone berserk. The colors inside it become brighter and brighter until they burst out of it and rise to the sky.

I can tell by the look on Satan's face that he wants to kill the colors. Blow them up or whatever. But he can't, because the wriggling rainbow lights are hovering above the protective circle.

Meanwhile, my eyes drift to the rogue angels standing behind the Devil. Their faces are filled with shadows, their wings pitch black, and the light that normally shines bright around them is a dull gleam. Although we can't hear the message coming from the pearl, I know the angels can. I can tell by their changing expressions. Everything except the glowing marble has become a blur to them.

After a couple of seconds, I'm starting to worry that they will not change their minds. Maybe they have been poisoned by Satan. Maybe… The angel in the middle is the first to transform. The gleam lights up from the inside and spreads to the wings, slowly at first but faster and faster. The angel shakes himself, and the shadows fall from his face. His eyes are suddenly a lot lighter too. He spreads his wings and pushes off,

295

shooting straight up into the air. With a soft whoosh, he lands behind me. There's no need to turn around. Even if we hadn't been standing in a safe zone, I would've known he won't hurt us. I can feel his light touching my back, soothingly, feeding me hope and strength.

Soon, the other six angels follow. The Devil doesn't even glance over his shoulder. He stands perfectly still, as if this doesn't bother him at all.

When the seven angels have taken their place behind us, the colors drop down and are absorbed by the pearl. It stops spinning and lowers itself back into the cloth. I wrap it and put it back in my pocket.

When Satan meets my eyes again, I smile as lazily as I can manage while my heart pounds in my chest. Sure, this is a win for us, but the fight hasn't even started yet. A lot can still go wrong.

When the Devil doesn't move, I cross my arms over my chest.

His eyes start to twinkle. Fire comes to life within them. "That's it? Really?" He almost chokes with laughter. The sound rises from the ground and shoots up through his body. For a second, I think I even see the grass vibrate under him. But when I blink, nothing moves.

I try to hide my confusion by giving him my most furious expression. He's trying to tick me off-balance, *I tell myself.* He's still afraid of me. Of us. If he wasn't, he would've used his powers to blow us all out of the circle already.

He waves his finger at me. "Oh, my dear boy. Look at you." He shakes his head and tuts. "Such a powerful device at your disposal, yet you don't know what to do with it." His eyes scan the faces around me. "Well, I was hoping for some more resistance, some good old-fashioned battling, like I did with my brothers when I was kicked out of Heaven. But…" he shrugs, "if this is all you've got, it will have to do."

Suddenly, he grows to twice his size. His skin rips, and underneath it, the real beast becomes visible. Two sharp horns grow out of his head. His hands turn into monstrous claws, and when he throws them forward, the rocks that form the circle go up in dust. Tiny flames rise up from the salt underneath. I try to hold my ground as they reach higher and higher, but the heat scorches the skin under my clothes. I back up one step. The flames follow me, growing into giant claws.

I imagine a layer of ice as a shield around me. Immediately, the heat dies down. I brace myself for impact. Seconds before the flame claws reach my face, they swerve to the side and envelop Mom.

Her scream of pain shatters my self-restraint. The ice around me cracks as I turn to aim my powers at my mother. She crumbles to the ground, engulfed in flames. I conjure a wave of water when I'm hit by something solid. It knocks me over, and the wave making its way to Mom changes into a useless stream that dries in an instant.

While I fight off the demon that has landed on top of me, I keep my eyes on Mom. She's struggling to escape the flames by using Charlotte's powers. When she can't get them to work, she tries to roll away from them. But they cling to her, no matter what she does. Even Charlotte's powers provide no defense against the hungry, unnatural flames. They burn the skin from her hands and neck. When her face starts to turn black, she closes her eyes.

I reach out for her, screaming at the top of my lungs.
"Moooom!"

CHAPTER 29

My scream echoes through the mansion. Vicky throws her arms around me without hesitation, but I push her away and jump out of bed. I know it was a premonition, but I need to make sure Mom wasn't harmed in real life, because I can still feel the heat on my skin. I've stumbled out of the room and up the stairs to the top floor before Vicky can utter one word.

When I burst into Mom's room, she's already sitting up in bed with a startled expression on her face. No burn marks though. No blackened skin.

"Another premonition?" she asks.

I throw my arms around her but hold her at arms' length a second later.

Worry flickers in her eyes as I scrutinize every inch of her. "Was it that bad?"

I'm still panting from all the screaming I did

seconds ago, in the premonition as well as in real life, and from the running. My whole body trembles with fear, and I can almost feel the adrenaline coursing through my veins.

I can hear our friends entering the bedroom, but I don't look up. I'm afraid to let Mom out of my sight, and for once, I don't care about all the people staring at me. Even though I should be the strong one here, the leader.

"What did you see?" Vicky asks calmly. "Can we prevent it?"

I gasp for air and squeeze Mom's arms harder. "I'm not sure. He was so… powerful."

Mona, Charlie and Gisella file into the bedroom too. No one asks who I'm talking about. They all know who I saw.

"He broke the protective circle as if it was nothing, and… killed you." I bite my lip to hold back the tears that burn in my eyes. "There was nothing I could do. Charlotte's powers weren't strong enough, or maybe you didn't know how to use them yet. And the others…" I wave my hand at everyone around us, "… nobody intervened. I think he had us all pinned down somehow." I finally turn my head to face my friends. "We weren't strong enough." My voice is shrill.

Maël's eyes are full of sorrow, but she stands tall as always. Even with her golden cape still a bit wrinkled and the headpiece crooked on her head, she looks mighty. Her lips form a determined line. "Then we will train until we are."

I shake my head, and Vicky leans against me. The newfound heat of her body gives me a sliver of hope. I swallow the squeak in my voice and suppress the trembling of my hands. "We need more than training."

Charlie flattens the disheveled mess on his head. "You know, you get those premonitions for a reason. And they're getting more frequent. There must be something in there we can learn from."

Mom shakes me off gently and I let her, albeit reluctantly. "Tell us what happened, from the beginning."

It takes me a bit longer than usual to tell the whole story, since my throat keeps clogging up every time I mention Mom. When I finally finish, she puts her arms around me again.

"Now I understand why you were so upset. It must have been horrible to watch that."

Vicky kisses me on the cheek and strokes my hair. It's a little uncomfortable with everyone looking at us, but it's exactly what I need right now.

"No one blames you for being upset," she whispers in my ear.

I rest my head against her shoulder in gratitude. "So…" I clear my throat when only a hoarse sound comes out. "The only thing we learned from this, is that we're still too weak to take on the Devil."

"No," D'Maeo interrupts, "we've actually learned something else."

I breathe in Vicky's sweet smell before looking up at the old ghost. "Which is what?"

"The Pearl of Arcadia can do more than what we thought."

I go over my premonition again in my mind and nod slowly. "Right… I forgot about that."

"So did I," Kessley admits with a shy smile. "The rest of your story was so… overwhelming."

I wipe the wet trails from my cheeks. "It sure was."

Kess turns to the other ghosts. "How do we find out what else the pearl can do?" A light bounces around in her eyes. "Are we going back to… you know where?" Her excited smile warms the whole room.

"That's probably best," D'Maeo answers. "I don't think there will be anything about it on the Pentaweb, since this seems to be top secret."

Mona agrees with a nod. "I'd never heard of an additional function."

Charlie drops his hand, finally deciding his hair is a lost cause. "I know someone who will be able to answer our questions about the pearl without a doubt." He raises his eyebrows at me.

"Quinn." I gesture at the ceiling. "But he didn't come when I called him earlier. What makes you think that will be different now?"

"You never know. We can always try, right?"

I rub my face. "I don't know. It feels wrong to ask him for help again while we have done nothing to help Heaven so far."

"Ahum." Maël raises her eyebrows high when I meet her eyes. "There is no better way to help Heaven than to prepare for battle, like we have been doing. Quinn will understand this. He knows we cannot do anything without a proper plan and training."

"Not unless we want to get ourselves killed," Jeep mumbles. "For real, I mean."

"Exactly."

I pull Dad's notebook from my waistband and clutch the leather cover. "It still doesn't feel good."

After a short silence, Charlie groans. "Fine. If you don't want to call him, I will. You can blame it all on me if we interrupt something important." He clears his throat and lifts his head to the ceiling. "Quinn? Can you spare a couple of minutes for us?"

With my index finger, I follow the lines of the claw marks on the front of the notebook. I don't expect Quinn to answer. He's probably wrapped up in a fight with a bunch of demons or drifting somewhere between Heaven and Hell, searching for the missing angels.

My finger comes to a sudden halt when a bright light nearly blinds me. I press my hand down on the book. *Please don't ask me when we're going to help Heaven. Please don't be disappointed.*

It's weird how the bond between Quinn and me has changed. We used to be good friends—and we still are—but now I see him more like some sort of fatherly figure. In his human form—his disguise—he still looks like the friend that I've known for years. He's so much more than that, though. He's a lot older than one would think, for instance. And he's not the average guy I took him to be. And with average I mean: regular teenager with regular hobbies and regular worries. But then again, neither am I. I guess we're all a lot more special than I thought. I just can't get quite used to the knowledge that Quinn is actually God's right hand. As in: the most important angel of all.

"You called?" Quinn interrupts my thoughts.

"Yes, we were hoping to get some answers about a certain pearl," Charlie answers cryptically.

Vicky pats her endless pocket with a meaningful look at me. I reach in, take out the pearl and hold it up for Quinn to see.

Then, something happens that I've never seen before.

Quinn's jaw drops.

He reaches for the pearl and takes it from Vicky carefully. His chest moves faster than usual. *This pearl must really be something special.*

"The Pearl of Arcadia," he finally says in a stunned whisper.

After the tenth time of him turning it around before his eyes, my patience runs out. "A premonition told me this thing can do more than repeat the message that God gave the angels. Do you know what it is?"

"I do," Quinn says, moving his hand up as if he's releasing a bird. The pearl rises up and floats in our midst, halfway between the table and the ceiling.

I bite my lip to prevent myself from screaming at Quinn to 'Tell us what it does already!'

Finally, he starts to explain. "What you have here, is one of the most powerful calling devices in existence."

"Calling devices?" Kessley and I ask at the same time.

Quinn nods without taking his eyes off the pearl. "If you activate this, it will send a signal to every human being on Earth that will one day become an angel."

I shake my head in confusion. "What? How would it even know who to call? You said the choice to become an angel was yours."

He folds his hand around the pearl and gives it back to me. After one last look, I drop it into Vicky's pocket.

"I did," Quinn says. "Each potential angel has the choice once they die. They can either go to Heaven or become an angel. Sometimes they are asked to become one; sometimes the request comes from themselves. Either way, that pearl…" he points at Vicky, "has the power to gather a small army."

There's a stunned silence.

Maël adjusts her cape, which is completely smooth again. "I have never heard of such an object."

Quinn shows her his white teeth in a conspiratorial

smile. "That's because it's top secret."

Vicky slides to the edge of the bed, curiosity written all over her face. "What happens when the signal is sent?"

"Once the call reaches the potential angels, each and every one of them has to choose between death or becoming an angel. If they choose death, they will instantly forget the call and live out their lives, after which they will move on to Heaven. If they choose to become an angel, however, they will be obligated to answer your call."

"And they will fight with us as angels?"

"Yes, if you tell them to."

Kessley is getting excited again, bouncing slightly on her feet. "Does that mean Dante will be their master?"

"Until their task is fulfilled, yes."

Kess grabs Taylar for support. "You'll have a shield of thousands!"

"That's a bit optimistic," Quinn responds.

"Hundreds then?"

"About a hundred, maybe." He gives her a friendly smile. "People under fifteen will not hear the call. And don't forget that most angels were never human. You need a pure heart to become one, and not many people have that."

"I know lots of people with a pure heart," she counters.

"Are you sure?" There's a twinkle in Quinn's eye as he holds her gaze. "Did they ever bully anyone?

306

Exclude someone? Lie? Keep wrongfully given change at a store? Ignore people who were bothering someone else? Leave someone who had fallen?"

With every word he utters, Kessley's shoulders sag a little lower. When Quinn finishes his list, the sixth ghost crosses her arms. "You can't tell me people like that actually exist."

Charlie and I chuckle at the same time. My best friend slaps Quinn on the back. "Qaddisin here is exactly like that."

Kessley snorts. "Of course he is. He's an angel."

"True," Quinn says before either of us can respond. "But I was like that when I was still human."

Suddenly Jeep throws his hat against the ceiling, startling us all. Except for Quinn, who glances over his shoulder with a small frown.

"As fascinating as this all is," the tattooed ghost says, "the most important question here is... how do we activate the pearl?"

Quinn walks around my friends and halts at the door. He holds out his hand to Dylan, standing in the doorway. "Hi, I'm Qaddisin. Quinn for friends."

Dylan stares at him with wide eyes. He seems overwhelmed by the presence of an angel. I can't blame him, most of us never get to meet one.

His hand trembles when he shakes Quinn's. "D-Dylan. Dylan f-for... friends."

Quinn chuckles. "Nice to meet you." He studies the young mage from head to toe. "I have a feeling you have something to do with the sudden appearance of this pearl. Am I right?"

"Y-yes, sir. I had one of th-the flowers it c-came out of."

Quinn squeezes his shoulder. "There's no need to be nervous. We're all friends here."

"S-sorry, sir," Dylan stutters.

Quinn winks at him. "And it's Quinn, not sir."

Dylan gives him a trembling smile. He still can't take his eyes off him, and it's starting to get uncomfortable. Mona must sense it too, because she stands up from D'Maeo's lap and aims some sparks at the young mage.

When they reach him, Dylan visibly relaxes. His hands stop trembling, his shoulders loosen up and he blinks several times. "Thanks, Mona."

"You know, Dylan…" Quinn tilts his head. "Only a handful of people are able to receive a golden peony, like you and Dante did. You're special, Dylan. I should be the one trembling in *your* presence." He winks again.

Dylan laughs. "Thanks, but I'm not *that* special."

"Of course you are," Gisella counters immediately. "Have you forgotten what we found out yesterday?"

Dylan fidgets with the hem of his shirt. "No, but I'm still not sure I believe it."

"You'd better get used to it," Kessley says cheerily, "because you're part of the special squad now!"

"Hear hear," Taylar says half-heartedly, which results in a mean poke in his side from his girlfriend.

"Seriously, though." Quinn looks at all of us, one

by one. "I need to get back soon, so I'll tell you how to activate the pearl."

We file downstairs and Quinn is about to finish his instructions when there's a knock on the front door.

When I open it, the iele float inside. "Sorry we're early," Soimane, the leader, says. "But the marodium seem to be up to something."

Sfinte, the one of the left, wipes a gray lock out of her eye. "We think they want to expand their territory."

"Which means our chances of defeating them are shrinking," Mandre finishes.

They follow me into the kitchen where they repeat the bad news.

"We can go now," I say.

"Fine with me." Vicky stands up and wipes some dust from her leather pants. "But what about Charlotte's powers?"

I bite my lip. "Well, maybe *you* should transfer them to Mom."

Quinn shakes his head. "That's a bad idea. You should leave that to someone who excels at spells."

Vicky drops back into her chair. She looks tired. "Dante then. But we can't leave this house without him."

"You won't have to," Quinn replies. "Once you get back from Affection, there will be enough time to transfer Charlotte's powers and for Susan to train. That is, if you leave now."

Kessley stares at Quinn with her mouth open. "You know when our battle with the Devil will take place?"

Quinn stands up and spreads his wings, that pop out of his back. The feathers touch Mom and Dylan's heads, and they both close their eyes for a second.

"I can feel the battle drawing near," he says, while the light from inside him burns brighter and brighter. "And I can tell you, you need to hurry. We all do." And with that, he turns into a blinding flash and disappears.

CHAPTER 30

I stand up and rub my hands together. "Well, that settles it then. We're postponing the transfer of Charlotte's powers until after our visit to Affection. We'd better leave now." I turn to the iele. "I reckon you know the way?"

Soimane's nod makes her long hair flow up and down. It's mesmerizing, and it takes a couple of seconds for me to tear my gaze away from it.

Charlie stands up and bows lightly. "May I offer you a ride?"

Soimane gives him her most beautiful smile, and for the first time, I see a hint of jealousy on Gisella's face.

"Thank you," the leader of the iele says, "but we never take the car. We've got our own way of traveling." She slides over to the front door, as always followed closely by the two other fairies.

"Does everyone have their weapons?" I check.

Taylar disappears for a second and returns with a sword and shield in his hands. Vicky taps her right side. "Got it."

I frown at her, wondering if I'll ever find out how she hides a sword underneath those tight clothes. But in the end, I guess some things are better left a mystery. It would be like a magician revealing a trick: once you know how it works, it's not as mesmerizing anymore.

When everyone is ready, we say a quick goodbye to Mona and Mom and jump into our cars. The iele rise higher into the air, wait for both Charlie and me to hold up our thumbs, and take off.

Everyone is quiet. I think we're all thinking about Quinn's words: 'I can feel the battle drawing near.' We all know it's coming, but hearing an angel saying it out loud somehow makes it more real. Even Vicky is worried. A deep frown is etched into her forehead.

I focus on the road in front of me. The iele fly at lightning speed, but their posture is the same as before. It's almost as if they're hovering in one place, except that their hair and clothes move even more than usual. It's a weird sight and, to be honest, a bit distracting, because once again I have trouble tearing my eyes away from them. After I almost steer Phoenix into a tree or two, I ask Jeep to keep an eye on the iele and tell me where they're going.

Once we're out of the forest, the fairies rise higher. A quick glance tells me they're out of my sight. "I can't see them anymore. Have they left us?"

"Don't worry, I've got them," Jeep answers. His voice sounds far away, and when I turn my head, I nearly drive the car off the road again. Jeep's head is sticking out through the roof. To me, he's now a headless body.

"Wow, keep your eyes on the road!" Vicky yells from the backseat, and I yank the wheel to keep us from crashing.

We leave Blackford soon, and when it slowly gets smaller in my rearview mirror, doubt starts to prickle my neck. *What if we overestimate ourselves? These marodium monsters sound dangerous.*

"Maybe we should go over the plan again," I suggest.

When the ghosts in the backseat agree, I dial Charlie's number and put him on speaker.

We go over every detail of our strategy again, and the goosebumps on my neck and arms disappear.

"I think we're here," Jeep says, lowering himself back into his seat.

I slow down and see the iele floating closer to the ground. When they block my way, I park Phoenix and give her a gentle pat on the wheel.

"Try not to get hurt," I whisper.

Everyone files out of the two cars, except Vicky.

I open the car door and peer inside. "What's wrong?"

She's grabbing her head with both hands. Her jaws are clenched tightly. "It's happening again."

My heart stutters. "What is?"

She rocks back and forth. "A little bit was hidden deep inside my head. It's fighting for control."

I fling myself forward onto the back seat and pull her into my arms.

I didn't want to think about the possibility that we beat him too easily before, but now I have no choice but to face it. "Beelzebub?"

She rests her head against my chest. "Maybe you should leave me here. Lock me in with a spell."

"No, I'm not leaving you alone. What if he makes you hurt yourself?"

A rustle behind me startles me, and instinctively, I throw a lightning bolt at the shape that bends toward us.

Jeep goes transparent just in time to make it fly through him.

"Sorry," I say.

He waves my apology away and addresses Vicky. "You controlled it before, you can do it again. You're strong now, Vick, and one of the toughest girls I've ever known. I have faith in you."

I kiss the top of her head. "Me too." The moment the words leave my lips, I believe them. She can suppress Beelzebub's influence. "Use your new powers."

She sits up abruptly, almost giving me a head-butt. "You're right. I can't hold it back forever, but I can hold on for now."

She hops out of the car without opening the door

on her side, and I crawl backwards.

The others are watching with concerned faces a couple of paces away. Vicky holds up her thumb and relief washes over their faces.

Jeep and I meet Vicky at the back of the car. I grab her hand, and electricity pulses through it.

"Don't let fear get a hold of you, that's what he uses to take over control," Jeep warns her.

Vicky straightens her shoulders and lifts her chin. "I'll be okay. For now. Let's do this."

We gather behind the three fairies. Soimane points at a line of trees about a hundred feet away. "Do you know what kind of tree that is?"

All the info Dad fed me during camping when I was little comes back to me. "Douglas firs."

"Exactly. And do you notice anything strange about them?"

I shake off the last of my worries and narrow my eyes. "Eh…" More memories shoot through my mind. Then it hits me. "The branches and needles start too low on the trunk for a Douglas fir."

Maël points her staff at the trees in the middle. "But only those four look different."

"Well-spotted," Soimane compliments us. "That is because the trees in the middle are an illusion. They hide the entrance into town."

D'Maeo and Jeep are scouting our surroundings.

"Won't we be spotted if we go in through the main entrance?" D'Maeo asks.

"It's the only opening; the rest of the town is

sealed off." Soimane grins while she floats higher. "But don't worry, we'll create a distraction for you."

Without another word, they take off to a point high above our heads and soar toward the hidden town.

We wait patiently for a sign that we can go in.

After a while, Taylar tilts his head. "I can't even hear anything. How are we supposed to know when to go in?"

A loud rumbling freezes us all to the spot. It's followed by a blue buzzing in the air, like electricity. Sounds trickle through to us. Yelling, growling, smashing, and more. Birds rise from the trees, screeching in fright.

"I think they broke the sound shield around it," Charlie comments.

"That must be our cue," Gisella answers.

As one, we start running toward the line of trees. It's weird to keep going when we get close to the illusion. With the bark of the nearest tree only an inch from my face, my legs almost refuse. But I force them to keep going and squeeze my eyes shut for a second. When I open them again, I'm running through a hazy world. Sounds are muffled, and everyone on the other side of the illusion consists of only vague shapes and dampened colors. Then I break through and come to a halt to give my eyes time to adjust to the suddenly vivid colors and my ears to the loud sounds. Vicky stops next to me, Kessley is on my other side, gaping at the houses and vegetation around us. "It's beautiful here!"

I point at a picturesque farm with a large barn to our left. "The noise is coming from behind that house, so that's where we're going."

We start walking, fast but carefully, looking around and over our shoulders constantly. But this part of Affection is deserted; the iele have done a great job of luring the marodium away from us.

Maël reaches the barn first. She peers around the corner and beckons us. We follow silently, Taylar pulling Kessley along because she keeps gaping at the gorgeous flowers that line the whole street.

We're halfway across the cobblestone driveway when Jeep whistles softly. Dylan bumps into me when I come to a sudden halt and turn back to face the tattooed ghost.

Jeep points at the barn wall next to him and then at his ears. *He heard something.*

We retrace our steps, and I put my ear against the wall. Whispers drift toward us. They cling to me, wrap around my head, but not in a threatening way. It's more like a soft touch.

"That's weird," I whisper. "Should we go check it out?"

Could it be a trap? I try to signal with my eyes.

Vicky places her hand on the wall and frowns. When she lowers her arm, her jaw sets. "Prisoners."

"We can free them once we've taken care of the marodium," D'Maeo says while he starts to walk away from the barn again.

"No." Vicky's voice stops him in his tracks. She has found a slit between the boards. She peers through it and backs up so fast that she almost trips over her own feet.

Jeep and I catch her.

"What is it? Are you okay?" With my eyes I ask her the real question that's haunting me. *Are you losing control?*

She blinks several times. "I'm fine. But... these aren't just any kind of prisoners. I think they're..."

"You think they're what?" I urge her.

"Angels," she answers, barely audible. "And they are in pain."

I rub my eyes and swallow a sigh. "So that's what the morodium were up to. They've captured angels."

Dylan walks to the wooden door. "We should free them."

I study him, while my brain goes in overdrive. There's an angry glint in his eyes that I haven't seen before, plus a lot of determination. *Is this a trick? Is this what he's been waiting for all along? To stop us from attacking the morodium and lock us in the process?*

I glance at Charlie and wonder again: what was going on earlier, at the table? Charlie wanted to tell me something, but Dylan stopped him. Something about the man who killed Dylan, Armando Accardi. Maybe he's waiting for us inside.

I shake my head. *No, impossible. Charlie would never turn against me.*

"What are you waiting for?" Vicky whispers in my

ear.

I lick my lips. "Nothing. Let's go inside and free those angels."

When everyone has joined Dylan at the door, I count from three back to one on my hand. On zero, Dylan opens the door. We file into the barn, me first and the others close behind.

It's dark inside, and the smell of burning lingers in the air.

"I'll make some light," I announce before I conjure a small lightning ball in the palm of my hand. When I find nothing close to us, I enlarge the ball slowly. As soon as it's big enough to make out the far wall, I let the ball float up to about seven feet above my head.

What I see when I take in the space is not at all what I was expecting.

There are six angels locked in the barn, standing upright, with their eyes closed and their lips moving restlessly. But there are no bars around them. No cages, no chains, nothing dark keeping them down.

Instead, dozens of human shapes surround them. Six or seven of them are moving in circles around each angel, closing in and backing down again. Taunting. Every now and then they grow a bit larger. Some are already looming over the angels, like giant shadows. When I step closer to one, I can hear the figures whispering.

"We're better than you."

"We're the most important species in the

universe."

"Bow to us!"

"Worship us!"

I turn to my friends. "They are turning these angels against humans."

Dylan is still standing close to the door. His hands are trembling slightly. "Why are their eyes closed?"

I study each of the trapped angels, noticing only now that none of them is reacting to the swarming shapes around them.

Vicky reaches out to the one close to me. She holds up her hand, trying to pick up the emotions coursing through his body.

"Anger, fear, resentment," she sums up after a couple of seconds.

"They have given them nightmares about humans." D'Maeo joins us, deep lines of worry in his forehead. "The marodium are building an army of angels. An army filled with hatred against humankind. An army that will do whatever Satan tells them to."

I open my mouth to ask him if he's sure. To beg him to tell me he's kidding. Angels that have gone rogue by themselves are hard enough to handle, but this… all this rage building up inside them, the images inside their heads feeding on the jealousy that some of them may already feel.

The first syllable that leaves my lips is drowned out by a sudden wave of noise. The whispers get louder, and the figures suddenly grow at double speed. I take a step back when the human forms rise above the angels one by one. They are shouting now, their hands pushing and shoving the angels.

Vicky grabs my hand. "What's going on?"

Jeep holds his hat in front of him, ready to throw it if the shapes decide to attack us. "I think we triggered some sort of fail-safe, that speeds up the process."

Maël pulls out her staff. "This is not good."

The hairs on the back of my neck stand up when the angel in front of me opens his eyes. He spreads his wings, sending the human shapes sprawling in every direction. All the light has seeped from his body. His eyes are as dark as the night, and his mouth is twisted into a menacing snarl. The feathers of his wings have turned into jagged shapes, his round jaw is now a square one, set in anger. The skin of his bare chest is torn. *No, this is not good. This is not good at all.*

* * *

Dante Banner returns in **The Ninth Angel** – the conclusion to the thrilling *Cards of Death* series.

The final battle is drawing closer at frightening speed. Will all their efforts to gain power be enough to beat the Devil once and for all? Or will Satan finally rule the world?

Turn the page for a sneak peek of the final book in the series!

Make a difference

Reviews are very important to authors. Even a short or negative review can be of tremendous value to me as a writer. Therefore I would be very grateful if you could leave a review at your place of purchase. And don't forget to tell your friends about this book!

Thank you very much in advance.

Newsletter, social media and website

Want to receive exclusive first looks at covers and upcoming book releases, get a heads-up on pre-order and release dates and special offers, receive book recommendations and an exclusive 'look into my (writing) life'? Then please sign up now for my monthly newsletter through my website: www.tamarageraeds.com.

You can also follow me on Facebook, Instagram and Twitter for updates and more fun stuff!

Have a great day!   Tamara Geraeds

Found a mistake?

The Eighth Mage has gone through several rounds of beta reading and editing. If you found a typographical, grammatical, or other error which impacted your enjoyment of the book, we offer our apologies and ask that you let us know, so we can fix it for future readers.

You can email your feedback to: info@tamarageraeds.com.

Preview

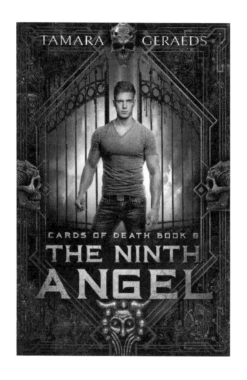

Cards of Death book 9

The Ninth Angel

CHAPTER 1

(first draft)

It's weird how, even when you're expecting it, everything can still spin out of control faster than you imagined. One second we're watching six angels being tortured in their sleep, the next we're faced with six creatures that don't resemble angels anymore, back-up by the nightmares that made them that way.

When one of them woke up, all aggravated and ready to attack the first human it saw, I thought there would be plenty of time to either wake it from its hypnoses or make a run for it.

I didn't expect the remaining five angels to wake up at the same time, and I certainly didn't expect the human forms hovering around them to focus on us. I figured they would disappear as soon as their job-to turn the angels against humankind-was done. Instead, they turned into all kinds of other monstrosities.

Gisella and Vicky react before anyone else does.

The werecat-witch throws her hands forward, creating a force field that knocks our enemies over. Or at least, it should, but the angels merely stumble to stay upright. The figures are blown back, but they recover quickly and with angry snarls and hisses.

Meanwhile, Vicky digs up two jars of salt from her endless pocket, and tosses them to Dylan and Taylar. "Create a salt line around the barn. Quickly!" she yells.

The two boys hurry outside and the rest of us form a line of defense in front of the only exit.

Gisella tries another blow, and when that doesn't work, she calls the shadows to her. There are lots of them in here, which is a good thing, because now she can send a shadow over to almost every angel and nightmarish monster in here. For a moment I think it's working too. Then the angels open their mouths and breathe out, sending the shadows back to their corners.

"Eh… I need some help!" Gisella calls out. The sliver of panic in her voice sounds unnatural. It sends a shiver down my back. If Gisella loses faith, the outcome doesn't look good.

There's no time to think of a strategy, because the angels and monsters are moving forward as one. Maël slams her staff against the side of a man that looks familiar. Taylar is jumped by his spitting image, save for the gruesome scars that line his face and the burn marks on his hands.

When I look at the other forms approaching us, I

realize the figures have changed into our worst nightmares. And although I'm afraid to face mine, I'm also curious. What does my worst nightmare actually look like in the flesh?

I conjure two lightning bolts in my hands and brace myself when I turn my head back to the incoming threats. The figure in front of me change shape constantly, as if it can't decide what it is supposed to be. I see Vicky's face changing into Mom's, and turn into a burning ball next. I almost smirk. *I guess there are too many fears in my mind to deal with?*

While it tries to find the perfect form to tip me off balance, I shower it with lightning, combined with rain.

I'm surprised it works, since I've never managed to create more than one meteorological phenomenon at time. The nightmare inducing monster shudders as electricity runs through its shadowy form. Around me I hear the clanging of metal, Maël's mumbling as she tries to slow down time, the whizz of Jeep's hat and Charlie's grease flying by and the whoosh of Gisella's catlike moves.

My confidence vanishes into thin air when I realize none of it is driving the angels back.

Then a voice calls out from behind us. "The salt is in place!"

"Retreat!" I yell at the top of my lungs.

Everyone backs up, and one by one they step outside.

I see multiple Kessleys melt back into one. Then it's only me and Gisella left. The dark figures have chosen one form as they close in on us: the form of Charlie. A smart move, seeing that he's my best friend and Gisella's boyfriend. It's hard to attack him, even though we know it's not him.

But they miscalculated Kessley's abilities. When both Gisella and I hesitate, my sixth ghost pushes us back and changes into a dragon the size of a small elephant. In response, the Charlies as well as the angels behind them charge as one.

I focus on a large wave, to hit them from the side, but Kessley opens her dragon mouth and breathes fire. The nightmare Charlies shriek and roll over to extinguish the flames.

Gisella grabs my hand and pulls me through the door, out into the sun.

Kessley shrinks back into her human form and follows us.

Taylar pulls her close and buries his face in her bleached hair. "That was so brave."

I don't hear her answer, because at that moment the first angel reaches the line of salt. When it bounces back slightly, it bares its teeth at us and tilts its head. "Well well, you found a way to trap us. But you forgot one thing." The words come out as a growl and the sunlight moves away from the door. The angel stretches his wings. "We are heavenly beings. Salt will not stop us."

I try to hide the sliver of worry that makes its way

up to my throat, by folding my arms. It takes all of my courage to stay where I am, about an inch from the doorway. It's a good thing Gisella and Vicky are standing beside me, or I would've stepped back for sure. Because if we're wrong about these lines of salt, this angel will crush me. I can see it in its eyes.

I envision a thick cloud above my side of the wooden door, filled with hail. I'm surprised at my ability to keep it in the air.

The angel folds its wings and steps forward so suddenly I flinch. Some hail escapes from the cloud above me.

It doesn't matter. The angel bumps into an invisible barrier. It lets out a surprised yelp of pain and bounces back.

The cloud above me dissolves. My lips twitch toward a smirk, but it's actually not that funny. These are angels and we need to wake them up somehow.

Kessley seems to read my mind. "Use the Pearl of Arcadia."

There's a loud rumbling from behind us, followed by a squeal of rage. It sounds a bit like a lion choking on a bone.

"Too late," Jeep says, pushing his hat back onto his head and moving his hands to find any skeletons hidden under the perfect lawns around us. "The marodium are coming."

I grit my teeth. "Okay, we'll come back to save the angels later."

"Don't bother, we're fine!" the angel calls from the

doorway.

I ignore him. "It's time for our plan, guys. Get ready."

Gisella turns to me and when I wrap my arms around her neck she somersaults to the roof of the farmhouse, where I hide behind the chimney.

"Good luck," she says, and she takes off in a blur.

Meanwhile, the others have split up too. They've scattered so fast that even I don't see them anymore.

"Okay, focus," I whisper to myself.

Even though I can't see the marodium yet, the approaching darkness above the houses tells me exactly where they are. The noise coming from the barn must have alerted them to our presence.

I can only hope our plan will still work, since we've got the angels and nightmare monsters to take into account now as well. If the marodium manage to free them from the barn, we're in trouble.

If only there was time to use the Pearl of Arcadia. But we can't risk it falling into the wrong hands. We need it for the final battle.

The darkness slides toward me fast. Heavy clouds accompany the sound of wet feet on the cobblestones. Light is sucked from the streets bit by bit. The trees and flowers shrink back. Trees and petals fold in on themselves, hiding from the approaching evil. The weird squealing gets louder with every second that passes.

I take on a more comfortable position and stare at the rays of sunlight in the distance. *I can do this, I can do this.*

The first marodium rounds the corner. I'm so stunned at its appearance that I forget what I'm supposed to do.

The creature is moving on all fours, even though it has a humanoid body. Slime covers all of its slick, uncovered skin. The head is big and bald, the shoulders muscular. When it pauses and stands tall to sniff the air, I get a good look at it. It has a giant mouth with teeth the size of crayons.

Its nose is nothing more than two holes, and when it lets out a hoarse high-pitched squeal I can see the muscles holding its jaws together move on the outside of its skull. The arms and legs look like they've been stretched thin. The fingers are extremely long and thin too, with sharp nails at the ends. The spinal cord sticks out of its back as if it's trying to break free.

I come to my senses when it drops back on all fours. The arms are so long that the wide shoulders are still pointing up.

When two of its congeners join it, I close my eyes. First, I try to drive the image of the horrendous monsters from my mind. Once I've succeeded, I imagine sunlight breaking through the clouds, shining brightly down onto the streets and into every corner of Affection.

The marodium let out a deafening shriek as the light hits them. They scurry to the side of the nearest house to find shelter, but Gisella pulls the shadows away. Their skin hisses and they burst through the door and disappear inside.

Soon, about two dozen more of them come sailing around the corner. They dive in all directions, shrieking in pain and fear as the sun burns them. Grease flies through the air, blocking their way, while Kessley appears in dragon form to make sure they don't flee back to the other side of town. The three iele come soaring from my left and with a combined arm gesture they send the fleeing marodium back to the middle of the road. Taylar, D'Maeo, Dylan and Maël close in on them from the right. With danger surrounding them on all sides, the monsters are left with only two options: stay and fight us while their skin burns away, or seek shelter in the house their mates have fled into.

WANT TO READ ON?

The final book in the series will be available October 2021.

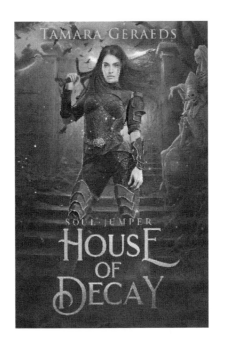

SOUL JUMPER
HOUSE OF DECAY

Welcome to Vex Monster Tours.
Please press PLAY to watch this video.

PLAY

Loading....

Loading....

Loading....

"Hi there, and welcome to Vex Monster Tours. If you're looking for an adrenaline-filled adventure, you've come to the right place. My name is Vex and…

You're laughing, aren't you? I don't blame you. I would too if I were you. But it's not my fault that I'm called Vex. My parents had a great sense of humor, or so they thought. They were both Soul Jumpers, of course, like me, and thought it was ironically funny to name me Vex, since they trained me to be a nuisance to any kind of monster.

Anyway, in case you don't know what a Soul Jumper is, I'll explain it to you briefly.

A Soul Jumper is a human with special powers, born and trained to kill monsters. We are stronger and faster than regular humans and have more endurance and agility and some other extras. When we touch the last victim a creature killed, a connection is made with the next target of that monster. When that target is attacked and about to lose the battle with the monster, our soul jumps into the target's body. From that moment on, our natural strengths are doubled, as are our senses. This gives us the power to defeat the monster before it kills another person. While we're inside the victim's body, they have no control over their moves but can still feel everything and talk to us. If they die, we jump back into our own body, which is protected by a flock of birds. Hawks, in my case. We have special Soul Jumper battle outfits, like I'm wearing now, connected to our souls to make them jump with us. They have some neat gadgets as extra back-up.

So, where was I?

Oh yes, Vex Monster Tours offers you the chance to see and fight any evil creature up close. To increase your chances of winning without my help, you get a day of training. That doesn't sound like a lot, but I'll give you a cupcake that contains a special mixture. It will give you the ability to pick up everything you learn a lot faster, and it builds up muscle at triple speed.

A blood vow is made between me and the monster of your request in which we agree not to attack before the arranged time. I will protect you the best I can while letting you fight the monster for as long as possible. Sounds cool, right?

But why, do you ask, would a monster agree to fight two people? Well, for one, most monsters are cocky, and two, these days, there are so many hunters roaming the streets that they have a hard time finding a quiet place to attack. They think they have a better chance for a meal when they're just fighting you and I… but we'll prove them wrong.

Have any questions? Feel free to email or call me!"

CHAPTER 1

I sense something off even before I see it. My muscles tense at the feeling that I'm not alone, like I should be.

Custos lands quietly on my shoulder while I peer left and right. Everything seems normal. There are no odd sounds, no footprints on the path or in the earth around the trees.

Then I notice it. The door to the training barn is ajar. It's just a crack, and there isn't enough wind to make it move, but I know something is wrong.

Custos cocks his head when he notices it a second later. He nudges my neck with his beak, as if to say, 'Go check it out!'

Slowly moving closer, my mind whirls around the possibilities. *Did I fail to properly close the portal after the last training session, making it possible for the monster to escape?*

I shake that thought off. Even if I didn't close it completely, the portal only lets monsters cross halfway. It's not really a passage; they can't get through to this world.

With narrowed eyes, I watch the creak in the door. My ears try to pick up a sound, any sound, that could give me an indication of what to expect. When they finally do, just as my hand moves to the doorknob, I freeze.

Custos lets out a disrupted croak as the pained whimper drifts toward us.

"That sounded human, right?" I ask him quietly.

He nods, and I wrap my fingers around the doorknob. "Good. That rules out the worst."

Before I get the chance to pull the door open, the leader of my protective kettle pulls my hair.

"Ouch," I whisper. "What was that for?"

The hawk swoops down to the ground and pulls at my pant leg.

A smile creeps upon my face. "Oh yes, good thinking, Custos."

I pull out the short blade hidden in my boot and wait for Custos to settle back on my shoulder.

"Ready?" I ask, and his talons dig into my shirt.

With one fast movement, I pull the door open. It takes me a millisecond to realize I won't need my weapon. No one is jumping out at me. The whimpering has stopped, but there's no doubt where it came from. Several of the traps that line the walls have been set off. Whomever broke into my barn managed to avoid the first trap, judging by the three arrows lodged into the wall on my right. Dodging them slowed him down enough to get doused with flammable liquid and set on fire.

I scan the floorboard in front of me. Yep, burn marks. The trail of black spots leaves no room for doubt about the intruder's next move. He dove for the bucket of water on my left, that has tipped over and is still dripping.

"And there it is," I say manner-of-factly.

Three small steps take me to the edge of what is normally a pretty solid wooden floor with no more than slits showing the dark void below. Now, the boards have moved aside and down, creating a large hole with a view of the endless blackness. Inches from the tips of my shoes, bloodied fingers are straining to hang onto what remains of the floor.

I lean forward so I can see my unwanted guest. "Hello there. How can I help you today?"

The man attached to the fingers is about nineteen years old. He has black hair covered in grease and green eyes that look up at me with a mixture of relief and despair. Scorch marks decorate his arms and face, and there are burn holes all over his shirt.

I study him shamelessly while he searches for an answer.

Custos scurries over and softly pecks at one of the fingers.

With a squeal, the man pulls back his hand, swinging dangerously by the other before wrapping it back around the floorboard five inches further to the right.

"Help me, please," he finally manages.

"Sure!" The fake smile on my lips almost hurts.

I squat down in front of him. "But first, I'd like to know what you're doing here."

One finger slips, and he groans. "I'll tell you everything. Please help me up."

"I will," I answer, examining my fingernails, "after you tell me."

"Fine." His voice goes up a couple of octaves. "I was hiking in the forest when a bear attacked me." My gaze drops down to his green shirt, which is streaked with red between the holes. There's a gash in the side that could've been made by a bear's claw, but it could also be the result of climbing the fence around my premises.

I frown. "Where's your backpack then? Did you drop it?"

"I did." He nods. His dark eyebrows are pulled together when he sends me a pleading look. "It fell into the pit. Please don't let me fall too. Please."

He sounds convincing, yet something about his story is off.

"Tell me exactly what happened with the bear."

He groans. "Please pull me up first. I can't hold on for much longer."

I stand up and take a step back. "I'm sorry, but I don't trust you. Your story doesn't make sense."

"Why not?" he exclaims. "I encountered a bear; I swear! I've never seen one so big in my life."

"What kind of bear?"

"A black bear, of course; it's the only one that lives here."

"Hmm." Anyone could know that.

And then it hits me. The thing that doesn't add up in his story.

"Bears never come close to my home. They sense

the monsters that visit frequently."

The muscles in his arms are starting to shake from the effort of holding on. "Please… I don't know what it was doing here. I'm telling you, it attacked me, and I figured climbing over your fence was my best shot."

I tap my lips with my finger. He is so full of bull that it's almost funny. Even if a bear would come close, climbing over the fence would trigger my alarm. *What are the odds of a bear approaching and my alarm failing on the same day?* And I'm not even counting the tripwires set up everywhere.

I cock my head. "You don't seem surprised to hear that monsters visit me on a regular basis."

He focuses on his fingers, trying to get a better grip. His breathing is fast, and sweat trickles down his temples and over the stubble on his cheeks. "Monsters are everywhere, why would that be a surprise?"

"No…" Slowly I shake my head. "You know who I am, what I am. You know what I do."

He clenches his teeth. "I swear-"

He yells in panic as his other hand slips from the edge. I drop back down quickly and grab it.

"Didn't your mother teach you not to swear?" I say. My voice is low with repressed anger. My patience has vanished. "Now, tell me the truth, or I'm throwing you in."

"All right, all right!" He swallows and licks his lips. His weight pulls at my arm, and I grunt.

"You better hurry."

"I know who you are. You're Vex Connor, a Soul Jumper, *the* Soul Jumper." He gives me a sheepish grin. "Everyone admires you. I just wanted to see how you did it all, you know. What kind of tools you use, how you live…" His voice trails off, and he breaks eye contact.

After a short silence, I shrug. "Well, that still sounds crazy but much more plausible than your other story." I grab his arm with both hands and haul him up.

He collapses on what remains of the floor and clutches his hands to his chest.

Custos shrieks, and I nod at him. "Yes, turn off the traps for a minute, please."

The hawk flies to the other end of the barn, close to the ceiling to avoid the booby traps that are higher up on the walls. I block the intruder's view as Custos picks up a rope, drops the loop at the end around the handle of the device I built and pulls.

With a sound like a collapsing bookcase, the floor boards pop back up until the black void below can only be seen through the cracks.

I stick out my hand. "Let's go. I'll give you a cup of coffee before you leave. You can wash up while the water boils."

* * *

Want to read on? Order this story on Amazon now!

IMPORTANT NOTICE

All *Soul Jumper* stories can be read in random order. You can start with the story that appeals to you most. It is, however, recommended to start with Force of the Kraken.

I hope you enjoy them!

ABOUT THE AUTHOR

Tamara Geraeds was born in 1981. When she was 6 years old, she wrote her first poem, which basically translates as:

A hug for you and a hug for me
and that's how life should be

She started writing books at the age of 15 and her first book was published in 2012. After 6 books in Dutch she decided to write a young adult fantasy series in English: *Cards of Death*.

Tamara's bibliography consists of books for children, young adults and adults, and can be placed under fantasy and thrillers.

Besides writing she runs her own business, in which she teaches English, Dutch and writing, (re)writes texts and edits books.

She's been playing badminton for over 20 years and met the love of her life Frans on the court. She loves going out for dinner, watching movies, and of course reading, writing and hugging her husband. She's crazy about sushi and Indian curries, and her favorite color is pink.

Printed in Great Britain
by Amazon

64422707R00206